PRAISE FOR *AYLIN*

"Aylin is like a chameleon, continually adapting to her new surroundings. But instead of coming across as a spoilt poseur, she is an attractive, warm character that fascinates and draws you in. Credit for this must lie in Kulin's excellent, exciting prose and the way she mixes facts with the re-creation of scenes, changes the subject of the story from Aylin to her male admirers to her patients and even changes the voice from the past tense to the present tense and allows the characters involved to tell the events of January 1995 from their own perspective." —Marion James, *Today's Zaman* (Istanbul)

PRAISE FOR *LAST TRAIN TO ISTANBUL*

"Ayşe Kulin is a clever writer. She draws the reader into the story of the life and loves of a Turkish family in wartime, and by the time the reader realizes that she has also cranked up the tension with a rescue plot, it is too late to put the book down unfinished. For aficionados of wartime novels, as well as for anyone glued to his or her seat watching the film *Argo*, this is a must read." —Helen Bryan, bestselling author of *War Brides* and *The Sisterhood*

"Kulin, a bestselling Turkish author, has penned this brilliant novel using the techniques of historical fiction. Her narrative with numerous characters and a number of subplots is handled deftly . . . The story is compelling up to the end and deserves a film adaptation. Highly recommended." —Historical Novel Society

"Truth is stranger than fiction, and I was on the edge of my seat from the very beginning." —Isabel Lachenauer, *The Cairene Diaries* blog

AYLIN

ALSO BY AYŞE KULIN

Last Train to Istanbul

Rose of Sarajevo

AYLIN

AYŞE KULIN

Translated by Dara Colakoglu

amazon crossing

Text copyright © 1997 Ayşe Kulin
Translation copyright © 2015 Dara Colakoglu

Previously published as *Adı: Aylin* by Everest Publishers in Turkey in 1997. Translated from Turkish by Dara Colakoglu.

Published by AmazonCrossing, Seattle

www.apub.com

Amazon, the Amazon logo, and AmazonCrossing are trademarks of Amazon.com, Inc., or its affiliates.

ISBN-13 (hardcover): 9781503948648
ISBN-10 (hardcover): 1503948641

ISBN-13 (paperback): 9781503948570
ISBN-10 (paperback): 1503948579

Cover design by David Drummond

Printed in the United States of America

For Aylin

She walks in beauty, like the night
Of cloudless climes and starry skies;
And all that's best of dark and bright
Meet in her aspect and her eyes.

Byron

FOREWORD

On Thursday, January 19, 1995, Aylin Devrimel Nadowlsky Goldberg was found dead by the cleaning lady, a car axle embedded in her chest. No concrete evidence suggested she had been attacked by an intruder. There were no signs of a struggle. Her hair was, as usual, immaculately coiffured. She lay flat on her back under her minivan, wearing a crisp, gray evening dress with a crescent-shaped diamond brooch on the collar and a diamond ring on her finger.

According to the autopsy report, Aylin had died two days earlier, on Tuesday night.

It was indeed a strange scenario. The police never identified a motive, and the unprecedented speed with which they closed the case raised many eyebrows. The official verdict was death by "freak accident."

Bedford, New York, was an upstanding community, full of wealthy and influential figures. The residents did not tolerate scandal or criminal activity.

No one could understand how a person lying diagonally under her car could accidentally die of an axle through the heart.

Aylin's family turned to private detectives to reopen the case. There were also rumors that the Turkish National Intelligence Service had started an investigation. However, no evidence could be unearthed. Some thought that Aylin may have been murdered by a clandestine organization. It was certainly a more likely explanation than "freak accident."

Only Porgy von Schweir saw what happened that fateful Tuesday evening. Only Porgy knew the whole truth. Unfortunately, Porgy von Schweir was a dog.

Aylin Devrimel Nadowlsky Goldberg lived a colorful and productive life, marked by achievement and fulfillment that few people experience. She was highly intelligent, multitalented, and very brave.

Nothing written can fully do justice to her character.

This book has been created with the help of those who loved her, so that her voice echoes through the world to which she was devoted. It is also a farewell to the many friends she left behind.

Had she lived, she would probably be the American ambassador to Turkey. Or perhaps she would be applying her innovative light therapy to the White House staff. There are numerous ways in which she could have succeeded, thanks to her incredible ability to learn and adapt, and to master any skill through diligence and altruism.

And had she lived, she would be soaring through life like the wind.

AYŞE KULIN

THE FUNERAL

There had been a downpour in the city that morning, but the dark clouds had turned into a penetrating cold, and the skyline leaned against a deep-violet horizon. At the intersection of Madison and Eighty-First, the windows of the Campbell Funeral Home were covered by a thin layer of frost. In spite of the freezing chill, the ceremony hall felt as if it had been heated by an invisible fire. An open mahogany coffin lay on the raised platform and a long line of people filed past, paying their last respects to the uniformed American officer before returning slowly to their seats. Everybody wept quietly, as was expected at a dignified military ceremony. Even the Turks, young and old, who traditionally found it hard to subdue their feelings, took care to rein in their emotions and abide by the solemnity of the occasion. Still, the tears came from deep within their hearts as they sat shoulder to shoulder, locked in their grief.

The woman who lay there among the flowers looked more like a Hollywood star than a soldier. She may have been in the uniform of a lieutenant colonel, but she was a Turk. There were red shimmers in her fashionably styled hair, and the contours of her face were flawless.

The subtle downward slant of her perfect lips seemed to be uttering, "There, you see. Once again I've done something you never expected." Her long, slim fingers were intertwined just below her bosom, so fragile, showing no sign of death. Death was too unbecoming for the woman who lay in this ornate coffin, decorated with garlands of colorful flowers. Even within its rigid walls, she had such a peaceful yet mischievous face. Death seemed so distant and alien that the scene taking place resembled a wedding more than a funeral. This ethereal figure looked as if she were waiting for a handsome prince to place a gentle kiss upon her lips and wake her—as if, any minute now, she would suddenly flutter open her eyes and start her incredible life anew. What a wind would blow then!

Breaking free from the suburbs and out to the shores of the Atlantic, reaching out to the Mediterranean like a mare's head and meandering in old central Europe, she would be a tempest, too strong to be crammed into a single country, too fast to spend a life with a single spouse or have a single profession. And yet that tempest could also be a calming and curing breeze, a tireless voyager that could not be held and could not rest.

Aylin!

Aylin Devrimel—a Turkish girl descended from a family deeply rooted in the Ottoman tradition—in the uniform of an American officer.

Turks filled the larger part of the hall—the childhood friends with whom she had shared school desks and whom she had never given up, her relatives, Turkish diplomats stationed in New York. They had all come to bid her farewell.

Aylin Devrimel Nadowlsky was one of the ten most renowned psychiatrists in New York. Many of her patients, their lives redeemed through her care, had come with their families to offer their final tributes.

A respected officer in the US Army, Aylin Devrimel Nadowlsky Goldberg was granted the rank of lieutenant colonel and awarded the Meritorious Service Medal within two years. Many of her fellow officers, of all different ranks, had come to pay their last respects to their extraordinary colleague.

Also present were her children—her dear niece Tayibe, and Mitch's sons, Tim and Greg—whom she had reared, educated, and influenced, whose problems she had shared. They were even closer to her than they were to their own mothers. They came to embrace her and bid her good-bye for the last time.

Her husbands, from her early years and her later years, her lovers, admirers, friends were all there, people acutely aware that they would never hear her vibrant voice again. They had been blessed by the joy of knowing her and now faced the sudden pain of losing her as she set off on her final journey.

She was the flippant girl who trapped herself in the golden cage of an Arabian prince many years ago, then managed to fly away from that same cage by her own will.

She was the hippie girl who hung around with the flower children in ratty jeans, got hooked on a physicist writing his dissertation, shouted, "Make love not war!" and tried to change her entire world.

She was the resolved and avid student who had chosen to study medicine at the relatively late age of twenty-six.

She was a successful doctor in that wild and splendid metropolis, New York, where competition ruled mercilessly but where incredible dreams were fulfilled.

She was the young woman who fell madly in love with the Afghan ambassador who was her father's age.

She was the dear wife of psychologist Mitch Nadowlsky, an immigrant from Istanbul.

Aylin. Aylin, whose soul could not be confined to cities and continents. Her great successes, deep solitude, and vast pain . . .

Her divorces, her yearnings, her new loves . . .
The army—
Samuel Goldberg, the last husband, the last grief . . .
The end!

After the viewing was over and everyone returned to their seats, they closed the mahogany cover of the coffin over Aylin's beautiful face.

A young woman at the piano softly played Verdi's *Requiem* as the speakers took to the podium one after the other.

The Turkish representative to the United Nations spoke first, and then Ahmet Ertegün stepped up. Leaning on his silver-headed cane, Ahmet Ertegün began his speech with a quotation from Byron.

"She walks in beauty, like the night
Of cloudless climes and starry skies;
And all that's best of dark and bright
Meet in her aspect and her eyes."

Byron had written this poem for Lady Wilmot, a woman he had fallen madly in love with. Aylin reflected everything beautiful in her eyes. She was now the owner of this poem.

Ertegün was followed by Talat Halman.

"In this ocean there is no death
No despair, no sadness, no anxiety
This ocean is boundless love
This is the ocean of beauty, of generosity."

Talat Halman recited these lines of Rumi's work, which he had translated into English himself. He told the listeners that this woman was molded of beauty, generosity, and love. She was to exist perpetually, like a drop in Rumi's ocean of eternal life. He spoke of Aylin's strange, catlike, hazel-green eyes. In one eye there was vigor and joy, he said, but there was always a slight shadow of grief in the other. "Una furtiva lagrima," he said. "A furtive tear drop." As he spoke, the melody of the famous aria "Una furtiva lagrima" from the opera *L'Elisir d'Amore* was heard from the piano. It was the opera Aylin had listened to in the last hours of her life.

It seemed as if an invisible hand blended the music, the poems, the tributes—though nothing had been planned. There was a balance and an order that inspired awe. Byron, Rumi, Donizetti, and Aylin had become one.

Tuesday, January 24, 1995: 12:50 p.m.

Two hours east of Manhattan, you will find Calverton National Cemetery, the burial ground for US Army officers.

There are crosses and crescents, Stars of David, and symbols of Far Eastern religions on the small gravestones that neatly line the emerald-green lawn that extends as far as the eye can see. Men and women of all beliefs, colors, and ranks lie here side by side as human beings who have come into and passed through this world. Their only commonality is their service in the US Army.

The funeral procession entered the cemetery at one o'clock sharp. A band led the soldiers as they slowly marched alongside the coffin, the congregation following closely behind.

At the entrance to the cemetery, an official stopped the cortege and asked Nilüfer which religious symbol should be inscribed on Aylin's tombstone. He held a booklet with nearly fifty options, and Nilüfer gazed in astonishment that so many religions, sects, and orders existed in the world.

She told him, "My sister stood above all religions. I do not want to reduce her to any one. It is better not to put a symbol."

But he was not to be deterred. "There must be some philosophy or system of thought she believed in. Please take a look and choose something. We must put a symbol at the head of the grave. There's even one for atheists."

"Aylin did believe in God. She was not an atheist."

The man was getting irritable. "Well, whatever she believed in, you need to choose one." Nilüfer called Tayibe to her side and they went through the symbols in the book. Tayibe spotted an emblem that resembled the wings of an eagle.

"Let's choose this one, mother," she said. "The bird's wings symbolize freedom. That is appropriate for my aunt."

Nilüfer said to the man, "We have chosen this." He looked at the symbol they were pointing at and ruffled the index pages of the book.

"This is the Sufi symbol. They did say that the lieutenant colonel used to be a Muslim."

"We have chosen the symbol with wings because it reflects my sister's personality."

Tayibe and Nilüfer strode over to the ceremony and stood at the front of the crowd that had gathered underneath a huge tent. The coffin was draped with the American flag as the band started to play the national anthem. The officers stood at attention and saluted. The civilians placed their right hands on their hearts. The Turks turned their palms to the sky and whispered prayers. Finally, "Taps" sounded from the bugle, echoing a heartbreaking, bitter lament against this heavenly judgment before fading away into silence.

With mechanical movements, two soldiers in uniform folded the flag on the coffin into a triangle, before presenting it to Nilüfer. Nilüfer pressed the folded flag close to her breast as if she were embracing her sister.

When the ceremony ended, the soldiers pivoted sharply on their heels, turned, and marched away in a row. The crowd started to disperse silently. Nilüfer stood motionless, arm in arm with her daughter.

Sam said, "We have to leave, Nilüfer."

"Aylin is not buried yet."

An officer approached. "The ceremony is over, ma'am. The burial will take place after you leave."

"I want to see my sister buried."

"That's against regulation here."

"I will stay until my sister is buried. I am not going anywhere."

"That's not possible, ma'am." The man smiled gently, loosely taking hold of Nilüfer's arm and directing her toward the car.

Sam, who had gone ahead, ran back when he heard Nilüfer's scream. Those by the gate turned. Nilüfer struggled desperately against the officer, whom Sam led a few steps away, where they spoke in hushed tones.

When they came back, the officer was grumbling.

The mourners, soiled with mud, returned to Aylin's grave. The rain had eased a little and the iron case started to descend into the pit. Nilüfer abruptly took a handful of earth and threw it on the coffin. This was a silent order. The Turks, Americans, Muslims, Jews, Christians, men and women, young and old all followed suit and kneeled, gathering the soil in their hands and tossing it onto the coffin. Earth, flowers, and leaves softly fell over Aylin's coffin.

It had finally stopped raining.

Tayibe and Nilüfer came to the gate of the cemetery. Nilüfer was utterly dejected. She had used her last ounce of strength to see Aylin buried and she was exhausted.

Suddenly, her daughter cried, "Look, Mother, look!" Nilüfer lifted her red, dried-out eyes. A river of light streamed out from behind the dark clouds. She turned back to Aylin's grave, where Tayibe was pointing. The sun—glimpsed for the first time since Thursday—was beaming directly onto the Sufi wings on Aylin's tombstone. The intensity of the light cut through the cold air like a sharp knife, bathing Nilüfer and Tayibe in a golden shaft.

Nilüfer blinked. Oh, this was a soft, peaceful light at last.

Mustafa Pasha of Crete

THE ANCESTORS

The years of political tumult that marked the decline of the Ottoman era still echoed throughout the empire. It was harder than ever to be a statesman, as the Christian community, triggered by France and Russia, started to revolt, and Greece lay in wait like a hungry wolf. The pervasive instability impacted even the highest official posts; Sultan Abdülmecid replaced his grand vizier twenty-two times during his twenty-year reign.

Born in 1798 in the town of Polyan in Thrace, Mustafa Pasha is remembered in history by the name Giritli, meaning "of Crete." He was just as renowned as the governor of Crete and had been subject to the mercurial Sultan Abdülmecid's constant dismissals. He was appointed and dismissed as grand vizier three times, but considered himself lucky compared to his predecessor, who had held the post and been dismissed from it six times.

Renowned for his bravery, Mustafa Pasha became famous during the Egyptian Campaign in 1821. He was still a very young soldier then, but was appointed military chief as a result of his heroic deeds. Indeed, he would display a remarkable talent for mastering difficult battles throughout his entire life.

One of God's luckiest creatures, he was educated in Egypt under the guidance of his maternal uncles. He studied hard, learned French and Arabic, and was rewarded with high-ranking posts in their entourage. Upon his uncle's death, he inherited a salary of 450 purses a year. The incredible courage he displayed suppressing the revolts in Egypt was also generously rewarded by an appointment as a guard to the governorship of Crete.

But a peaceful administrative post could not compare to the harsh military rule of the battlefields. Mustafa, used to the demands of war, soon tired of the placid life in Crete and volunteered to help suppress the revolt in Lebanon. Upon his return, he was rewarded the title of "governor of Crete for life" at the young age of thirty-two. From there, the road to Sultan Abdülmecid's court was paved for the unyielding pasha, and he was named grand vizier.

As grand vizier, he soon discovered that the principles he lived by on the battlefield could get him into trouble in court. As military chief, he had not needed diplomacy. But a statesman was expected to lead with precision, foresight, and sensitivity; Mustafa's rough and direct manner began to upset people. Soon, his title was enriched by a second: "Crazy."

Crazy Mustafa Pasha of Crete was appointed to his final office in 1866, his reputation restored once again by outstanding military achievements. He had hoped to settle the Cretan revolt but was summoned back to Istanbul before he could broker peace. He died with a broken heart, never witnessing the tolerant society he was determined to help foster.

But Mustafa would have gone to rest with immense peace in his heart had he known that his descendant would reprise his volatility, boundless courage, defiant spirit, and sharp intellect, that a little girl four generations later would bring his people great happiness.

HILMI PASHA

Mustafa Pasha of Crete was rumored to have had forty concubines, seventy thousand gold coins, ninety-nine farms, and two hundred houses. He also had eleven sons. Hilmi and Veli were the most handsome and cleverest among them. Appointed ambassador to Paris at the age of twenty-two, Veli Pasha preferred to make use of his inherited courage to engage in debauchery rather than battle. He flirted with Napoleon's wife, Eugenie, audacious enough to give her a ring with a *V* made of diamonds to wear alongside the ring the emperor had engraved with an *N*. As opposed to Veli—or, as the Parisian ladies called him, "Le Beau Veli"—his brother Hilmi spent most of his life observing his father's tumultuous career in Istanbul.

He had no interest in flirting with the Parisian aristocracy. He lived just as fully in Istanbul, where he had seen the ins and outs of a cosmopolitan lifestyle and known prosperity when his father was grand vizier. He was erudite and cultured, speaking various languages and studying French art. As the son of a nobleman, he was used to lavish extravagance. He did not need Paris. Besides, Hilmi Pasha had made a very fitting choice for the son of a grand vizier by marrying the daughter of the minister of protocol. She was a prize—noble and well schooled in all the ways of the court—and Hilmi insisted on treating her as such. He commissioned the architect Garnier, the man behind the Opéra de Paris, to design their home on the shores of the Bosphorus. Hilmi called for nothing less than a mansion, big enough to accommodate his extensive family and, naturally, a splendid banquet hall.

Years later, one of Hilmi Pasha's daughters, Melek, met her young neighbor Hasip at the age of seven, as they played hide-and-seek in the grove. Children, of course, are notorious gossips, and the rumors that Melek would marry Hasip when they grew up reached the ears of her mother, who kept the news a secret from her husband. Hilmi had inherited his fair share of his father's fierce nature, and his wife did not want to be on bad terms with the Bayndrl family, as it was said they were descended from the Prophet. Moreover, little Hasip's uncle lived in Paris, and the family planned to send Hasip to his uncle within a year to be educated like a westerner. Mrs. Hilmi did her best not to block the path of a perfect prospective son-in-law, but the wings of fate would not grant her wish for a long time.

Hasip took his time returning to Istanbul. Life in Paris was so exciting that he arranged for a clerkship in the Turkish embassy, where his uncle had served as ambassador. Hasip grew to be tall and handsome with deep-green eyes and a wrestler's physique. He also fit in well with the aristocrats thanks to his family's influence. He fenced with the founder of the Olympic Games, Baron de Coubertin, took long walks with his dog at the Bois de Boulogne, and made appearances at all of the elite parties. The French knew him as "the handsome man with the handsome dog," and the Turks called him "the young, vigorous, and crazy Hasip." He had left Melek, the lovely grandchild of another crazy man, far behind and forgotten her.

. . .

In the meantime, Melek blossomed into a coquettish and attractive young girl, though she was quite petite. She was fluent in French, English, and Greek and was an accomplished pianist. She was descended from aristocratic lineages on both her mother's and father's sides. The matchmakers worked tirelessly to find her a far more eligible suitor than the youth next door—now a distant figure in Paris. That suitor was the Nizam of Hyderabad, who sent his prospective bride a box full of jewelry instead of the customary sweets.

Mrs. Hilmi was wild with joy. The richest man in the world was pursuing the daughter she had always found a little small and frail. But although Melek was born under a rising star, a secret power seemed to pull that star down. Tragically, the Nizam of Hyderabad drowned in a shipwreck on his way home from England before ever laying eyes on his fiancée.

At once, the matchmakers went back to the drawing board; this time landing on a candidate who could not be disregarded, despite the fact he was not as wealthy as the Nizam—Prince Mehmet Ali of the Egyptian dynasty.

Melek was not given the chance to weigh in. In those days, if a suitable husband emerged, the girl's opinion was not considered, even in the most modern of families. When her dowry was complete, Melek and her family gathered on an autumn day at the Tophane wharf, where they saw her off to Egypt. On board, Melek leaned against the rail and waved her handkerchief to her mother and father until they were no longer in sight.

Three years later, the same crowd gathered to welcome Melek on her return home. The potbellied Egyptian prince had turned out to be impotent.

That summer, a love story shaded by memories was rejuvenated in the groves of Emirgan.

Hasip returned to his country because he had run out of money and grown tired of the hectic pace of life in Paris. He was twenty-eight with shiny red hair—a very handsome bachelor. One day, he was wandering the grounds when he came across his childhood love in her garden. Twenty years later, she was still pure and untouched, despite all the storms she had lived through. Melek's mischievous glance and cherry lips had not changed, but her face seemed shadowed by a mysterious sadness. It was as if God had saved this girl for him, keeping her protected until he was ready.

Melek and Hasip were engaged soon after. Hilmi Pasha gave his consent only after he learned that the young man was an excellent hunter. Shortly after the wedding, Melek's mother died suddenly of a heart attack, as if she had only been waiting to secure her daughter's happiness. She bid farewell to this life at a party she threw at the Grand Hotel in Vienna, her lifeless body supported by her dancing partner as the Viennese Waltz played on.

The Bayndrl Sisters

Once married, Hasip made use of his education by founding the School of Agriculture in Istanbul, where he lectured for years. From there, he was appointed advisor to the General Administration of Agriculture in Istanbul.

Melek and Hasip lived happily in their spacious home on the Sea of Marmara until the First World War. They were blessed with five children, three daughters—Esma, Leyla, and Ecla; and two sons—Esat and Hilmi. The war stripped them of the prosperity that had ruled in their grandfathers' days, bringing misery and famine to everything it touched. Although the Bayndrl family did not suffer from starvation, Hasip had to sell some of his property to allow his family to continue living in the manner they were accustomed to. Indeed, the youngest of the family, Hilmi, was born in a villa far simpler than the mansion on the bay where his older siblings were born.

The Bayndrl house was a study in contradictions. Hasip reared his children with the ironclad discipline of a typical Turkish patriarch, but he also encouraged them to develop a European mindset. He was proud of his Parisian upbringing and thorough education in European culture, and he was keenly involved in overseeing a similar education for his children. He focused particularly on their knowledge of foreign languages and did not discriminate between the girls and the boys. All of the Bayndrl children spoke Greek, French, and English in addition to their native tongue. Hasip favored Greek because his paternal grandmother was the daughter of a priest from the island of Chios. There were always at least a few Greek servants at home, as well as a Greek nanny. The children also had a governess who taught them French.

Despite the turmoil of raising five children, Melek and Hasip's household never lacked parties filled with music and dancing. The guests ranged from former pashas, ministers, and ambassadors, to members of the diplomatic corps and contemporary artists. But when the visitors took their leave, Hasip transformed into a tyrant. The family had to take its place at the dinner table at seven o'clock every day. If there was even a five-minute delay, Hasip's silver-handled cane began to dance, usually across the back of his older son, Esat. His daughters also got their share if he was really furious.

When Hilmi came down with pneumonia, Hasip, who was very fond of the boy, had Hilmi's bed brought to the living room so he would not get bored. That same day, Esma invited a young French naval officer, the grandson of the Duke of Rochefoucauld, who was visiting Istanbul, for tea. When Hasip returned home and saw that a guest had been ushered to the room where his sick son lay in bed, he got so angry that his cane fell on the young girl's face like a thunderbolt. Still, in some ways he was tame, never meddling with his children's fashion choices or their friendships with the opposite sex.

As teenagers, Esma, Leyla, and Ecla pranced from one party to the next with the English and French officers who were abundant in Istanbul. But their revealing outfits and modern lifestyle led to gossip among the old families of Istanbul. While most other daughters found suitable husbands at a young age, the Bayndrl girls had to wait until their late twenties.

When Hasip's sons were of age, they followed in the family tradition and went to France to continue their education. But thanks to the defeat of the Ottoman Empire in the First World War, Hasip's financial situation was worse than ever. They had sold the villa and moved to a flat in the city with only a distant view of the Bosphorus. Hasip continued to lecture at the School of Agriculture, trying hard to feed his extensive family while still giving his sons the best opportunities. By now, the girls had left behind the exuberant lifestyle of their youth, and Melek had come to terms with the sad fact that her daughters were still unmarried and would soon be considered old maids.

But then something unbelievable happened: the Republic of Turkey was founded, and many of the empire's oldest traditions fell out of favor along with the dynasty. Ankara became the capital, and a new era blossomed in which well-educated youths with a mastery of foreign languages were suddenly in demand for the recently established state offices. The government built new schools and recruited young engineers to Anatolia to construct bridges and dams. New railways spanned the country from west to east, north to south.

As for Hasip, he was invited to the inauguration of the School of Agriculture in Adana and stayed to deliver a number of lectures. The Adana elite organized dinners, teas, and card games to keep their visitors from Istanbul entertained. At one of these parties, Hasip played a game of bridge with a young lawyer who had just opened up an office. His name was Zihni. When Hasip realized that his companion came from a respected family and spoke fluent French, he thought of his daughters, still waiting for good suitors in Istanbul. He asked Zihni why he remained a bachelor.

Zihni had not been able to find the girl of his dreams, someone modern and cultivated who spoke foreign languages, at least in Adana. When Hasip told him about his own daughter, Esma, Zihni could not believe his ears. Would this noble gentleman introduce his daughter to a young lawyer such as himself? Indeed Hasip would.

When Hasip returned to Istanbul, an air of excitement filled the Bayndrl house. The blue-eyed and handsome lawyer was to visit Esma in ten short days. Esma had flirted with many young men from various nations and carried on daring relationships for her day. She was a bright girl, extremely active and talkative. Yet she could not help but be carried away by the idea of this new potential suitor. According to her mother, this was her last chance. Melek had the walls painted and the curtains sent to the dry cleaner, Esma began a strict diet, and her younger sisters, who were far more beautiful, were sent away on the day Zihni was due to arrive.

When Zihni saw Esma, he was instantly sure that she had been created just for him. God had given him three times what he had wished, for Esma was fluent in French, Greek, and English; well versed in music, painting, and art; and always had a quick retort. She epitomized the new Turkish values with her modern mannerisms, a jewel for a man wishing to make the most out of his career.

Indeed, a few years after they married, Esma attracted the attention of the first president of Turkey, Atatürk, at a party. He convinced her to join the national assembly, and she became one of the first female deputies, not only in Turkey but in the entire world. She represented Turkey at many international conferences throughout her life. Her husband, Zihni, went on to become the notary of Ulus, the most respected neighborhood in Ankara at the time.

Just as Esma was married off, Hasip's older son, Esat, began to make a living, alleviating Hasip's finances a bit. Now, his most beautiful daughter, Leyla, was to have her turn. She was his favorite, resembling her father most in both looks and character. She was tall and robust, had the same reddish-blond hair and green eyes, and a personality just as difficult to handle as her father's. She had adapted to their financial struggle with the greatest poise of anyone in the family, wearing old dresses without complaint.

A cousin lined up many of her husband's friends for Leyla and the youngest daughter, Ecla, but neither sister would settle, and the young suitors did not particularly want to marry the snobby girls, who were approaching thirty. That is, until Cemal Bey entered the scene.

Cemal worked at the State Railways in Ankara and met Leyla over dinner at her cousin's house. He was one of the most attractive men she had ever met, tall with green eyes. They could have almost been siblings. They made up their minds almost immediately that night, and Leyla accepted his proposal without hesitating.

Cemal came from Ibrad, a village nestled in the peaks of the Taurus Mountains just off the Mediterranean. The inhabitants of Ibrad descended from strange stock. According to legend, a polytheistic Roman tribe that settled there accepted the Islamic faith before switching to Christianity. They decorated their houses in the Italian style, and their dialect included many Italian words. They preferred not to trade abroad or marry their daughters outside the tribe. One proverb stated, "Why should a stranger take our best and see our worst?" Cemal was one of the first of his generation to venture outside his insular community and marry a girl not from Ibrad.

And so a second engagement was celebrated in the Bayndrl house. Soon after, Cemal left his fiancée in Istanbul and returned to Ankara to look for a house. They would begin preparing for a wedding once he found a suitable place. But an appropriate home could not be found, despite Cemal's good salary. Instead, he spent the whole of his income on leisurely pursuits and was seen flirting with the young daughter of a colleague. Still, he had no intention of giving up the charming Leyla, whose attentions he positively relished.

Month after month, Leyla waited proudly as Cemal offered excuses, claiming there was too much construction in the city. And though Cemal would visit his fiancée, marriage was never mentioned. Three years went by like this. Cemal received two promotions, many buildings were completed, and finally Leyla heard of her fiancé's debauched reputation in Ankara.

Back in Istanbul, Leyla's cousin nagged her husband about setting her cousin up with a man like Cemal until he organized another dinner to introduce a friend who was intent on finding a wife. Leyla and Ecla were among the guests to welcome him that evening.

Nusret Kulin was the son of the Kulinoviç family, who had immigrated from Bosnia to Istanbul during the Austro-Hungarian tumult. He had just returned home from studying mechanical engineering in Germany. Leyla observed the spectacled young man's buoyant nature with a careful eye, noting his frequent bursts of laughter and storytelling skills throughout the evening. They even chatted and danced for a while. Leyla grew fond of the young man, thinking him smart and optimistic. But unfortunately, Nusret Kulin's heart settled instead on her dark-haired sister. Soon, the Kulin family visited the Bayndrls to ask them for Ecla's hand.

And so the youngest, most coquettish daughter became engaged to the dashing young engineer. Melek was elated to learn they would be married within a few months, although the situation looked rather strange. Leyla was the older sister and had been engaged for three years, yet Ecla would marry before her. Hasip felt very sad for his favorite daughter, now in a bind, but Leyla would not allow her father to have a frank discussion with her fiancé. In the end, she was the one who came up with a solution. She convinced her father to let her take a day trip to Ankara. Both saw fit to keep it a secret from the rest of the family.

Cemal was startled when his fiancée appeared at his door early one morning. Leyla began talking before he had a chance to speak. She had been waiting for three full years, she said. Maybe Cemal had changed his mind about this marriage, but she needed to preserve the honor of her family. Everyone in Istanbul was gossiping about the never-ending engagement. Her mother was extremely upset, and her father had lost his confidence. To resolve the issue, they needed to get married immediately and divorce two months later.

Cemal was astounded to hear this offer, but Leyla insisted she was very serious. She felt compelled to save her father's hurt pride and was ready to give Cemal any guarantee he needed that the divorce would come through, as long as they were married before Ecla's wedding. Cemal listened to Leyla in disbelief. What a tough person this serene girl had turned out to be. He felt suddenly guilty for disregarding her feelings and her family's honor for such a long time. He agreed that Leyla could set any wedding day her heart chose.

Leyla's trip ended in victory, and she triumphantly shared the good news with her father when he picked her up at the station. Two Bayndrl daughters would be married, only ten days apart. Their parents were thrilled, but the relationship between the two sisters became tenser than ever as they immersed themselves in the urgent business of securing dowries.

Leyla had hoped for a modest wedding with only family members present, but Hasip Bey rejected the idea of a small ceremony and planned for the event to take place at the Acacia Hotel, where her sister would also be married. The newlyweds would honeymoon for ten days at the hotel, participate in Ecla's wedding, and then leave for Ankara. However, on the day of her sister's wedding, Leyla was still distressed by her forced marriage and secretly envied Ecla for finding a man who actually wanted her. Leyla told her husband she was ill, and because Cemal refused to leave his young wife alone with a fever, he did not go to Ecla's wedding, either.

Leyla and Cemal left for Ankara the next day. The new bride and groom settled into lodgings provided for them by the State Railways, a cute little house with a garden right behind the station. Cemal had kept his promise and married Leyla, so he returned to his former lifestyle with a clear conscience. Though he no longer flirted with the French engineer's daughter, he left Leyla alone every night to join a game of poker with his friends. At home, Leyla turned on all the lights in the house and the garden and read for hours. When she heard her husband's footsteps, she ran to her bed and pretended to be asleep. Husband and wife lived under the same roof without any quarrels for two months. For Leyla, there were no grounds for any discussion. She had made an agreement and was simply waiting for its expiration date.

Two months later, when Cemal returned home, he saw three suitcases by the door and assumed that someone had arrived from Istanbul to visit his wife. But the luggage belonged to Leyla. The young woman quietly told her husband that their two months were up, and she had reserved a ticket on the train to Istanbul the following day. She would summon her lawyer to draw up the divorce papers as soon as she arrived.

Cemal Bey could not believe his ears. He had not thought for a single second that Leyla's bargain was in earnest. But here she was, without any sign of anger or regret. He tried to object but was once again taken aback by her determination. She thanked him for sticking to his promise and declared that it was time for her to follow through with her end of their agreement. Cemal was so disturbed that he couldn't sleep the whole night through. He knew he had failed to appreciate his good-natured, proud, intelligent, and beautiful wife. He begged her to give him another chance, another two months to prove he was worthy of her love. At last, Leyla consented to a trial period of one additional month. But the conditions of the contract would be different this time around. Cemal Bey was to come home every night like all the other husbands, dine with his wife, and go out with her, not other people. In short, they were to live like a normal married couple. Should Cemal find himself getting bored with this lifestyle, then he was to share his feelings frankly. Cemal accepted, finally realizing the good fortune that had almost slipped through his fingers.

In the end, the husband and wife lived together not for one month, but for a lifetime. In fact, Leyla would have a far more harmonious marriage than either of her sisters, despite its inauspicious beginning.

Leyla and Cemal's first child, Nilüfer, was born after a very difficult delivery when Ecla's daughter was six months old and Esma and Esat's children were both three. With so many grandchildren, the Bayndrl family had finally found happiness and peace.

No one could have predicted the dark clouds of disaster that would gather just a year later, when the very healthy Hasip, an avid hunter who had not even swallowed an aspirin until his sixty-sixth year, fell ill and needed an operation. Unfortunately, during the procedure, the surgeon made a rare error and pierced Hasip's bladder. Hasip—who hated hospitals—had to tolerate all the indignities that recovery entailed. The wound had to be dressed continuously, and he was told it would take six months for the scars to heal. In despair, Hasip chased the nurses and doctors out of his room with his silver-headed cane, cursing them all. In the end, they brought him home to wait patiently for those six months to pass by.

Several weeks later at their home, Melek was playing French songs on the phonograph at top volume for her husband to enjoy. When she called for him and heard no response, she grew uneasy. Entering their bedroom, she found him sitting upright in his armchair with a bullet hole in the right side of his forehead. His pistol had slipped from his hand and fallen to the floor, a thin red stream flowing from his brow. Trembling, she reached for the piece of paper on his knees. It read:

> *I don't have the patience to bear this misery for six more months. I am taking my own life.*

Aylin

When Aylin was born in August 1938, she already embodied many of the traits of her forefathers. Although the pain inflicted by her grandfather's suicide had started to subside, his story was still told often.

The little girl grew up hearing about her very proud, very peevish, unbending grandfather yet never knew that her love of weapons and her daring courage later on in life were most likely thanks to the genes she inherited from him and from her great-great-grandfather Mustafa Pasha. Indeed, she was to have the kind of fearlessness that surpassed all common boundaries.

When Aylin was born, her older sister Nilüfer was seven. The year 1938 was full of new experiences for Nilüfer. She had moved from a house with a garden to an apartment, started school, and her mother was expecting another baby.

One day, Nilüfer was sent to a friend's house for the night. When she came home the next morning, she found her mother lying in bed with a baby girl who was even smaller than Nilüfer's dolls. The baby stretched her tiny hands out from her bundle, eyes like two thin lines. She had absolutely no hair and a wrinkly face.

Her mother said, "Look, Nilüfer, I made this little girl for you. She is all yours." From that moment on, Nilüfer considered herself Aylin's protector and would intervene in her sister's life without moderation. But Aylin never took offense and loved Nilüfer all her life.

The apartment the family moved to just before Aylin's birth was in the most modern building in Ankara at the time. It had four separate entrances facing the tall clock right in the middle of Kizilay Square, the nicest area in the city. The majority of the tenants were well-off bureaucrats who socialized most evenings. Soon, these adult friendships trickled down to their children, who formed long-lasting bonds.

When Aylin began first grade, Nilüfer finished middle school and was sent to Istanbul to study at the French high school. In her absence, Aylin became closer than ever to her best friend, Betin. They also played with Ayşe, the daughter of a young engineer whose elder brother was Auntie Ecla's husband.

Nilüfer missed out on those days. She was a big girl attending high school in the big city, and it was apparent that she was becoming a young woman of incredible beauty. When she visited Ankara for the holidays, everyone on her street gathered at the windows to witness her loveliness. Besides her staggering looks, she also possessed great intellect and was deeply interested in metaphysics.

Leyla was uneasy about her older daughter's dream to study at the university. She thought a girl should get married and have children once she finished high school. The good suitors that lined up at the door in a young woman's youth could very well disappear by the time she graduated.

Just as Aylin's parents enrolled her at the American school in Istanbul, Nilüfer finished high school and returned to Ankara for the summer. It would be many years before the sisters crossed paths again.

Nilüfer began to experience the exhilaration of being a pretty young girl in Ankara. As Leyla watched her daughter turn into an exceedingly beautiful woman, she became alarmed that Nilüfer might get carried away with the wrong man and tie herself to a bad marriage at a very young age. Nilüfer was well aware of her beauty and the privilege it afforded her. In fact, it appeared that she had a monopoly on Bayndrl beauty. Aylin looked like a beanstalk, and her other cousins were either too dark or too short.

In spite of Leyla's warnings, Nilüfer began to flirt with Aziz, the son of a rich businessman. Aziz fell in love with Nilüfer at first sight. When Leyla realized that she could not stop the youngsters from seeing each other, she begged them to get engaged, but Aziz's father vehemently rejected this idea. His son was still a student. Aziz stood his ground, professing his undying love for Nilüfer until his father agreed to give his consent once Aziz finished his studies in Scotland and took over the family business. In the meantime, Nilüfer continued her friendship with Aziz in spite of both families' objections. After three years of studying economics in Scotland, Aziz was called to military service for two years, postponing the young lovers' marriage even further.

Just before Aziz started his service in September, the lovers went to the registry office and got married without informing their families. Nilüfer had left home with her swimsuit dangling from her hand, and when she came back three hours later, the wet swimsuit was wrapped in a towel.

"Where did you swim today?" asked her mother.

"At Tarabya Beach."

"As if there's no sea right in front of your house."

"I was meeting friends."

"Was it crowded as usual?"

"No. Very few people. It was so romantic." They sat face to face on the terrace, in the big armchairs that looked out to sea. Leyla lit a cigarette. Nilüfer reached for the pack, pulled out a cigarette, placed it between her lips, and lit it.

Her mother said, "You should wait till you become Mrs. Tansever before you smoke a cigarette right in front of my eyes, young lady."

"Pardon? Didn't hear you."

"Oh, yes you did, Nilüfer. Young girls don't smoke. You must wait until you can call yourself Mrs. Tansever."

Nilüfer exhaled. "Very well, then I can smoke my cigarette."

Now it was Leyla's turn to be astonished. "What do you mean?"

"I am Mrs. Tansever, Mother, as of three o'clock this afternoon."

Leyla could not decide whether she should feel angry or happy about the news. Her new son-in-law was the only son of a very wealthy man. Furthermore, he was getting a very good education and was sure to have a secure future. She did not object to Aziz; she was simply against her daughter's dating someone without getting engaged. Now her daughter just stood there, married. In her heart, she felt relieved.

After his military service was over, Aziz returned to London to finish his studies, his young wife at his side.

THE RECKLESS
YEARS OF YOUTH

As Nilüfer enjoyed London as a newlywed, Aylin continued her studies at the American School for Girls. She never studied hard yet always managed to pass her classes with the highest grades. As boarding students, Aylin and her classmates enjoyed wonderful freedom after daily lessons were over. They often went to the Plateau if the weather was nice, a three-acre field with a view of the Bosphorus flowing at its feet. When the linden trees flowered in spring, it became a kind of heaven on earth. The girls went for long walks, lay on the grass and chatted, or studied in the shade under the trees. If the weather was poor, they would study in the study halls, spacious rooms with huge tables for eight where girls could work on their homework. There was a desk in each room where a young teacher would sit, ready to maintain order. On the first evening of her third year, Aylin sat in the study hall with fifty other students. Young Miss Dean, an American teacher who was new to the school, was there to stand guard.

Miss Dean appeared at precisely nine o'clock and took her seat at the desk. All the girls rose with military discipline.

Miss Dean said, "Sit down, ladies." But the girls continued to stand and started to sing the national anthem. Miss Dean stood up and put her right hand on her heart as a gesture of respect. When the song was finished, Miss Dean sat down. Yet the girls started to sing the school march. Miss Dean rose again. The school march was followed by another march. Then came "Yankee Doodle" and "Humpty Dumpty." Finally, Miss Dean realized how ridiculous their behavior was. So she started to yell at the top of her voice but could not make herself heard over the din. As the girls' concert moved on to the "When the Saints Go Marching In," Miss Dean slammed the door and left.

When the headmistress arrived, all the girls were immersed in their books. She screamed, "What a disgrace! Who will explain what's going on in here?" The girls sat motionless in their chairs, silent. "Who planned this?" asked Miss Ashover. "If you don't answer me, you will all sit here till three o'clock on Saturday."

A tall, reedy, and freckled child rose to her feet.

"We wanted to give Miss Dean a welcome party. We thought she would appreciate it."

"Devrimel, of course. Always the ringleader."

"We just wanted to make her happy."

Miss Ashover threw up her hands and left the classroom. There was nothing she could do. The moral policy of the school emphasized telling the truth. She was surely not going to punish the only student who had the guts to do so. But Aylin was not quite finished.

Weekend dinners were ceremonious affairs at the school, and the girls were encouraged to dress up. Waiters laid out white tablecloths and dishes much tastier than any of the students had at home. After the day students left the school grounds on Friday, the boarders enjoyed special menus. Aylin belonged to this second group because her family lived in Ankara. She loved the roasted meat with gravy on Saturday nights and

Sunday breakfasts of kedgeree and eggs or strawberries with whipped cream, depending on the season. She dreamed of poaching the school cook as her own personal chef, if only she could one day catch a rich husband like her sister. But her chances were pretty low considering she was not half as beautiful as Nilüfer.

In her second year at the school, Aylin had found herself in the midst of an identity crisis. All of a sudden there appeared another tall, skinny, freckled, ponytailed girl named Aylin.

"People keep confusing us. We must each choose a nickname," said Aylin to the intruder.

"You are my carbon copy, so that should be your nickname," said the other Aylin.

"You are *my* carbon copy; I was here first," said Aylin.

"But I am much darker than you are."

"So?"

"Carbon copies are always paler than the original."

Aylin was speechless for the first time in her life, and the namesakes became good friends from that moment on.

While tucked up in their dormitory beds at night, the girls whispered to each other about their dreams for the future. Some wished only for a happy marriage and plenty of kids, some wanted to be rich and live in a large mansion by the sea, some sought fame and others success. At her turn, Aylin said, "When I grow up, I would like to have butlers with white gloves to serve at my table." There was a loud roar of laughter.

When someone asked her why, Aylin answered, "Because having a white-gloved waiter serve you at the table is a sign of wealth and good manners. It indicates that you know how to live well."

One of the girls said, "You have to catch a really loaded guy for that sort of thing."

"A freckled girl who looks like a beanstalk! What rich guy would ever marry you?" asked another heartless youngster.

Aylin's heart was heavy, but she whispered in a low voice, "I'll earn my own money to hire my servants."

As the years passed, Aylin started to blossom. She transformed from a beanstalk into a very attractive young girl who made heads turn when she strolled down the street. And in her senior year, she finally had an admirer, the first romance of her life. Her mother wrote to Nilüfer in London to share the news.

Leyla was a clever woman. She had not forgotten the tension she caused by getting between Nilüfer and Aziz, and she and was not willing to take the same path with her younger daughter. As a result, Aylin enjoyed the freedom and pleasure of flirting. After the first admirer, she made friends with another student who had white-blond hair and light-blue eyes. Together, they could have passed for a Swedish couple.

When Aylin graduated, her photograph in the yearbook appeared next to the following write-up:

Hobbies: Dark glasses and driving.

Likes: British cars, journeys to Ankara.

Dislikes: Being called "sophisticated." Blond men.

Future plans: Too many to be included in a page.

Philosophy of life: Veni, vidi, vici.

A possible interpretation—she was impressed by the lifestyle her sister had in London. In spite of Aylin's exuberant life in Istanbul, she missed her family in Ankara. She was loath to be sophisticated even in those early years, and her relationship with the blond boy was over. She was ready to conquer her lively, colorful, and multifaceted future.

From Elysium to Adversity

Aylin spent the summer of 1958 in her uncle Hilmi's new villa on the Sea of Marmara. Hilmi had bought the large piece of land surrounded by pine and fruit trees, and commissioned a mission-style house inspired by visits to California.

Because Uncle Hilmi was childless, he treated Aylin as though she were his own daughter. Though he was willing to pay for Aylin's university tuition, Leyla still wanted her to get married and have children. Aylin did not agree with either of them. She did not want to fall back to the books from which she had just broken free or tie herself down in marriage. She was swayed by the dolce vita; she went to parties in low-cut dresses with puffy skirts, high heels, and dangling earrings. When summer ended, she decided to go stay with her sister in London.

Nilüfer and Aziz ran with a highly intellectual milieu. Nilüfer tried to convince Aylin to study in London, but the English universities would not accept her diploma from the American School for Girls.

Aylin started to think harder about how she would spend the coming year. She came across an advertisement in a fashion magazine and was at the door of Lucie Clayton's Modeling Agency on Bond Street the very next day. It was not difficult for her to attract the agency's attention, since her height, measurements, and red hair made her an ideal candidate. Her mother objected, but Hilmi came to her rescue and paid the tuition for modeling classes so Aylin could begin this new phase of her life.

In just three months, Aylin went through an amazing transformation. Her long, sleek hair was cut short and dyed blond; she learned to swivel like a mannequin, shadow her cheek bones, and emphasize her eyes with expertly applied makeup. If her family had approved, she would have been one of the most sought-after models in London. But her mother insisted that Aylin marry rather than accept a job that would ruin her name in Turkey. Nilüfer agreed with her mother, so Aziz started to invite Turkish university students with promising futures over for drinks at their home. Yet no eligible suitor emerged. Aylin still had bigger dreams.

As spring bloomed in 1959, Aylin visited her uncle Hilmi, who had just moved to Geneva and wanted his beloved niece to enroll in university courses. He even bought her a little sports car to persuade her. Such a bright person should not waste her talents at absurd places like modeling school, he said. Aylin did not think she had wasted her time at Lucie Clayton's. In fact, she had learned many useful skills. Her mysterious air and her makeup techniques would prove to be very fruitful.

Aylin conceded, and, as promised, her uncle paid for her tuition at the Sorbonne. She was to stay in Geneva and improve her French until the semester began, then settle in Paris to start her education. Hilmi wanted his niece to study economics and take over his business. He was a wealthy businessman, a major importer with a number of offices around the world. Ecla's son had already said no, and Esma's son had gone to America. Only Aylin was left to fulfill his wish.

Unfortunately, Aylin did not stay in Geneva until September. In July, Nilüfer and Aylin learned that a tumor had been discovered in their mother's breast, and that she needed an operation immediately. They flew to Istanbul, where Leyla had been diagnosed with cancer. Her husband was inconsolable and her daughters refused to believe their ears. The pillar of their family—their talented, forceful, and beautiful mother—had fallen prey to a nearly incurable disease. They were devastated for their mother, but they worried just as much about their father, who was utterly shaken by the fear of losing his beloved wife.

As always, Leyla tried to pull her family together with her boundless strength. She was going to recover. She knew a lot of people who had beaten cancer. She still had so much to do; she had yet to marry off her younger daughter and she still had no grandchildren. She did not have the slightest interest in releasing her hold on life.

After the operation, Leyla recovered at the hospital for two weeks and then went home. Aylin did not want to leave her recuperating mother and return to Geneva, but Leyla was vehement that her health not interfere with her daughters' lives. In the end, Hilmi persuaded his sister to continue her recovery in Switzerland. Aylin and her mother returned to Geneva together. Hilmi was hopeful the Swiss doctors could help, but unfortunately they could do no more than their Turkish colleagues. It was too late, they said. All they could do was try to keep the patient comfortable.

When she started classes in Paris in September, Aylin was distraught. She had not improved her French and could not stop thinking about her mother, who was consistently getting weaker. The following year, when Uncle Hilmi sensed they were approaching the end, he sent Leyla to Paris to be with her daughters before she returned home to Istanbul. By then, Nilüfer and Aziz had moved there, when Aziz completed his studies at the University of London and accepted a job at NATO.

In Paris, Leyla seemed better. The city did her good. She was in good spirits and felt less pain. The girls began to think that their mother could make it through.

Ten days later, after their mother had returned home, they received the dreaded call from Istanbul. Their mother was dying. They rushed to be by her bedside. Leyla lay in her bed like a pale, withered flower, trying to hide her suffering. Her face was white and she had grown so thin that she looked lost under the sheets. Nilüfer tried to ease her grief by taking refuge in Eastern religions. Aylin, on the other hand, revolted against everything and everyone. Even God. She experienced the first deep pain of her life. One day, Nilüfer found her sister sobbing on the floor. Aylin tried to speak between her sobs as she leaned into Nilüfer's embrace.

"Nilüfer, if one of us were a doctor, we could stop her suffering. Oh, Nilüfer, I wish I were a doctor!"

Leyla died in the fall of 1961. The girls remained at their father's side for a month before returning to Paris. Aylin fell back into her courses, but she did not want to go to school. She didn't want to do anything.

PARIS AND THE PRINCE

After Leyla died, Nilüfer enrolled in a few archaeology and art history courses at the Louvre. She and Aziz had settled in a nice house in Passy.

Aylin, on the other hand, dropped out of the Sorbonne. The loss of their mother had been a blow for both sisters, but Aylin had taken it harder. She had always had a special bond with Leyla, perhaps because Leyla had been too doting on her younger daughter when Nilüfer was away at school. Whatever the reason, her mother's death devastated Aylin. Within weeks, she seemed on the verge of a breakdown. Worried, Nilüfer invited her to move in.

Tall, slim, chic, and elegant, Aylin would often wander along the Rue de St. Honoré, down the Champs-Elysées, and through Saint-Germain on the Left Bank. Aylin and Paris were a good match. The two sisters had explored the city together when Aylin first arrived there. They went in and out of galleries to gaze at paintings and sculptures; they sat at cafés and soaked in the most beautiful city in the world. In the wake of their mother's death, they felt no urge to do anything but linger in the streets. It was as if, without their mentor, they had lost their way. They had no one to praise or support them. Nilüfer pulled herself together first. She started to insist that her sister make plans for the future, encouraging her to look into the many art courses offered in the city.

Aylin said, "I want to study medicine."

"How will you manage a career in medicine, Aylin? That's not child's play."

Aylin said, "You sound like Mother. I know what it takes."

"Really? You are twenty-three now. You'd study for six years, and then you'd need just as long to complete an internship."

"I don't care how long it takes."

"You don't know what you're talking about. You couldn't even finish your economics course."

"Nilüfer, don't be that way. You know why I had to stop."

Nilüfer paused, "Well, things have changed. At least now you can start where you left off."

"I didn't like economics. I can't study that."

"You didn't like economics, but you'll like medicine. Is that so? Medicine is a lot more difficult."

"That may be, but it's what I want."

Nilüfer scoffed. "This is just a pipe dream. Why waste your time chasing ridiculous dreams when you can study art, history, something easy that only takes two or three years?"

Aylin said, "It's medicine or nothing."

Finally, Nilüfer exploded, "Aylin! Our mother is dead. You can't bring her back even if you do become a doctor."

Aylin asked, "Do you want me to return home?"

Nilüfer sighed. "No. Stay here as long as you wish. Continue living aimlessly! Put on your fancy dresses, your makeup, have dinner at La Coupole! But for God's sake, do you think that will satisfy you?'

That spring, their aunt Esma visited Paris to attend the board meeting of the International Council of Women. As soon as she checked into her hotel, she invited her nieces for tea. The girls sat in a corner of the crowded lobby and waited for their aunt, watching the people go in and out. Suddenly, the air seemed to stir. Two men wearing loose pants and turbans ran ahead to make ready for a man with his pants tucked into short golden boots. He wore a gold-embroidered caftan and a fez, and entered the hotel with a large entourage at his heels. As he strode by the girls, Aylin met his gaze for just a second. His dark eyes lingered on her with a piercing look. And then, he was gone.

Nilüfer said, "Who are these people in such strange outfits? They must have come from the Middle East."

Their aunt joined them a few minutes later, and they settled in the tea room.

Her aunt asked, "How are you coping, Aylin? Do you feel better?"

Aylin replied, "I feel much better, Auntie."

"Listen, my dear child. You cannot die with the deceased. You must put aside your grief and choose a path for yourself. Your mother would want you to get married, but since there are no suitors in sight, I think you should go to school."

"I want to study medicine."

"At this age? You're a bit too late, Aylin."

Nilüfer said, "My mother, may she rest in peace, used to say that a long course of study is for ugly girls."

"Am I not the ugly duck of the family?"

Her aunt said, "You were! But now, you are like a butterfly that has just left its cocoon. You are beautiful."

All of a sudden, there was another stir in the air. The strangely dressed men entered the tea room and sat down at the next table.

Nilüfer gulped. "Oh, they are here now."

"Who?" Esma asked.

"The Arabs we saw in the lobby, Auntie. They are just behind you."

Esma said, "Good! I don't like Arabs. Much better not to have to look at them."

They chattered away. After a while, Nilüfer said, "That man with the fez keeps staring at us." Aylin turned and met those piercing jet-black eyes again.

Esma said, "Of course he'll look. In his home country, the women hide their faces behind a veil. Can you blame him?"

Aylin commented, "He must be admiring Nilüfer's beauty."

Nilüfer said, "Sorry, Aylin, but he is looking at you, not me."

Esma said, "Come on, girls. He's an Arab. I'm sure he is looking at all of us." Aylin tilted her head a little in the man's direction again.

Then a waiter came with tea and began serving them. Nilüfer leaned over and asked, "Do you know those gentlemen wearing caftans over there?"

"Yes," replied the waiter. "They come quite often. The gentleman in the black caftan is Sheik Rahim Ben Tallal, a prince from Libya. The others are his entourage."

Aylin gulped. "Oh, a prince!"

Esma interrupted, "C'mon dear, everyone's a prince in Libya. The king of Libya probably has five hundred sons. Don't act like he's the prince of England." When she finished her tea, Aylin rose to go to the ladies' room. With her head upright and her tummy drawn in, she swayed across the room like a swan, just as she had learned at Lucie Clayton's.

Her aunt asked, "What's wrong with Aylin? Why is she walking like that?"

Nilüfer replied, "Oh, she's doing the model walk."

Her aunt said, "All for that Arab she takes for a prince? He's not worth the effort." She leaned toward her niece and said, in a serious voice, "Nilüfer, now that your mother is gone, you need to take care of your sister. Do insist that she enroll in a reasonable program. Before it's too late, dear."

Nilüfer said, "I'm trying my best, Auntie. But our mother's death rocked her and she's grown a thick skin. She'll be all right with time."

"You know, time tends to pass. Then you look up and see that you're too old to study and too late for marriage or motherhood." She paused and added, "That last one was for you, Nilüfer."

"We do not want a child, Auntie."

"But why, dear?"

"Aziz is deeply attached to me. He fears that my attention for him would wane with a baby."

"And what about you?"

"Well, it's something that we both have to agree on. We must both want the child." Her aunt started to speak, but Nilüfer hushed her, "Oh, where is Aylin? Auntie, let me tell you something. As Aylin was walking to the ladies' room, that Arab got up and followed her."

"Run after her and see what's happening. Go, go, my dear girl. Why didn't you tell me before?"

Just as Nilüfer rose, Aylin appeared. She swayed toward them and took her seat.

Nilüfer asked, "Where have you been?"

"In the restroom."

"Is anything wrong with your stomach?"

"I was powdering my nose."

"Did that Arab follow you?"

"You mean the prince?" asked Aylin.

Esma replied, "How do you know he's a prince? You're taking the waiter's word?"

Aylin said, "Auntie, you're being very suspicious. Not to mention racist."

Her aunt said, "I've never liked the Arabs."

"But you like the French, the English, and the Italians, don't you?"

"Yes, I do. Europe is the cradle of civilization." The waiter returned, and Esma asked for the bill.

He said, "It has been paid, madame."

Esma looked surprised. "Who paid it?"

"The gentleman at the table behind you."

"I don't know that gentleman. Bring me my bill at once."

Aylin blushed a little. She said, "Auntie, please don't make a scene."

"How can I not make a scene?" She turned around to see that the Arab was gone.

"Auntie, don't make such a fuss," said Aylin. "Besides, you will get to know that Arab very soon. I'm going to marry him."

Soon after, Nilüfer and Aziz's house started to fill up with the most exquisitely perfumed flowers. When Prince Rahim Ben Tallal came to pick up Aylin in his black limousine, the neighbors crowded at their windows to watch. All of a sudden, Aylin found herself in the middle of a fairy tale.

Nilüfer did not know what to do. She could not believe a chance encounter outside a restroom could have led to this.

When the prince had followed her, Aylin had told him she was not in the habit of speaking with strangers.

The prince had asked, "Even if that stranger's intentions are very serious?"

"How serious?"

"Serious enough to propose."

Aylin said, "Well, in that case you will have to speak to my family." But she had already made up her mind when she gave him Nilüfer's address. If this so-called prince did propose, she was going to say yes. Her mother had drilled Napoleon's words into her head: "When you get your chance, take it. Otherwise, it'll slip through your fingers."

Nilüfer's conscience told her that it was wrong for her sister to marry someone with such an alien language and culture. Aziz did nothing to interfere, but the girls' aunt resisted with all her might. Esma believed if her sister Leyla were still alive, she would never have given her consent. Yet when she told Aylin's father that a Libyan prince had proposed to his daughter, he merely wished her the best. Leyla's death had shaken Cemal to the core. He was dealing with his own crises. Still, Esma did everything in her power to convince Aylin to take a step back. She talked to her niece every day until she was exhausted and scolded a friend who compared Aylin to Cinderella.

"Aylin descends from a long line of high officials who advised the sultans. It's that baggy-trousered Arab who should feel lucky."

Nilüfer tried to console her aunt. "Look, Auntie, not every girl meets a prince. Let's not interfere."

"Who knows how many other wives he has? He is as old as her father!"

"The man was educated in France. He's civilized and well mannered."

"That's fine, but what if he throws her into a harem? How will she escape?"

The girls waved away their aunt's protests, knowing she had been biased from the start. So Esma enlisted the wife of the Turkish ambassador. She, too, tried to persuade Aylin to give up on the idea of marrying the prince.

"Why do you insist, dear? Coups d'état happen in Libya almost daily. Each prince is the enemy of the others. We've obtained diplomatic intelligence on this Tallal. He had to flee the country because he sided with the party that supports good relations with the West. Being around this man might be dangerous."

"But I like a little danger."

"Danger is for films and novels. You cannot live this way in real life."

"I have the courage to try."

"What about your difference in age? You are twenty-three and he is forty-six."

Aylin said, "I have always found the men my age to be very shallow and boring." Indeed, Aylin would always favor men at least fifteen or twenty years older in the years to come.

"This marriage will not last, dear."

"It'll go as far as it can. If you don't give your consent, then I'll elope, like Nilüfer."

Esma said, "At least have a long engagement so that we can get to know the man." But the prince would not delay. The wedding ceremony was planned in Libya according to his traditions. Esma was angry. "If this man wants to marry you, he should ask your father for your hand. In the meantime, we can prepare your dowry. How can one get married in such haste?" she said.

Away from Aylin's ears, Nilüfer reassured Esma. "Auntie, if we keep on at her, she'll marry out of spite like I did. Let her enjoy it for a while. She'll give up, don't you worry."

Esma departed Paris with a heavy heart. And Nilüfer, hoping that Aylin would soon tire of the prince's ostentatious courting style, left Paris for her summer vacation in Istanbul.

Uncle Hilmi learned of Prince Tallal only days before the wedding. His niece simply called and said, "Uncle, I'm getting married and no one from my family will be by my side. Will you come?"

Uncle Hilmi met the groom the day before the ceremony. He put his head in his hands and moaned, "How could this happen to us?"

There were very few people at the wedding. The only Turks present were Uncle Hilmi and his new wife Rozi, and the Turkish ambassador with his wife. Rahim Ben Tallal arrived with his entourage. Even in the July heat, he wore a gold-embroidered caftan of wine-red velvet. Aylin had chosen a pink linen suit with a miniskirt and a small beret. She looked like a little girl beside the prince. The mayor performed the ceremony with no mention of religion. After the wedding, they all went out for champagne. The prince presented his new wife with an emerald ring and earrings.

On their wedding night, Aylin's husband approached her as she undressed. She had bought a cream-colored silk nightgown to wear and withdrew into the bathroom to change. She admired her long, narrow silhouette in the mirror, jumping when she saw the bright black eyes behind her.

"You don't need this," said the prince. "Your lovely skin will do." Her husband had taken off his clothes, and Aylin saw him naked now for the first time. Without his loose caftan and his heeled boots, he had been stripped of his grandeur. Now, he was just a puny, elfin man with a bald head and dark skin. Without his fez, Aylin could finally see that he was five inches shorter than her. Still, his eyes had that piercing gaze. Aylin's excitement mingled with fear and remorse. She gulped. *He has very impressive eyes,* thought Aylin. *I like his eyes. This must be love.*

After the wedding, they traveled to Istanbul, and Aylin introduced her husband to her family. She enjoyed the headlines that appeared in all the local papers and often invited her friends to her hotel suite or the tea room. These were the nice things in her marriage.

When they returned to Paris, Aylin's new life was extraordinary, with all the mysterious splendor she had read about in novels. They lived in a splendid hotel, and every day, Rahim Ben Tallal stayed in bed till noon, read the papers in French and Arabic after a long breakfast, spent the whole afternoon with his countrymen, and finally descended to the lobby around seven to join Aylin. Aylin did not understand a single word the men said, and sometimes her head ached. She often stayed overnight at Nilüfer's house. Her husband did not object as long as he knew she was with her sister. He himself did not return to the hotel some evenings. Aylin presumed he was gambling.

Aylin's early married life was flush. The prince left her heaps of money every morning, and she would shop to her heart's content, inviting her friends to eat or have tea with her.

But after a while, the prince limited her allowance. Rahim Ben Tallal started to give Aylin less and less, claiming that the money his family sent did not always reach him. And the splendid Libyan wedding ceremony he had promised never took place. There were rumors that his family's enemies had infiltrated the government. Traveling to his home country would be too big of a risk. They also couldn't go to Algeria, where most of his relatives now lived.

Aylin began to question whether the man she'd married was a real prince. Though he no longer gave her money, they dined out every evening and went afterward to discos, nightclubs, or casinos, entertaining armies of friends. He would shower Aylin with jewels, then send them to the lobby to lock them in the safe, never to be seen again. Eventually, Aylin told her husband that she wanted to find a house for them. They searched for a villa worthy of a prince, but he refused each one over some little defect or another. Just as Aylin started to believe that she would never escape the hotel, a majestic apartment at the Bois de Boulogne won Tallal's approval. They immediately moved in and hired a servant and a cook. Finally, Aylin could live like a normal newlywed. She hoped to share her Turkish recipes with the cook and host dinner parties for her friends, but her husband became even more of a stranger once they settled in. Sometimes he disappeared for days, claiming he was engaged in very important political affairs. Thank God, Nilüfer was also in Paris and Aylin could confide in her.

Nilüfer once asked, "Don't you ever question him?"

"I know that I won't get an honest answer."

"Do you think he visits other women?"

"I don't care in the least."

"Aren't you jealous at all, Aylin?"

"Actually, I prefer it. I sleep more soundly alone."

Nilüfer suddenly realized how tragic her sister's life had become. "You don't love this man."

Aylin did not answer.

"Do you want a divorce?"

"He will not accept it."

"So our aunt was right. You've locked yourself up in a golden cage."
Aylin said, "The cage is not even made of gold."

The beautiful apartment in the Bois de Boulogne did not last long. In less than a year, Aylin found herself back in the hotel suite. The prince did not give an explanation, but she heard from one of the bodyguards that the prince felt more secure at the hotel. Aylin started to spend more and more time at Nilüfer's.

One morning, she appeared at Nilüfer's door with a face as white as chalk.

Nilüfer said, "What's the matter, Aylin? You look like a ghost."

"Nilüfer, something terrible has happened. Help me."

"What is it? What's wrong?"

"I'm pregnant, Nilüfer." Aylin started to cry.

"Does he know?"

"No. He will never know. If he finds out, I will never escape him. We must have the child aborted."

"Yes," said Nilüfer, "but it's very difficult in Paris. You must go to Istanbul immediately."

"He won't let me. I've told him that father's ill, but he didn't believe me."

"What shall we do?"

"He might go to Algeria for the weekend. There must be some doctors here who do abortions. Please find out."

"How? Are you mad?"

"Ask your friends, ask your servant, talk to the janitor's wife, anything. Nilüfer, please!"

When the prince left for Algeria, the two sisters went to see a doctor who had done an abortion for their janitor's niece. Aylin's knees shook, fearful that the doctor would refuse. Nilüfer was scared her sister would have complications.

"I cannot perform this abortion in a hospital," said the doctor. "If they ever found out, that would be the end of my career."

Aylin interrupted, "But if you do not abort this child, this would mean the end of my life."

"Allow me to explain," said the doctor. "I will place something in your uterus before you go home today. You should start bleeding later this evening, at which point you will call me and meet me at the hospital. I will transfer you to the emergency ward and intervene because of the bleeding. It will be a necessary abortion, madame."

That night, Aylin stayed at Nilüfer's. Aziz had no knowledge of the plan, and when Aylin knocked on their bedroom door at midnight, he was worried. He rushed his wife and his sister-in-law to the hospital but could not understand why Aylin had chosen a second-rate doctor. Aylin had not wished to keep it a secret, but Nilüfer insisted.

It all happened as planned, and Aylin used her maiden name for the hospital records. Besides, the skinny girl trembling in her miniskirt and cotton blouse looked nothing like a princess. After spending the night in the hospital, Aylin went home to Nilüfer's. When Tallal called, Nilüfer told him that Aylin's stomach was upset from some bad mussels, and that she would take care of her for a few days.

After the abortion, a melancholy air descended upon Aylin. Nilüfer had thought she would be relieved, but Aylin had faced her reality on that operating table. She was not a princess. She was a slave. Aylin needed to do whatever she could to slip through the bars and escape. Only then could she beat her wings toward a blue horizon—the life that awaited her.

When Tallal returned to Paris, Aylin proposed a divorce. Wouldn't the prince be happier with a Libyan woman who spoke his own tongue and understood his culture? Tallal cut her speech short. "Divorce is not possible."

Aylin said, "But Islam will acknowledge a divorce. Even a woman can ask for one."

"When did you learn the rules of Islam?"

"You seem to forget that I am Muslim, too."

The prince said, "Islam may allow divorce, but my family does not."

Defeated, Aylin asked to visit her father in Istanbul for the summer. Fortunately, Rahim Ben Tallal was preoccupied with political conflicts in Libya and had no time to protest. He permitted her to travel with Nilüfer, and soon they were headed home. Back at her father's house, Aylin called her old friends and cousins. One of them was getting married that summer. Istanbul's socialites had been preparing for the party for weeks. Aylin wanted to look chic at the wedding. Everyone should see what a happy princess she was. She had picked out the perfect Dior dress, but unfortunately her jewels were still locked away in Paris.

She had not realized how much she missed her relatives, even the ever critical Aunt Esma. She spent time with Betin and their childhood friends almost every day, trying hard to return to the carefree days of her youth. Betin had married and was expecting a baby. Aunt Ecla's daughter Semra had also married, moved to Ankara, and had two children. Ayşe, Semra's cousin and Aylin's friend from Ankara, now lived in London and was expecting her second baby. Aylin's carbon copy from the American School was also living in London with her young husband. None of her friends was a princess, but they all had husbands they loved, and the freedom to divorce should that love ever end. Aylin, on the other hand, had never felt that mysterious thing called love and had married a man she could never divorce. How swiftly time flew. How quickly those carefree years passed by.

Aylin was determined to enjoy the summer in Istanbul, unaware she would meet the love of her life just a few weeks before returning to Paris.

Polat

One late summer night, Aylin and her friends were invited to a party at a garden on the Bosphorus. A group of young men and women danced to romantic songs on a terrace washed by moonlight. Aylin leaned against the garden wall, soaking in the magnificent view.

Suddenly, she heard the host approach. "Hey! Parisians! Have you two met?" Aylin turned and saw a spectacled young man beside her.

"No, we haven't."

"Well, let me introduce you. This is Polat Saran, a gentleman studying at the Sorbonne, and this is Princess Aylin."

The young man asked, "Do you belong to the Ottoman dynasty?"

"I am not as noble as that. I'm only the wife of the nephew of the king of Libya."

"And where is your prince?"

Aylin said, "In Paris."

"Oh," said Polat. "Would you dance with me then?"

Aylin walked to the terrace where the other young couples were dancing. Polat embraced Aylin's slender body and spoke softly in her ear, "I wish you weren't married to a Libyan prince. I wish you were just a student like me, Aylin."

"I was, only a year ago," replied Aylin. "Isn't it amazing how fast things can change?"

Polat Saran called Aylin the next day to see if she would join him for a swim at the sandy beaches of the Black Sea. The day after that, Polat came to collect her with a bunch of friends Aylin knew from her school days. For the rest of the summer, they swam at a different beach every day and went to the trendiest bars and clubs at night. Aylin was having a wonderful time with people her own age. Nilüfer said, "You'll miss these days when you return to Paris."

"My life should have been like this, Nilüfer."

"You shut your ears to everyone who tried to tell you."

"I was still reeling from my mother's loss."

"Don't you dare blame my mother, may she rest in peace."

"Stop scolding me, will you? I know I made a mistake."

Nilüfer said, "Well, let's see if you can get out of this mess." She was well aware that her sister had trapped herself, but did not think Aylin deserved to be punished for life. She was too young. Nilüfer also felt responsible for not having been more proactive. After all, her mother had entrusted Aylin to her on her deathbed, as she had done when Aylin was born. "You will be her mother after I'm gone, Nilüfer. Always take care of her and never leave her side." Nilüfer needed to find a way to free Aylin of Tallal. For now, she refused to spoil her sister's joyful summer. In those blissful last few weeks, Aylin finally learned the meaning of love.

Polat was the son of one of the most successful shipping magnates in Turkey. His family sent him to Paris after high school, where he was accepted into the Sorbonne. He had great depth of character, immersing himself in literature, philosophy, and the arts in addition to his commercial law studies. He was a special young man, and in Aylin, he had found an equally special woman.

It was as if she did not live by worldly dimensions, as though she acted on an imaginary stage. Her approach to people, events, and situations was entirely unique. And as to her failures and mistakes—she felt she had none! These words belonged only in the dictionary, not in real life. She was different: a philosopher endowed with an amazing aesthetic; a comedian who could excavate humor from anything. Polat laughed and enjoyed life with her like with no one else before. He saw neither a princess nor a married woman in Aylin. She resembled no one. Even her beauty was beyond description. Some found her disproportionately tall and thin, while some thought her flawless, like a model. Some found her hazel-green eyes sad and dreamy, while some found them treacherous or mischievous, like a cat's. For Polat, Aylin was simply the magical person he had fallen madly in love with.

Back in Paris, Aylin left her hotel every morning and walked to Polat's house in Saint-Germain, where she listened to music and read books while Polat was in class. Afterward, they took their lunch in their favorite little restaurant and went back to Polat's apartment together. Aylin would stay there till nightfall if Polat didn't have lectures in the afternoon. Every evening, she returned to her hotel, exhausted by loving. There she'd climb into a foamy bath to cast off this new identity and emerge from the tub a slave ready to bear her punishment.

At this point, Rahim Ben Tallal had not been intimate with his wife for three months. Each night that she claimed she had a headache or an upset stomach he simply gave her a piercing glare. In turn, Aylin stopped asking where he had been on nights he did not come home, complaining about the bodyguards who filled the suite with smoke, or asking for money to spend in the boutiques. She had turned into an angel since her summer in Istanbul and demanded only one thing from her husband, "I want to complete my education."

The answer was short—"No!"—and Aylin never asked again. The prince thought she would insist on it and waited for her to protest. But she did not. His wife had changed, and he noticed.

One night, the doorbell began to ring incessantly. Polat headed for the door, thinking a friend might be dropping in with his girl to take advantage of his home's many bedrooms. But when he saw the turbaned Arabs at the door, he turned pale.

One said, "Are you Monsieur Saran?"

Polat tried to remain calm. "Yes, that's me. What could you possibly want at this hour?"

"We have a message to deliver to you."

"Listen gentlemen, why don't you come at a more suitable time? I have an exam early in the morning."

"Let's go inside," one of the men said.

Fearful they might get rough, Polat ushered them in. "Do you know Princess Aylin?"

"I have a friend with that name."

"Since when?"

"We grew up together. We both used to spend summers on the Bosphorus."

"Are you still in contact?"

"We see each other now and then."

"Does she ever come here?"

"Listen, gentlemen. I am a bachelor. Lots of young women visit me. Some are sweethearts and some are just friends."

"Princess Aylin will not set foot in this house again," one of the men said. "If she does, you'll pay."

"If she does, I'll give her your message. However, you may want to tell her yourself. We Turks do not traditionally drive away our guests."

One of the Arabs said, "We're warning you for the last time. You will not see her again!"

"You have been misinformed. She is just an old childhood friend."

The Arabs saluted Polat with their hands on their guns. Polat recognized the threat. After they were gone, he stood paralyzed at the center of the room, not sure what to do. He had to send an urgent message to Aylin; she could not come to his home for a while.

It was close to midnight. He decided to call Nilüfer, though he was aware that she did not like him. When they met in Istanbul, Nilüfer had been cool and distant. When he had gone to Nilüfer's home in Paris to pick up Aylin, Polat could see the look of disapproval on her face. But he had to reach her. Reluctantly, Polat dialed Nilüfer's number.

Back at the hotel, Aylin was also having a hard time. The prince had ordered dinner to their suite and drunk only soda water instead of his usual glass of wine. He hadn't said a single word during their meal. Aylin was tense. As soon as the waiters had cleared the table, he said, "We have to talk."

"About what?"

"About your improper behavior."

"I do not understand."

"Oh, yes you do. You refuse to fulfill your marital duties, yet you make inappropriate visits every day. This must end immediately."

"I don't know what you're implying, but I could also complain about unfulfilled duties."

"Like what?" The prince was taken aback.

"You disappear in the evenings without saying a word."

"I'm a man."

"You promised me before the wedding that we would be on equal footing, like any civilized man and wife."

"You have betrayed me, Aylin."

"You have betrayed me, too, sir. We never had a wedding party, and you also promised me a house."

"Don't forget that I am in exile."

"I didn't ask for a palace; I asked for an apartment. As to my wifely duties, I have no doubt that you have others who can fulfill them."

"You have an active imagination."

"So do you."

"I have concrete proof."

"Your men spy on me? How degrading!"

"You asked for it."

"I ask only for my freedom. Ours has not been a successful marriage. Please allow us to get a divorce."

"Never!" said Rahim Ben Tallal, and banged the door as he left the suite. When Aylin tried to leave, she realized that the door was locked. She was terrified. She couldn't call Polat. It was too dangerous. Instead, she called Nilüfer.

"Don't bother asking the concierge to open it," said her sister. "Tallal must have bought them all off. Wait for morning. We can have breakfast together."

TRAPPED IN THE CAGE

Nilüfer had just hung up when Polat called. "Polat, you've already caused a huge mess for my sister. Leave her alone before things get worse."

"I understand why you're angry, but things have gotten out of control. I'm very anxious about Aylin. Please don't let her come here," begged Polat.

"She is not going anywhere, and under no circumstances should you call her. I will get in touch when I have more information."

Nilüfer was in the lobby of the hotel at ten o'clock, but by noon, Aylin still had not showed. Finally, Nilüfer called her.

Aylin picked up, her voice trembling, "Where have you been? I've been waiting for hours."

"I was waiting in the lobby. I was scared that Tallal would answer if I came to your room."

"He's not here," said Aylin. "He never returned last night. The door is still locked."

"I will come up right away." Luckily, Nilüfer found a maid on Aylin's floor and bribed her to open the door. The sisters embraced. Nilüfer told her about Polat, and Aylin shook with fear.

"I can't stay, Aylin," said Nilüfer. "The prince can't know that we have unlocked the door. I will ask the maid for a duplicate of the key."

"Please don't forget to call."

"Don't worry, we'll find a way out. You must be patient." Rahim Ben Tallal returned to the hotel that evening but barely spoke to Aylin. They dined silently. After dinner, he left and locked the door behind him. This happened for several days.

On the fourth day, Aylin burst out. "How long will this captivity go on?"

"Until you come to your senses."

"I'm about to lose my senses. I haven't breathed fresh air in days."

"We can dine out tonight. You love going out," Tallal said in a mocking tone. Aylin did not answer. She finished dressing and the couple left the hotel, two bodyguards at their heels. There had been five bodyguards before, Aylin noticed. She wondered whether her husband was running out of money. They ate silently, but Aylin was glad to be among other people.

She said, "Don't lock me up in the room tomorrow. I promise I won't go out."

Tallal said, "I will think about it."

The sisters spent the week uneasily, speaking on the phone for hours about Polat. Nilüfer hated him like poison but was afraid he and her sister would contact each other.

Nilüfer called Tallal and invited him and Aylin to dinner that weekend. She was surprised to hear him accept without hesitation and prepared a special dish with couscous she thought the Libyan would appreciate. Aylin and Tallal did not speak during dinner. It was clear that they were both very angry.

Finally, Nilüfer said, "For God's sake, what's the matter with you two?"

"Your sister says that she is not happy and wants a divorce."

Nilüfer let out a shrill little laugh. "You must be kidding, Prince. My family would never allow it. Even joking about it is frowned upon. Don't let my father hear you."

Tallal threw a swift glance at Aylin. "It's the same in my family."

Nilüfer said, "Matrimonial disputes are to be solved in private."

"Your sister does not agree."

"I'll talk to my sister." She turned to Aylin. "Shall we have lunch tomorrow?"

Aylin looked to her husband.

Tallal said, "Where will you have lunch? My chauffeur will take you."

Nilüfer said, "Let's go to Lipp; it's been such a long time."

To Aylin, Tallal said, "Well, be ready at half past twelve."

When the sisters met the next day, Aylin started to cry. "Nilüfer, I thought I would never get out of that hotel room. I can't go back there."

"Today you must. It will take a lot of patience to free yourself of that man. Aziz has consulted a lawyer. It won't be easy."

"Did you talk to Polat?"

"Leave him out of it. I'm trying to save your life, but your mind is still somewhere else."

In the end, Nilüfer convinced her sister to go along with her plot. Aylin was to pretend she had given up on the idea of divorce. Then maybe Tallal would allow her go to Istanbul with her sister for a brief holiday.

"There's something else: I don't want to sleep with him. When he insists, I feel like jumping out of the window."

"You should have thought about that before you married him. What about those piercing dark eyes?"

"Don't poke fun!"

Nilüfer said, "Aylin, just please no more pregnancies!"

Polat was still a concern. Nilüfer made Aylin swear numerous times that she would not contact him.

Over time, Tallal calmed down. He continued to let Aylin go out with Nilüfer, as long as they were accompanied by his chauffeur. But he still locked Aylin in the hotel room when he went out, which was most nights since Aylin had told him she would not sleep with him until this captivity was over. She took her pillow and blanket and slept on the wide couch in the living room.

Nilüfer quickly made friends with the maid who cleaned the rooms on Aylin's floor. She explained the situation and offered her quite a lot of money to make a copy of Aylin's key. She promised not to tell anyone how she came into possession of the duplicate. Finally, the maid agreed.

Aylin started to visit Nilüfer weekly, returning to the hotel after a few hours. The moment she stepped through Nilüfer's door, she'd grab the phone to call Polat. Once, she had begged to see him so much that Nilüfer called him to her house a few hours before Aylin's visit and kept him there for a long time after she left out of fear of his being discovered in their home. Finally, Nilüfer could no longer handle the stress and told Aylin that she was not going to allow Polat in her home anymore. Desperate, Aylin began trying to meet Polat in different places around the city.

Once, she told the driver that she wanted to shop a little at the Galeries Lafayette on their way back to the hotel.

The driver said, "I cannot stop here, madame."

"Drop me off, drive around, and come back later. I'll wait for you here at the entrance."

She jumped out of the car without waiting for an answer and dashed into the teeming crowd. She met Polat on the ladies' floor, where he tucked a few facial creams and a bottle of perfume in her hand. "I didn't want you to waste time picking these out."

They snatched a couple of skirts and blouses and rushed into a dressing room. Finally back in Polat's arms, Aylin kissed him passionately. When she stepped through the door a few minutes later, her hair was disheveled but she had a smile glued to her face. She waited at the entrance and then waved at the car approaching her.

The driver said, "Do you know how many times I went around this block, madame?"

Aylin replied, "Well, women lose track of time when they shop. And the line was long."

The man said, "Don't tell the prince about this. He'd get very angry with me."

Aylin said, "Good God, I can't see why shopping should be forbidden. But if you insist, I promise to keep this between us." She let out a breath and took out her mirror to tidy her hair and reapply her lipstick.

Love was wonderful, even when one's life was at stake.

The lawyer Aziz consulted had hired a detective to spy on Tallal and photograph him with different women in nightclubs. In the meantime, Nilüfer asked her uncle to help them. Ever the doting uncle, Hilmi flew to Paris to assess the situation more closely. He could see that his niece was miserable—she had lost weight and looked like a bundle of bones. Her captivity had to end immediately. Uncle Hilmi consulted a new lawyer, Turkish this time. It was possible for a Turkish citizen who wed in France to obtain a divorce through the Turkish courts as long as the embassy in Paris acknowledged the marriage. The law was finally on their side. They rushed to the embassy with Aylin's marriage certificate.

Their plan was coming together. They just needed a day when Tallal would not be in the hotel.

They waited. But Tallal stayed at the hotel every night during that first week. Aylin became more and more nervous. Finally, the following Wednesday he said, "I'm going out tonight and may not come back. Order your meal before I leave."

Aylin ordered soup. Once the waiters left, Tallal got dressed, locked the door, and was gone. Aylin called Nilüfer ten minutes later.

"Tonight's the night."

"Check your key."

"Nilüfer, I checked it at least a hundred times."

"Don't leave a suitcase out; he might come back."

"Don't worry. I'll be at the door at seven in the morning. If you don't see me, it means that he's come back."

"Should we leave tonight?"

Aylin said, "No, let's stick to the plan and get as far as possible. If he stays the night elsewhere, he won't return before noon tomorrow." She sounded cool and unruffled.

"What if he does come back?"

"He won't. He hasn't been out in over a week. You don't know this man's libido like I do. I'm sure he will not be back till noon."

Nilüfer stirred all night, but Aylin slept soundly. When the alarm rang, she rose, switched off the bell, and got dressed. She tucked a pair of trousers, a blouse, and one or two pairs of underwear in a bag. She retrieved her passport and marriage certificate from the corner of the lowest dresser drawer. Tallal had hidden them away in a big envelope. He did not know that Aylin checked them every other day. She unlocked the door at five to seven and hung the "Do Not Disturb" sign on the knob before locking it behind her. Not willing to wait for the elevator, she took the stairs. In her slacks, T-shirt, spectacles, and ponytail, she looked like a skinny, freckled student instead of the beautiful, chic princess who lived in the third-floor suite. She slipped out of the hotel like a ghost. As discussed, Nilüfer and Aziz were in the car parked across the street. She climbed into the backseat.

Nilüfer said, "Move it, Aziz."

Within a few hours, they were at the Swiss border. When they were safely across, they began to scream with excitement.

This was the most exciting journey of Aylin's life. She was getting closer to freedom with every mile. She began to sing at the top of her lungs in the backseat. All of a sudden, her face went white. "Aziz, please stop!"

Aziz said, "Do you need to use the bathroom?"

"I have to throw up."

Aziz pulled over and Aylin lurched out of the car. She retched on the side of the road before returning to the car and lying down on the backseat.

Aziz said, "The poor girl's whole system is in shock."

Nilüfer said, "Listen Aziz, stop at the first drugstore."

They stopped for the night in Trieste. Neither Aziz nor the girls had the strength to go farther. Aylin's nausea had gotten worse. Nilüfer asked to share a hotel room with her sister. When they were finally alone, she turned to her sister. "Are you pregnant again?"

"I don't know, Nilüfer."

"How can you not know? You said you didn't sleep with Tallal!"

"I didn't."

Nilüfer said, "Well then, it must just be anxiety."

Aylin did not answer and slipped into the bathroom. Nilüfer followed.

"Why are you running away?"

"I'm not."

"I know you. Why are you keeping secrets from me?"

Aylin gave no answer.

"You slept with Polat? How could you? How could you risk your life? How many times? Where?" Nilüfer started to cry, throwing everything within reach at her sister.

"When we get to Istanbul," Nilüfer said, "I will show that reckless man what a fool he has been. I'll talk to his father and have him cut off."

Aylin said, "Calm down, Nilüfer. I'm not pregnant, I promise."

They arrived in Istanbul three days later. When they pulled up to their father's house, it seemed as if the nightmare might really be over. Aylin's nausea had subsided by the time they reached the Turkish border. Nilüfer still felt guilty about her outburst.

On Monday, they rushed to meet with their uncle's lawyer, and Aylin gave him power of attorney for her divorce. The lawyer appealed to the court with photographs of Tallal and other women in clubs around Paris. They then sent the request to France, which sued the prince for the "disharmony" his cultural differences had caused.

The lawyer warned Aylin to wait patiently until the divorce was final. She could not risk being seen with anyone. Whenever she went out at night, she was chaperoned by a family member.

Aylin called Polat, who had arrived in Istanbul weeks before. He was very happy to hear that Aylin had broken free, but her other piece of news dampened his spirits. As Nilüfer suspected, Aylin was pregnant. They had no other choice but to abort. Polat was the son of an extremely conservative family, and since he had just started his education, marriage was out of the question. Aylin did not fault him. She only wished to keep Nilüfer in the dark. She had already burdened her sister with too much. Polat arranged for a doctor, and Aylin went through with the procedure alone.

When Nilüfer came home that night, she assumed Aylin was already asleep. She was in bed reading a book when she heard Aylin call. When she went into Aylin's bedroom, her sister was sitting in bed in a pool of blood. She looked like she was going to faint.

"Nilüfer, get a doctor fast."

Nilüfer gasped.

"Quiet. Don't wake Father."

"You were pregnant, weren't you? Oh, Aylin. Did you have an abortion without telling me?"

"Yes, today."

"Who arranged for it? That horrible man."

"Now is not the time to discuss it."

"He needs to see what he has done to you." Nilüfer walked over to the telephone.

"Nilüfer, please don't. There's a big party at his house tonight."

Nilüfer got even angrier. "He is busy with a party while you are dying here?"

"Let's take a taxi and go to a hospital."

"He will come," said Nilüfer. "He is responsible for it."

Aylin did not look well, and the bleeding was getting worse.

Nilüfer said, "Give me the number quick. I promise I will be civil."

After she hung up, Nilüfer helped Aylin get dressed. Her legs were smeared with blood and she was too weak to stand. They heard their father's voice in the other room.

Nilüfer called out to him, "Daddy, go back to bed. Aziz is coming to take both of us out. We will be home late."

Polat was at the door within fifteen minutes. He swept Aylin into his arms and rushed her to his car. Within ten minutes, they were at the emergency room. As the doctors whisked Aylin away, Nilüfer lit a cigarette.

"How could you do such a thing, Polat? What if Tallal had found you? He could have killed you both."

"You are right, Nilüfer. But Aylin was in such a miserable state, I wanted to cheer her up. I thought she might go mad, and I didn't want her to think that I had deserted her. I am sorry."

"Does your family know?"

"No, not even my friends know anything."

Nilüfer said, "Good. Let no one hear of this."

It was dawn when they left the hospital. Polat brought the girls to their house and headed back to the Bosphorus, thinking of what he would tell his party guests.

Aylin's health recovered within a few days, but her heart felt heavy. Her life was a total mess. Although she was no longer a captive, she was not yet a free woman and had no idea how long the divorce would take or what Tallal would do when he found out that she had run away. This reckless marriage had brought her nothing but a few newspaper headlines. What was she to do? Aylin knew that Polat's family would resist his marriage to a divorced woman who was two or three years older than their son. She was not willing to go to war with the Saran family. She just wanted peace.

Soon, they heard that Tallal was searching for Aylin in every corner of Paris. He called her family in Istanbul every hour of every day. Finally, Aylin's father spoke up.

"This man is your legal husband. You cannot evade him forever. Either answer the phone or write him a letter. Tell him why you are not going back."

Aylin wrote a long, carefully worded letter outlining the reasons she needed to end their marriage. She hoped her husband would understand that a divorce would be the best solution for them both. Tallal sent a flood of letters in reply, sometimes begging, sometimes making threats. Aylin lived in fear that he would come to Istanbul. He never showed up, but the summer of 1964 was nevertheless a nightmare.

At the end of September, Nilüfer and Aylin went to Geneva. Aylin had decided to study medicine, and this time no one could change her mind.

Aylin applied to many universities in France and Switzerland but received rejection after rejection. Finally, she was accepted by the University of Neuchâtel, just before the birthday that would have made her too old to enroll there.

JEAN-PIERRE

Aylin was twenty-six when she entered the University of Neuchâtel. She had shoulder-length hair and severe bangs. She tossed out all the Lanvin, Dior, and Balenciaga outfits, along with her royal pretenses. She started to wear narrow slacks, tight T-shirts, and flat shoes, and ran in and out of the school's stone halls without any makeup on, clasping her thick medical textbooks like a teenager.

Uncle Hilmi's friend Toby von Schweir had persuaded Aylin to take a thousand dollars from him when she left Geneva for Neuchâtel. Aylin created a meticulous budget for her new life. She put aside her tuition fee, placing her living expenses in one box and her pocket money in another. In any case, there was no place in the small college town to spend money, and her lectures were so difficult that she found herself studying until two o'clock in the morning. She just needed to get through the first year, when most students dropped out. She'd heard the ones who made it through year one graduated no matter what. Aylin was determined to keep up her grades so she could transfer to the University of Lausanne. She worked like mad not to miss her chance.

A year later, her hard work paid off. Lausanne accepted her application, and she enrolled in October 1965.

The lectures at Lausanne were much more difficult, but she didn't care. She was happy with life as a student. It was the era of the flower child, and the city was filled with young people. Hoards of guitar-playing youngsters in ratty jeans sang in the gardens, parks, open-air cafés, and city streets. This generation had no notion of fashion or luxury. Luckily, simplicity suited Aylin's new budget just fine.

Nilüfer visited her sister for Christmas vacation. She barely recognized Aylin at the train station. Aylin wore faded blue jeans and no makeup, blending in with those around her.

When they got home, Nilüfer turned to her, "What's the matter with you? Are you totally broke?"

"No, no! I manage."

"Your hair . . ."

"I don't go to the hairdresser."

Nilüfer said, "Let me take you to one tomorrow."

"What shall I do with a hairdresser, Nilüfer? Everybody's hair is like this at school. I'm a student, remember?"

"Right. What about your lessons? You said they were difficult."

"I'm having problems with physics. I've forgotten a lot since high school."

"Maybe you should take private lessons."

"Oh, I already do."

"Do you have enough money?"

"Lessons are free."

"Really?" said Nilüfer.

"An assistant professor of physics named Jean-Pierre instructs me."

Nilüfer said suggestively, "I would never have thought a Swiss man would give free lessons."

Aylin said, "Well, he does."

Nilüfer looked at her intently. With her plain face, freckles, and glasses, Aylin did not look like someone who could seduce a physics professor. Still, Nilüfer could not suppress her sharp tongue. "I hope this physics assistant will not demand some other kind of payment."

Aylin laughed and said, "Come to campus tomorrow. I'll show you around. If we find Jean-Pierre, you can meet him."

The next day after the tour, Aylin brought Nilüfer to a row of offices. She knocked on a door and entered. A bespectacled young man sat at the table with thick books piled on either side of him.

Aylin said, "Jean-Pierre Egner, meet my sister." The young man rose from the table and seemed to get longer and longer, like a beanstalk.

Nilüfer said to Aylin in Turkish, "I think this guy is even skinnier than you are. I take it back. This boy is not likely to demand anything from anyone."

They shook hands, he welcomed Aylin's sister to Lausanne, and the sisters moved on.

Aylin said, "Don't misjudge him by his looks; he is a genius."

Aylin had adapted to her academic life beautifully. She no longer looked like a young woman who had put up with an abusive marriage, two abortions, and a divorce. She just looked like a teenager who was born to study medicine. Her whole world consisted of lectures, books, exams, and the university. And she was incredibly happy. Nilüfer left Lausanne with a light heart. She leaned down from the window of the train to kiss her sister for the last time before she departed.

"You know what," said Nilüfer, "you're like a chameleon. You can adapt to any situation."

That summer, after exams were over, Aylin brought Jean-Pierre to Istanbul. They arrived covered with dust and dirt from traveling in his run-down car, visited family for a couple of days, and went on an Anatolian expedition. They planned to tour the whole Aegean and Mediterranean coasts and brought a camping tent with them.

Aylin's friends, who had seen her just two or three years earlier as a princess, could not believe the change. Only Betin didn't find it odd.

She knew her friend's soul would never change no matter what role she slipped into.

Jean-Pierre fell in love with Turkey. Peasants welcomed them in their homes and shared their soup and bread and sour milk; even modest villages embodied the rich history of the Hellenistic and Roman ages, reaching as far back as seven thousand years. They discovered untouched, captivating ruins and enjoyed a wonderful climate, crystal-clear seas, the sun, sandy beaches, and fertile meadows. Aylin rediscovered the majesty of her homeland through Jean-Pierre's eyes.

That summer was full of happy memories Aylin would never forget. She gained new insight into life, into the world, into her heart. The Aegean towns had a magical, wild, and natural beauty totally different from the civilized worlds of Paris, London, and Geneva. The people in the small towns they traveled through had a humble and serene wisdom, so different from the bourgeois culture Aylin had grown accustomed to. In her homeland, Aylin found peace within herself.

After her journey, Aylin experienced another shift when she found out that Nilüfer wished to get a divorce.

She could not believe her ears. "What are you talking about? Nilüfer, is there someone else in your life? Other than Aziz?"

Nilüfer said, "Yes. I'm a human being like you, and I fell in love."

Aylin realized that until that day, she had only known her sister as the wife of Aziz. Her sister had always been beautiful, but conservative. Now that Aylin looked at her under a different light, she saw a young, beautiful, sensitive woman glowing with excitement. Aylin was astonished.

"What will you tell Aziz?"

"I'll tell him the truth."

"But he will die."

"No, he won't. He must have been expecting this for some time now."

"Weren't you on good terms all these years?"

"Yes, we were on good terms. But we haven't been happily married. Aziz had affairs now and then, and I think I have always been waiting for the right man."

"And you kept your eyes closed."

"Yes."

"But why, Nilüfer? Didn't you love your husband?"

"I did."

"What kind of love is that?"

Nilüfer said, "Love is not black and white."

"Who is the new man? Do I know him?"

"You've heard of him," said Nilüfer.

"Will you divorce Aziz? Do you want to marry this man?"

"As soon as we return to Paris, I'll do everything in my power to get a divorce, and as soon as I get a divorce, I will get married."

"Who is this man?"

Nilüfer took a deep breath, looked Aylin in the eyes, and said, "Mr. G."

"*What*?" Aylin rocked with laughter. "Stop messing around and tell me the truth. Who is it?"

Nilüfer remained silent, her expression serious.

"You're mad. Mr. G. is as old as your grandfather. No, as old as your grandfather's grandfather."

"Didn't you marry an older man?"

"He wasn't that old. Mr. G. won't marry you. He has been a bachelor since time began! And he's busy with his work as the politician of the people!" The sisters had switched roles. Now it was Aylin's turn to criticize.

Nilüfer said, "When you get to know him, you'll like him. But I will never be able to like that pasty, pale-eyed beanstalk, Jean-Pierre. Don't ever marry him."

"Are you poking your nose into my affairs again? Mind your own business! How did you get acquainted with Mr. G. anyway?" asked Aylin.

"At the home of another politician. I met him at Aunt Esma's."

"Did he make a pass at you?"

"What a remark! Don't be rude. We had met at a cocktail party at Auntie's years ago and chatted for a long time. Then we met again this summer. I asked, 'Are you still a bachelor?' He said yes. Then, when I said, 'Who are you waiting for?' He pointed his finger at me. Of course, I didn't take him seriously. I planned to go to the beach with friends the next day, and he must have heard us because he showed up! He started to call every day. He is an incredibly well-educated and interesting man. Aylin, don't you know what love is?"

Aylin replied, "Nilüfer, I could tell you everything you told me when I wanted to marry Tallal."

Nilüfer shook her head. "It was always in vain. Don't you waste your time, too. No one actually listens. People have to find happiness through their own trials and errors."

When they returned to Lausanne, Aylin and Jean-Pierre moved in together. Toby von Schweir's money was disappearing fast, although Aylin had been very frugal with her living expenses. She used the money her uncle sent to pay her tuition, and had no interest in asking him for more. He had already spent too much on her divorce proceedings.

Jean-Pierre had a nice apartment close to the university, and after moving in, Aylin spent most of her evenings there with him. They were very good friends, and the young man was undoubtedly her greatest help when it came to her physics and chemistry studies. He was also teaching Aylin to appreciate nature. On weekends, they cycled in the mountains or went skiing, drinking mulled wine in front of a chalet fireplace, enjoying the little things together.

One day, as Aylin reviewed her budget, she said, "Jean-Pierre, this will be another hard month; the anatomy books cost a lot."

"Buy the secondhand books."

"That's what I've been doing! They're still too expensive."

Jean-Pierre began pacing the room. "Aylin, I want to say something, but please don't misunderstand me."

"What is it?"

"Did you know that you don't have to pay tuition if you're Swiss?"

"Yes. I also know that I'm not Swiss."

"You could be."

"This is not like converting to Christianity, darling."

Jean-Pierre said, "You could marry me."

Aylin was speechless. In a hoarse voice, she asked, "What are you talking about?"

"I'm only asking you to marry me."

"Just so I can study free of charge?"

"No, I want to marry you because I love you, because I'm happy with you, and because we're already living together."

"When do you want to marry me?"

"Right now."

"Yes, yes, yes," shrieked Aylin. Jean-Pierre took her in his arms, and they whirled around in the room. Suddenly, Aylin pulled away.

"Damn it, Jean-Pierre, I just remembered something you will not like."

"What?"

"I'm already married."

Two summers ago, Aylin's lawyer had been overly cautious not to provoke Tallal by pressing the French courts to finalize the divorce. Even if the wheels were set in motion again immediately, she told Jean-Pierre, it might be a while.

.   .   .

Meanwhile, Nilüfer had convinced Aziz to give her a divorce. Aylin was sad to lose Aziz, whom she had loved like a brother for almost twenty years.

She begged her sister, "Nilüfer, please don't rush into another marriage."

Nilüfer said, "I've made up my mind."

Aylin said, "If you get married to that grandpa, I'll go ahead and marry the beanstalk."

Nilüfer laughed. "I wish you the best of luck and happiness with the beanstalk."

The sisters faced a turning point in their relationship as the age gap closed. Aylin was maturing, learning to judge things from different angles. For the first time in their lives, she was worried for her older sister. Nilüfer was like a teenager in love. As soon as she obtained the divorce, Nilüfer got married for the second time. The wedding ceremony was very simple.

When Aylin received the good news she had been waiting for from her lawyers, she called her uncle immediately. "My dearest uncle, at last I'm as free as a bird. I got the divorce decree. Now tell me when you can come to Switzerland, so that I can set the date for my next wedding."

Her uncle exclaimed, "But you are free as a bird! You really want to jump into a new marriage so soon?"

Aylin replied, "'Jean-Pierre and I have been living together for two years now. This time I'm sure that I'm doing the right thing."

Uncle Hilmi was quite taken by the idea that his niece was to marry a young nuclear physicist who had gained a reputation at the university for his intellect. Aylin needed a husband who would take the burden off his shoulders.

Only the Egner family, Hilmi, and Hilmi's wife Rozi attended the ceremony. Rozi thought that Aylin was the simplest bride she had ever seen. She wore a light-green suit without even a hat on her head.

As the years passed, their marriage changed not only Aylin's appearance but also her inner nature. While Aylin lived with Jean-Pierre, she discovered the true scientific depths of medicine and learned that richness did not lie in the outer world but in the inner labyrinth of the human soul.

New Horizons

On a terribly hot day in July 1971, Aylin stepped into New Rochelle Hospital. She had just graduated from medical school and jumped at the chance to become an intern so close to a bustling metropolis like New York City.

Jean-Pierre had received an invitation he could not refuse from Los Alamos National Laboratory in New Mexico. Aylin did not want to go to the desert. New Rochelle had been her first choice for an internship, despite the long distance.

Jean-Pierre and Aylin never considered divorce, but they were fully aware that their marriage would no longer function as they reached this crossroads. Neither would prioritize domestic happiness over a career. They were both extraordinarily talented people with bright futures. As they set off in their respective directions, they granted their marriage the freedom to take its own course, shook hands, and parted ways. They still had their memories and a deep and abiding friendship.

Aylin immersed herself in her new job. Young psychiatrists worked the night shift during the first year of their internship, and many of the patients under their care needed constant attention. New Rochelle was a very busy hospital with a large number of patients, and Aylin's hands were full day and night. She worked hard and felt tired at times, but there were also pleasant surprises. For instance, the wife of her young Pakistani colleague, Azim, turned out to be Zeynep, a friend since childhood. Aylin's apartment turned out to be close to Zeynep and her husband's. The two childhood friends began to spend time together almost every day.

One night in the winter of 1972, Zeynep persuaded Aylin to join her and Azim at a cocktail party at the Afghan embassy. Aylin enjoyed the city's nightlife very much, but as she prepared for the cocktail party, she had no idea that she was about to encounter the love of her life, someone she would travel around the world to pursue.

When Aylin first spotted him amid the crowd in the embassy's central hall, everyone else seemed to disappear. He was standing in front of a window, an elegant pillar of dark skin, curly hair, and penetrating green eyes. He was smoking.

Aylin turned to Zeynep. "Who is that man?"

"Who? Oh, Haidar. The UN ambassador to Afghanistan. He's a very attractive man, isn't he?"

"Introduce me to him right now."

"Aylin, take care, Haidar is married!"

"Zeynep, introduce me to him." Zeynep and Aylin walked over to Haidar. Haidar saw a luminous, long, slim, mysterious-looking young woman approach him as if in a dream. He thought she looked as if she had stepped off a cloud, still dressed in dew.

Zeynep said, "I would like to introduce Aylin to you, Your Excellency."

Haidar said, "This is the first time I have been introduced to such a beautiful and elegant American."

"I'm Turkish, Your Excellency."

Haidar's admiring glance locked onto Aylin's hazel-green cat eyes. Aylin could never remember what happened next that night. All she knew was that in the weeks after she found herself in a dream she did not wish to end.

Haidar spoke English with a perfect Oxford accent and French like it was his native tongue. He was a poet, and Aylin felt she understood every word of the poems he recited to her in Pashto. Haidar opened up the world of the fine arts and taught her to appreciate culture. Aylin devoured the books he gave her to read and enjoyed the concerts and exhibitions he chose for them. In return, Haidar fell madly in love with Aylin. He found everything he desired in this enchanting woman who was almost as young as his daughter. He found in her not only a great depth of intellect but a deep sense of humor and a boundless energy. Aylin inspired a new sense of life in a man who had already left middle age behind.

Aylin never asked a single question about his wife, although she knew she lived in his homeland and that they had three grown children together. These issues quickly became taboo. Haidar also knew that Aylin had a husband but never asked questions, either.

Although they lived separately, Aylin and Haidar started to spend three or four nights of the week together.

In the second year of her internship, Aylin began to take care of private patients in addition to her patients at the hospital. She also began to work with patients who were hospitalized for non-psychiatric issues, like appendicitis, but who suffered from things like insomnia and depression. Because her schedule was busier, Aylin and Haidar spent less time together in the second year of their courtship, but when the summer came they traveled to Turkey and then to Afghanistan. At home, Aylin introduced her sweetheart to all of her relatives. It was as if the family had grown accustomed to the men who suddenly appeared in Istanbul with Aylin. They thought Haidar was far more cultivated and elegant than the Libyan Tallal, yet could not help but wonder what would come of the affair.

Aylin was not introduced to Haidar's family in Afghanistan. Still, she was very happy to visit her lover's country, to see and feel the colors, the aromas, the tastes, and the customs around which he had grown up.

Toward the end of 1973, Haidar was given a new appointment in London, and Aylin felt that her happiness was being stolen from her. She applied to hospitals in London to be near him but received an incredible offer from Roosevelt Hospital, one of the best hospitals in New York. Zeynep begged Aylin not to resign and indulge in another mad affair.

For once, Aylin decided to follow a friend's advice and chose not to leave New York. She would travel to London frequently and spend holidays with her lover.

Aylin flew to Europe four times within a year. The physical distance between her and Haidar did not cool their mutual passion; in fact, it only rekindled it. Every three months, they met in Paris, Rome, or London. Haidar continued to romance Aylin with roses, gifts, poems, and whispers of love.

In 1974, Haidar was reappointed again, to India. Aylin realized that fate was making things more and more difficult for them both. Aylin knew she was facing a major decision: she could either follow the man she loved across the globe, or she could prioritize her own career. Could she give up on love for the sake of a job? Just as she prepared to say no, she was appointed head of the Department of Psychiatry.

Aylin could foresee the many opportunities this appointment would open up for her, but she was loath to abandon Haidar. Why, she asked herself, couldn't she be Haidar's second wife, given that they were both Muslims?

Zeynep reacted violently to this idea.

"The second wife! Would that suit you? Shame on you!"

"I would even veil myself for Haidar's sake."

"And examine your patients from behind the veil? Are you mad, Aylin? How many more years can you run after a married man who gets appointed to a different corner of the world every two years?"

"Zeynep, you don't know what love is."

"If it makes me as dumb as you are, then I don't want it!"

In the end, Aylin's common sense triumphed over her feelings. She gave up the idea of following her lover to New Delhi, at least for the time being. She pulled herself together and immersed herself in her job. She was so preoccupied with her work that she rarely had enough time to even think about Haidar. Soon, her research took her to Istanbul to work at the main psychiatric hospital there for three months.

Despite this frantic life, it was still not possible to push Haidar entirely out of her mind. When he sent Aylin tickets to come to New Delhi, she traveled happily to meet him.

During one of these trips, they went to Kathmandu together. Aylin was completely bewitched by the country and got carried away with the magic of the East. She arranged for a job at the city hospital in New Delhi and sent a telegram to Zeynep asking to meet her at the airport when she flew back to New York.

Zeynep was endlessly astonished by Aylin's willingness to waste her talents. She was furious with Haidar for giving Aylin his total support in her plans. Haidar's son-in-law was about to become the minister of finance in Afghanistan, and Zeynep reminded Aylin that the family could not tolerate such a scandal, that they would all hate her like poison. Zeynep couldn't believe her childhood friend was on the verge of sacrificing everything to remain the mistress of a married man.

In a last desperate attempt, Zeynep invoked her own romantic misfortune. Her husband had moved out when Aylin was away in India. She begged Aylin to come live with her during this time of loneliness and despair. Aylin agreed.

Soon after, Zeynep invited a few bachelor friends over for a spaghetti dinner. Bayram was a young doctor from Turkey, a friend from

Zeynep's school days. He brought along a colleague, Mitch Nadowlsky, a psychologist from Turkey, and an attractive one at that.

MITCH NADOWLSKY

The evening of Zeynep's dinner, Mitch and Bayram left the hospital together. They picked up a couple bottles of wine and walked the few blocks together, chatting all the way. Bayram filled Mitch in on the woman he was going to meet at Zeynep's place. She was a doctor of psychiatry with a brilliant future—talented, tall, redheaded, and witty. She looked more like an American than a Turk. He added that she was rather morose at the moment because her lover had recently moved to India, and Zeynep thought they could cheer her up.

Mitch visualized a big, plump woman. Certainly such an accomplished woman must be average looking, otherwise she would have been surrounded by suitors.

Bayram said, "Actually, she has been. She is a divorcée." He knocked and Zeynep answered the door, welcoming her guests. Mitch walked to the kitchen with the wine. When she heard someone come in, the woman in front of the stove turned, and their eyes met. Later, describing that moment, Mitch would always say, "I was struck."

Her eyes had a mischievous sparkle. All night, he followed her everywhere. It was as if a magnet was pulling him in Aylin's direction.

When the party was over and the guests were gone, Zeynep turned to Aylin excitedly. "What do you think about Mitch?"

"Oh, I suppose he's okay."

"What do you mean?"

"You know, just an average person."

"Don't you think he's good looking?"

"Maybe. But he's nothing compared to Haidar."

"Oh, forget Haidar," said Zeynep. "Don't you think he's smart and attractive?"

"I think he tried a bit too hard." Aylin rose and walked to the door.

"Hey, where the hell are you going? We're chatting!"

Aylin said, "I have to call New Delhi."

Two days later, Mitch invited Zeynep and Aylin to dinner at a Chinese restaurant. Afterward, they went to a jazz club.

The next day, he brought over a book for her and ended up staying for dinner. After he left, Aylin told Zeynep, "Good God! I thought he would never leave. I kept Haidar waiting for my call."

Aylin's annual vacation was approaching, and she had made plans to go to New Delhi again. On top of her work in the Department of Psychiatry, she had also begun lecturing at Cornell's medical school, which was affiliated with her hospital. Aylin's days were hectic.

On a searingly hot Sunday, Mitch called Zeynep to tell her that there would be a new Ingmar Bergman film on TV that night. There was no cable TV in Zeynep's house, so the girls went over to Mitch's place. On their way, the girls got caught in the rain. When they arrived at Mitch's apartment soaking wet, he gave them towels to dry off. Aylin's red hair dripped water, and Zeynep looked like a soaked mouse. They all laughed and stretched out in front of the television. By the middle of the film, Zeynep was terribly bored. "Sorry, I can't stand this any longer. I'm going home to bed."

They called a cab and Mitch said, "I'll take Aylin home when the film ends."

At three thirty, Zeynep woke up and realized she hadn't heard Aylin come home. She rose to go to the bathroom and snuck a peek through her friend's bedroom door. The bed was intact. Aylin wasn't back. Zeynep went back to bed with a huge smile.

Mitch opened up a brand-new life for Aylin. There were a thousand things they could share. Mitch knew all the songs from their childhood, from the traditional ballads to the hits of the fifties and sixties, not to mention all the French chansons. When he sat at the piano at house parties, he stole the spotlight with his husky voice. They had many mutual friends to meet for nights out, dinner parties, and dancing. At the piano, Mitch was always happy to sing whatever anyone requested. His voice had that peculiar charm unique to Istanbul natives. When they made love, quarreled, cried, or rejoiced, Aylin and Mitch did so in Turkish. They were two of a kind, able to understand what the other meant in the wink of an eye.

After so much time loving a man many years her senior, Aylin felt as if she had woken from a dream. She was now grabbing at life with a young man who shared her enthusiasm. She had become so accustomed to the secrecy of her relationship with Haidar that she had to adjust to the noisy crowd encircling her now. She felt as if she were on a fantastic holiday. She'd gotten carried away with Mitch without even realizing it. As for Mitch, he was madly in love with her.

Aylin cancelled her trip to New Delhi as Mitch, who had separated from his wife a year earlier, waited for his divorce certificate to finally come through. Aylin wrote to Jean-Pierre and asked for a divorce. Jean-Pierre had been expecting her call for a long time and filed the documents immediately.

Mitch and Aylin moved in together. There were three bedrooms in their apartment, and they turned the two spares into offices. Mitch's sons, Timothy and Greg, who were nine and ten respectively, stayed at their place two or three nights a week. The boys adored Aylin. The poor kids had been torn between their mom and dad in the midst of the divorce, and were relieved to finally have some peace. Aylin became an incredible stepmother, playing sports with them, making up games, and balancing their father's strictness. She was careful never to make a comment about their mother. The boys were very proud of the looks Aylin drew at the beach or the swimming pool. They loved the way she oversaw their lessons and listened to their problems. Tim and Greg were very supportive of their father's relationship with Aylin, and they were hardly alone. Mitch and Aylin were meant to get married and live happily ever after.

There was only one person who fiercely opposed the marriage, and that was Nilüfer.

Nilüfer declared a merciless war against Mitch, to the extent that Aylin's close friends, like Betin, did not even want to see her anymore. Aylin, however, did not blame Nilüfer. She did not particularly care what Nilüfer said and did. Since birth, Aylin had been inured to Nilüfer's self-righteousness, and that would continue all her life. She could never be angry with her sister.

However, some got caught in the crossfire.

One day, Mitch's brother Rafa, who lived in Istanbul, received a call from Aylin's sister. Nilüfer wanted to pay him a short visit to discuss an important matter. Rafa was surprised. Could it be that Aylin's family wanted to help plan their daughter's wedding?

He said, "Certainly, whenever is convenient."

Soon after, Nilüfer arrived at Rafa's house with a few other people. Without shaking hands, she walked straight by him to the sitting room and took a seat. She refused Rafa's offer of coffee or tea with a sharp nod of her head and began speaking without preamble.

"I came here to ask you to stop this marriage."

Rafa sighed. "I cannot interfere with the lives of adults over thirty."

"Aren't you Jewish?"

"Yes!"

"Aren't you worried about your brother marrying a Muslim woman?"

"No."

"What kind of a Jew are you? I'm extremely concerned about this union."

Rafa said, "That is your problem."

Nilüfer said, "You also have a little problem." She pulled a folded newspaper from her bag and extended it to Rafa.

"Read this carefully. Mitch, you, and your family are in trouble. If I were in your shoes, I would do anything I could to stop this marriage."

Rafa shook the paper out and read it. It was a ridiculous newsletter written by the radical right. On the second page, there was a picture of a bearded Arab and a caption that stated Sheik Tallal planned to track down his Turkish wife, who had divorced him without consent, and punish her for daring to marry a Jew.

Rafa felt faint, but he forced himself to appear unmoved. Nilüfer's companions did not utter a word. Instead, they sat with downcast eyes, like lackluster actors in a school play.

Nilüfer rose and walked to the door, the men of her group at her heels. Rafa could not stand to see her out—he felt trapped in a horrible nightmare. Once she was gone, he placed a call to New York. He needed to get in touch with Mitch even if it took two days.

But when Mitch finally answered, he did not react in the way Rafa had expected.

Mitch said, "How could you ever believe anything in that joke of a newspaper? If the Libyan really wanted to find Aylin, he would have done it by now. She even married a Christian husband after she left the sheik."

"But Mitch, I saw the paper with my own eyes."

Mitch said, "The editors probably published a fake issue for Nilüfer's sake. Don't be scared, Rafa. Relax!"

Zeynep was also on the offensive again, though not on Nilüfer's level. She had worked hard to get Aylin to move on from Haidar, and strongly supported her relationship with Mitch. However, she did not think it appropriate to enter into a third marriage so quickly. One day she invited her friend to lunch for a serious talk.

"You're mad, Aylin. You never take life seriously. First a Libyan, then a hippie, then you waste all that time with an old married man!"

"That time was not wasted, Zeynep. Those were the most beautiful days of my life."

"Fine, but why get married again? Would it be so bad to just go on like this for a while and be certain of what you really want?"

"I know what I want. I want Mitch. I want to get married and have children. Time is running out."

"You would get married to someone just to have kids?"

"You know that I'm not marrying just anyone."

"Aylin, think about the future. You are a psychiatrist, while Mitch is just a psychologist. You're already so much more accomplished professionally than he is. Eventually, he'll get jealous and start to resent you."

"How can you say such things? Why would Mitch envy me? He's one of the best in his field."

"He's lower on the totem pole than you are."

"Is this the army, for God's sake? What has that got to do with it?"

"You are used to men who are more accomplished than you, like Haidar."

"You did everything in your power to get me to leave Haidar and take up with Mitch. I don't understand you at all, Zeynep."

"Haidar was a mistake; that's why I pushed you to Mitch. But I forgot how quickly you fall head over heels in love."

Aylin said, "Haidar was a dream, a fantasy. This time I know what I'm doing; I'm marrying Mitch because I love and respect him and want to spend my whole life with him. He is an enlightened man; he will not care a wink about which one of us is more successful."

There was such an intense sincerity in Aylin's voice and eyes that Zeynep gripped her friend's hand.

"Okay, forget this. Everything will be all right."

At this point in her life, Aylin wanted a child, but with two children already, Mitch did not want any more kids. Besides, he and Aylin were very busy professionals at the peak of their careers, working very long hours. Aylin was nearing her forties and Mitch was already there. He did not want to face a crying baby at his age. Yet he could not get Aylin to give up the idea. Finally, he resorted to his last defense.

"Listen, Aylin," he said. "I'm not a fanatic, but I respect my religion very much. I don't want my children to grow up without Judaism."

"Then we can raise our child as a Jew. All religions are sacred to me."

"Well, there are two obstacles to that. First, a child belongs to his mother's religion. You are not Jewish. Second, Nilüfer would never recognize a Jewish niece or nephew—she would rather poison the child!"

Aylin was shocked into silence. Then she burst out laughing. "I'll take care of everything."

Mitch and Aylin got married in a simple ceremony at their new apartment, accompanied by close friends and his children. It was a perfect day for both of them.

Aylin had surprised Mitch with a real Jewish wedding. She had secretly converted.

Mitch was in awe of what Aylin had done for the sake of their future baby. All he had to do now was say yes.

The bride and the groom stepped under the huppah; prayers were said, glasses were shattered, songs were sung, dances were danced, and Aylin and Mitch entered married life surrounded by those they loved.

Aylin was filled with joy when she soon became pregnant. But in her third month, when she went to the hospital for heavy bleeding, she knew that she had lost her baby. She tried again and again and again. At one point, she lost so much blood in a miscarriage that she nearly died. Aylin had six miscarriages in all, each worse than the last. She suffered great physical and mental pain, not to mention grave disappointment. Finally, she gave up on the idea of having a baby.

Aylin traveled to Turkey that summer to meet her husband's family and to introduce Mitch to hers. Mitch was hesitant to confront Nilüfer, but after Aylin's traumatic miscarriage and subsequent depression, he was willing to do anything to lift her spirits.

Nilüfer had sent a letter inviting them to her home in Ankara. As the trip approached, Mitch grew even more apprehensive.

Aylin said, "This will be a good opportunity for you two to reconcile. Why would she reach out if she didn't have good intentions?" Aylin's father went to Ankara ahead of them. He wanted to talk to Nilüfer and prevent the damage he knew she was capable of inflicting on Mitch. Nilüfer's husband also begged his wife to behave. Nilüfer listened to their pleas with blank eyes fixed on the ceiling and said nothing.

Aylin decided they should go to Ankara before Istanbul so as not to further anger her sister. Nilüfer's chauffeur met them at the airport and took them directly to Nilüfer's villa. As they rang the doorbell, Aylin's heart raced. The butler ushered them inside, and they proceeded to the study where Nilüfer, her husband, and her father awaited them. Aylin's brother-in-law embraced her and shook hands with Mitch. "Welcome to my house, sir." Nilüfer kissed her sister and turned to face Mitch, who extended his hand. She looked at him as if he were a repulsive insect and groaned before turning away. Her father stepped swiftly in front of her, kissed Mitch's cheeks, and said, "Welcome, my son," directing him gently to the inner hall of the home. Mitch was breathless. He thought of leaving, but his gentlemanly father-in-law begged him to ignore his insolent daughter.

"Please," he wheezed, "please overlook her behavior. Ever since the car accident, she has been like this. We can hardly believe that she is still alive. God has given her back to us, so we accept everything as it is."

Mitch noticed that his wife's lips were trembling. He had nearly lost Aylin to anemia after her last miscarriage; there was no way he would let her be upset by her childish sister.

"I don't care what Nilüfer does," he said. "I'm not going to risk my wife's health with this nonsense. C'mon, Aylin, let's go unpack." Mitch would never forget the look of gratitude she gave him, and vowed not to let Nilüfer disrupt their vacation.

The whole household worked hard to be excellent hosts to Aylin and Mitch, especially the young servant, Hulusi, who trailed them everywhere to serve them. Aylin's father was happy to have a respectful son-in-law who spoke his native tongue.

Aylin's niece, Tayibe, was thrilled to see her dear aunt and uncle. The little girl, accustomed to her cold mother, soaked in her aunt's love and affection as much as she could. She would be lonely again when they left.

Nilüfer did not say a single word to Mitch in those fifteen days. In turn, Mitch acted as if Nilüfer did not exist. Although they moved around each other, they did not see, hear, or touch each other. In the beginning, Mitch found this unbearable, but soon he started to enjoy this strange situation. The farce ended when Aylin and Mitch went to Istanbul with Aylin's father. Mitch felt like he had passed the most difficult and ridiculous examination of his life.

Indeed he had, because Nilüfer sent Tayibe and Hulusi to New York that summer. They had enrolled Tayibe in a five-week language course. The little girl had just turned nine and didn't know a word of English. When her course was over, the Nadowlskys rented a beach house on Fire Island.

As soon as the children got out of bed, they dashed to the beach and had their breakfast on the sand. They spent the days fishing, racing bikes, or swimming until late in the evenings. Aylin usually placed a huge bowl of shrimp in front of the children at noon. Tim, Greg, and Tayibe ate more shrimp and ice cream that summer than they did for the rest of their lives. In the evenings they cooked on the grill—hamburgers, sausages, or fish—and afterward they took another dip. Tim and Greg were grateful to see this extraordinary change in their father, who had never wanted to do anything on vacation before but listen to classical music.

That summer they also made some serious family decisions. Tayibe was going to continue her education in New York after she finished elementary school in Ankara. Hulusi would stay on for the next year until Tayibe came back in the summer. Since both Mitch and Aylin worked during the day, he could stay in the house to care and cook for her once she returned.

At the end of that unforgettable summer, Tayibe returned to Ankara, the boys to their mother, and the Nadowlskys to their apartment in New York with Hulusi. There was a lot to do. Their lease was about to expire, and they had to find a new house and office for themselves. Mitch and Aylin dipped into their savings and bought an apartment on the Upper East Side with a fantastic view. As they both had private practices, they opened an office just up the block. Happily settled into their new home and office, they hosted endless parties all winter long. Aylin was a very sociable person and had many friends at the hospital where she worked. Their home thronged with visitors, and the social status their new address afforded them soon rippled through their professional lives.

At one party, the director of Aylin's hospital asked Mitch if he would consider transferring. Joining his wife at a hospital close to his home seemed like a dream.

Mitch was hired on at Cornell's medical college as an instructor, and in their private practice the Nadowlskys were flooded with new patients. They soon managed to pay off their new apartment.

Other than her miscarriages, there was nothing to upset Aylin in their first few years of marriage. Mitch adored her. They had a beautiful home. Turkish friends visiting New York always dropped in for drinks. They enjoyed time with colleagues and friends. In fact, another couple from Istanbul, Leyla and Ivan, lived on the same block, and the Nadowlskys saw them almost every day. Aylin found a maternal figure in Leyla, who conveniently shared her mother's name. She was a bit older than Aylin and very bright. Aylin consulted her about almost everything over their daily morning coffees. It seemed as though Aylin had attained the kind of peace she had yearned for.

Their happiness only grew with Tayibe's arrival. The child God did not grant her Nilüfer now gave her, just as her mother had handed Aylin to Nilüfer so many years ago. She was to give Tayibe all her love, attention, and affection, treating her with the same care and patience a true mother would.

Tayibe came to New York in September after spending her summer vacation with her parents. Aylin was ecstatic, and Mitch was happy to see her with a child at last. His sons were also excited to see their friend from two summers ago. Mr. G. was sad to see Tayibe go, but wanted his daughter to become fluent in English, and also felt it wise to send her away from Nilüfer, who had begun to neglect her.

As Aylin's father mentioned, Nilüfer had not been the same since her horrible traffic accident in Saudi Arabia a few years back. Her hip bone had been fractured and her face disfigured. She was in a coma for months, but just as the doctors had given up all hope, she returned to life. But that beautiful face of hers was never restored, and one of her eyelids continued to droop. Her recovery was long and very painful. Nilüfer found solace from her suffering in religion, devoting herself to Islam. She even veiled herself for a while, completing the daily prayer five times from dawn till sunset. She was in constant contact with her

Muslim teachers. Tayibe was subjected to religious training, too. Nilüfer made the child memorize prayers and do the ritual washing. She gave Tayibe a prayer rug, a prayer kerchief, a rosary, and a Koran when she left for America.

As Aylin drove to the airport to pick up Tayibe, she felt uneasy. The husband of a very close friend had died, and a prayer chanting was scheduled for later that day, which she felt compelled to attend. Such rituals had a deeper meaning for people who lived far from their homeland. Aylin had two choices: she could either rush to drop Tayibe at home, or take her to the prayer. But how could she bring such a young girl to that gloomy, grief-stricken place? Yet she did not want to leave her young charge alone.

Tayibe emerged at the customs gate with her two braids and willowy body, and aunt and niece embraced each other tightly. Aylin was reunited with her surrogate daughter at last. When they got in the car, Aylin explained the situation to the young girl with a heavy heart.

She replied, "I would like to come, Auntie."

"Darling, I must tell you that this is not very suitable for a young child. If you get bored, you can go to the bedroom and watch TV in silence."

"I won't get bored, Auntie."

Aylin pulled up to the house.

"Auntie, would you please open the trunk?"

"Why?"

"I need my scarf and Koran."

Aylin thought for a moment that she had misheard. She blinked at Tayibe. The child looked very grave. She took out Tayibe's suitcase, and the girl pulled out a rosary along with the scarf and the Koran.

They entered the house, where everybody was sitting in chairs against the wall. The prayer chanting had already begun. Aylin was wearing a flowery summer dress. She wrapped her Hermès scarf around her head. Tayibe wrapped her head with her white muslin prayer kerchief.

Only her small, thin face peeked out. She opened her Koran on her lap, took her rosary in her hand, closed her eyes, and started to silently recite the eulogy. People in the room began to notice and nudged each other in her direction. Everybody stared at the young girl. It was clear that Tayibe knew everything by heart, and they were deeply impressed. Aylin was so startled she didn't know whether she should laugh or cry.

As they drove back home, Tayibe told Aylin about her mother's religious lessons. Would it be all right if she prayed on the prayer rug every morning?

Aylin said, "You do know that praying is not enough to be a good-hearted, proper individual, don't you, Tayibe?"

"I know, Auntie."

"God will love you if you're a gentle, decent person even if you don't do the daily prayers."

"I know that, too."

"Well then, decide for yourself. It is your choice."

"Auntie, there is just one reason for me to do it."

"And what is that?"

"I gave my mother my word."

Aylin stopped the car and hugged Tayibe tightly. "Tayibe, you are the purest servant of God in the world. I'm sure He loves you very much."

Hulusi was thrilled to see his friend Tayibe again, and immediately led her to the boys' room, where she would sleep. When Tim and Greg came on Wednesdays and weekends, they drew a curtain in the middle to separate the room. But they had so much fun that Mitch often had to tell them to quiet down.

The Nadowlskys had a very strict routine. On weekdays, Aylin and Mitch were usually at the office by seven o'clock, and Aylin received her first patient around seven thirty. Since Mitch was only a psychologist and could not prescribe drugs, he often referred patients to his psychiatrist wife. They had lunch together at the small restaurant just across the street from their office, or in the dining hall at the hospital, and discussed their private consultations. Their afternoon appointments usually lasted until six or seven, and twice a week they lectured at the hospital's medical school.

With the little girl's arrival, their lifestyle became more family oriented. Tayibe was always the first to return to the apartment in the afternoon. She did her homework and chatted with Hulusi as she waited for Mitch and Aylin to come home from work. When Mitch walked through the door, he always put on his classical music and helped Tayibe with homework for at least an hour. Over dinner—delicious Turkish dishes prepared by Hulusi—the family discussed what Tayibe had learned at school that day, then listened to some more music or watched TV before bed. Tayibe's TV allowance ended strictly at a quarter to ten. When the boys joined them on Wednesday evenings and on the weekends, life became even more colorful. They would go out with friends often and continued to rent a beach house in the summers.

On special occasions, like birthdays, Christmas, and Thanksgiving, Aylin prepared the meals with utmost care and attention. Aylin was born a Muslim and became a Jew, but she loved to celebrate the joyous Christian feasts the most. She had a cross and a Star of David together with a *Mashallah* charm on a chain around her neck. According to Aylin, God was for everybody. She loved all human beings, no matter their religion. She had taken an oath as a doctor not to discriminate and respected every person equally, and Mitch adored her for it.

Aylin may have had a deep love for humanity, but she also had a wild temper when she believed an injustice was being done to someone. There was nothing she would not do to protect that person.

One Wednesday evening, Mitch, Aylin, and the youngsters went out to a little restaurant for dinner. As they strolled down the sidewalk, a black Cadillac bumped straight into a tiny Volkswagen waiting for the green light. A young man stepped out of the Volkswagen, left his wife in the car, and approached the Cadillac. Within seconds, two burly men dragged him into their car and slammed the doors. Aylin was at the Cadillac's side in an instant. She kicked at the doors, banged on the windows, and yelled like mad. The light changed and the car screeched off. Mitch ran to her side.

"Have you lost your mind? Those guys could have killed you!"

Aylin said, "I would have killed them!" The genes of Crazy Mustafa raged through her bloodstream.

Aylin was also unafraid of taking on challenging patients, the patients other doctors had rejected. When Lucy Crewe was referred to her, Mitch begged her not to accept.

"Do you really think you can cure someone who has attempted suicide twelve times? This girl is a hopeless case."

"Did you see the girl, Mitch?"

"I've studied her case notes, Aylin. I beg you, don't do it."

"She's young. She's angry. You'd know if you saw her."

"No doctor wants the burden of a patient committing suicide. Patients line up for you, Aylin. Don't waste your precious time on this girl."

"There was something in her eyes, Mitch. She is crying out for help. I think I can cure her."

Mitch said, "You'll never change, Aylin."

When Aylin started seeing Lucy, she thought only of saving her from her suicidal tendencies. She never could have foreseen that one day this young woman would heal and end up supporting her in return. Aylin had a young girl in her care now. How could she refuse another girl who had just left adolescence behind? Doctors were not supposed to love their patients—indeed, it was forbidden. Doctors were supposed to heal, direct, and soothe—nothing more. But it was impossible to convince Aylin to do anything but build a caring relationship with each patient, no matter how much it infuriated her superiors. In Lucy, Aylin invested not only her academic expertise, she invested her heart.

Tayibe never could have dreamed her aunt would become the mother she never had. In Aylin, she confided all her problems. They had great fun together, and Aylin was immensely tolerant in every respect, even as she was strict about Tayibe's studies. She did not permit bad grades and insisted on checking homework. Other matters, like bedtime, shopping, movies, and TV were Mitch's responsibilities.

Nilüfer occasionally visited her daughter in New York, although she still did not talk to Mitch under his own roof. For her, it was her sister's home. Mitch did not let it bother him; he had convinced himself that she was nuts and was determined not to hurt Aylin's and Tayibe's feelings. Still, they had their occasional clashes.

On one visit, Nilüfer suffered from jet lag and could not fall asleep until very late. If she wanted anything in the middle of the night, she knocked on Hulusi's door. But Hulusi slept like a log and did not wake easily. One night, her incessant knocking woke Mitch. He got out of bed to see what was happening.

"What is it? Are you ill?" he asked.

"No."

"Why do you need Hulusi?"

"I want some tea."

"It's three o'clock in the morning. Let him sleep. I'll make your tea."

"I want Hulusi to make my tea."

"Hulusi is my employee. I don't want him up at this hour."

"No, he is mine."

"Nilüfer, I've been paying his salary for years. I don't want you to wake him. I will make your tea."

Nilüfer said, "Hulusi is my houseboy, but if you insist, make the tea dark." She flounced back to the living room. Mitch made the tea and brought it to her on a tray.

Nilüfer took a sip. "It's not dark enough."

Mitch swallowed hard and said nothing. When he returned to bed, Aylin asked him what had happened. Mitch tried to tell her but fell into a fit of laughter, tears running down his cheeks. In the morning, she said to her sister, "You are killing him, Nilüfer. My husband is this close to losing his mind because of you."

When Nilüfer left, life went back to being peaceful, maybe even a little monotonous. Mitch worshipped his wife. The kids were happy, and he was indeed the happiest member of the family.

But Aylin began to get bored with so much harmony. Her friend Leyla was the first to spot the symptoms.

Leyla's husband Ivan often took long international business trips. She was sick and tired of her teenage daughter's attitude and was fed up with being left alone. When Aylin was over for coffee one day, she wailed about her husband's absence until Aylin interrupted her.

She said, "Leyla, at least you have space to breathe. What would you do in my shoes?"

Leyla was startled. "Aren't you happy, Aylin?"

"I can't say I'm unhappy, but sometimes I feel suffocated."

Leyla sat speechless. She was scared she would hear things she did not want to know.

Aylin said, "Don't misunderstand me. Nothing's wrong with Mitch; I'm just tired of the same old routine. I feel like a machine."

Leyla said, "Why don't you take a vacation?"

"I don't think this is something a vacation can settle. We are together all the time. We go to bed and rise together; we work and come home together; we eat together. I want to do some things separately."

"Like what?"

"I've no idea. I almost wish there were another woman in Mitch's life."

"Aylin, are you mad?"

"You know what, Leyla, I'm fed up with sex, too. If he had someone in his life, Mitch wouldn't be so cross with me when I reject his advances."

"Do you have someone else in your life?" asked Leyla, fear in her voice.

Aylin said, "No. Never. I could do without love and sex for a time. I'd just like to be by myself."

Neither woman really thought that such a thing would ever happen. Leyla remembered their talk that day as neighborly venting about their husbands. She didn't take what Aylin had said seriously. Meanwhile, Aylin started to listen to her inner voice, and their beautiful, harmonious home began to dissolve.

First, Mitch and Aylin argued about their summer plans. Aylin wanted to rent a beach house in either Southampton or Fire Island, but Mitch claimed they could not afford it on top of school tuitions.

Aylin said, "I want to get away for the summer. We've always managed it no matter what. That's how I grew up."

"Then go to Istanbul for the summer."

"Don't be obtuse, Mitch. You know that I cannot leave my patients."

"Well, you know that I can't rent a summer house until the boys finish school."

As a solution, Aylin proposed they visit her friends on Long Island every weekend, but Mitch did not want to suffer through the summer traffic.

Aylin shouted, "For God's sake, don't you want to enjoy nature, the sea, the trees?"

Trying to remain calm, Mitch answered, "No. I don't need such things to rest. I can find peace—"

"Just sitting between these four walls with that goddamn music at top volume?"

Mitch strode out of the room, and that weekend Aylin took Tayibe to Boston to visit a friend. When she returned, she found the apartment littered with elaborate bouquets. Apparently, Mitch wanted her forgiveness. Aylin did not hold a grudge. They reconciled. But the seed of discontent had been sown.

When Mitch came home and played his classical music on the turntable, Aylin now took a glass of wine to her room and closed the door tight. In response, Mitch started to bristle when Aylin poured a drink every evening after work. Mitch did not tolerate alcohol. Aylin's single glass of white wine was enough to make him furious. When she started going out on weeknights, he complained because he had to get up so early in the morning.

At long last, Mitch wanted to face the tension enveloping their home. "Aylin, you are clearly unhappy and it is affecting our marriage. Is there someone else in your life? Do you want to get a divorce?"

"No."

"What is it, then?"

"Why don't we give each other some space, Mitch? We have spent more time together in five years than most married couples do in fifteen. It's too much."

"So you want to separate our offices?"

"No."

"Can I be honest, Aylin? I think this is about my money. I will never be able to give you the life you want. But I don't want to have a summer house, a weekend house, or a fashionable car. I'm content with what I have, but you are not, and your dissatisfaction has changed you into an irritable person. You don't enjoy sex. You're drinking too much. I'm telling you this because I love you and want to help."

"I want a change, Mitch. I'm so bored."

"Do you want a divorce?"

"No," screamed Aylin. "I don't even want to hear the word! I love you, too, but please, let's try to make a change. We're both mature people. Let's have a trial separation."

"How?"

"Let's give each other two days a week."

"Two days to do what?"

"To be free. You could go to dinner with someone, and maybe I could go to the opera."

"But why not do those things together?"

"The whole point is to take some time apart."

"But we are married, Aylin."

"Our marriage is wearing out, Mitch. I'm asking you to help me save it."

"So you will allow me to dine with someone else, is that right?"

"Of course."

"Then what? Maybe we'll go dancing."

"Sure. Why not?"

"By then, we'll be tipsy. Can I invite her back here?"

"No, you wouldn't bring her here. But perhaps you could go to her place or a hotel."

"What about you? Will you do the same?"

"Why not?"

"And then?"

"There's no 'and then.' You know I haven't felt like sex lately."

"What if your feelings change?"

"I'll come to you."

"So, in short, you will allow me to be with another woman?"

"Yes."

"You won't be jealous?"

"Not in the least."

"You are sure?"

"Positive."

Mitch bowed his head. "Well then, you don't love me anymore, Aylin," he said in a sad voice. "In that case, divorce is the best way to go."

Aylin looked helpless and began to cry. She tried to change his mind, but Mitch rejected the idea of separating just as she rejected divorce.

In the end, Mitch's threats were just a reality check. He decided to let things take their natural course. Aylin knew Mitch would never betray her. He was the man she had trusted, leaned on, believed in, and loved for so many years. She could never give him up. Yet she still felt this peculiar sense of ennui. She felt as though her soul had wings that beat but could not take off. Maybe she needed her own psychiatrist. But all the doctors in the area were their mutual friends.

Finally, Aylin chose her close friend Emel as her confidante. Like Leyla, Emel had been watching this thunderstorm roll in for some time. Ever since Aylin and Mitch's wedding day, Emel and her husband had been among their closest friends. They always had wonderful times together, but lately it felt like it was all in the past. People were getting older and more complacent; their lives revolved around routines. But Aylin did not want that. She wanted to fly toward the highest peaks. In a sense, she had. None of her friends had come close to her professional success. She had become one of the most esteemed, expensive, and sought-after psychiatrists in New York City.

Emel asked, "Aylin, can't you be satisfied by your professional success?"

"And ignore my private life? What about my feelings, my desires?

"Your private life is wonderful! You have a handsome husband who loves you and is devoted to you."

"I wish he weren't so devoted. Maybe if he could just give me a chance to miss him, things could change."

"You're swimming in dangerous waters, Aylin. There are many women who would jump at the chance to tear Mitch away from you. You'll be sorry then."

"I know he won't leave. We are deeply committed to each other, but I sometimes feel like I'm being strangled. Help me, Emel."

"What do you want me to do?"

"Introduce him to single girls."

"Are you mad?"

"For God's sake, Emel. You're my dear friend. I cannot ask this of anyone else. Introduce him to someone he will like. It'll do us both good to get a little space."

Emel said, "Aylin, think it over once more. You will regret this."

The two-nights-a-week plan was put into effect. Mitch still considered it nonsense. Nonetheless, he agreed to tolerate it for a time because he knew it would fail. Who knows, he thought, maybe it would solve their crisis. It was worth a shot.

On Wednesdays and Fridays, they spent the evenings apart. Aylin usually took the opportunity to take a patient to a bar and observe them under different conditions. She enjoyed the chance to order a glass or two of wine away from Mitch's judging looks. Mitch did not mind the alcohol so much as the fact that she was fraternizing with patients in her care. There were strict ethical rules concerning the issue, but Aylin had never been one to care for rules. And if she believed her patient needed special care, she paid those rules even less attention. Strangely, those patients she saw outside the office improved at an incredible pace.

For the first few weeks the plan was in place, Mitch stayed home alone, but eventually he was coaxed out by his colleagues, who had accepted this silly arrangement as just another of Aylin's whims. Mitch started to take a female doctor or friend out to dinner now and again. Aylin and Mitch told each other about their free evenings in great detail the following morning. Aylin demanded honesty. If either of them felt an emotional connection to someone else, the other party had to be informed. This was her way of keeping the situation under her control.

At the beginning of December, Aylin learned that one of her dearest friends back in Istanbul, Suzan, had breast cancer. She was mad with grief, remembering her mother's battle with the malicious tumor. Since the diagnosis was grim, she decided to spend the holidays by Suzan's bedside. Mitch did not mind spending the holidays alone, but he refused to share it with Nilüfer, who had booked her trip months earlier. Desperate, Aylin called Emel to see if she would host Mitch at her country house in New Jersey. "If I leave Nilüfer and Mitch alone at home, someone will end up dead." Emel accepted gracefully.

"Could you also invite a friend for Mitch?"

"Aylin, I told you I would not interfere."

"Emel, don't you want to have an equal number of men and women at your table? It would be nice for him. I don't want him to feel lonely."

Mitch happily accepted Emel's invitation. He was looking forward to playing bridge with her husband, Paul. He dropped Aylin off at the airport, bought a case of Beaujolais, and headed out to New Jersey.

Emel and her husband had invited a few friends to dinner that evening. Mitch struck up a conversation with Barbara, a brilliant, merry, and slightly plump blond. She'd divorced many years earlier and now worked as a movie critic for an arts magazine. Both Mitch and Barbara had fun showing off their piano skills, singing Christmas carols, and dancing.

Barbara went home at night but came back the next day to play bridge and Scrabble. So as not to run into his sister-in-law, Mitch stayed on at Emel's until the New Year, and Barbara found excuses to stop by again and again. This did not go unnoticed by Emel.

She decided to say something.

"Both you and Aylin are very close friends of ours, Mitch. We feel guilty for introducing you to Barbara."

"Did you know that Aylin has been pushing me to meet someone?"

Emel did not answer.

"I've done what Aylin has asked me to do. I've found a girlfriend."

"You can't be serious, Mitch. I think you're doing this to punish Aylin."

Mitch said, "I'm very serious. It wouldn't be fair to use Barbara like that."

That day, he moved into Barbara's house.

A week later, Aylin returned to New York and found Nilüfer alone at home. Emel had suggested that something was up, but Aylin hadn't taken it seriously. When Nilüfer left two days later, Mitch had still not come home. When they returned to work after the holidays, they walked back to the apartment together after their last appointments.

Aylin said, "Well, did you have a good time? What did you do?"

Mitch said, "I did what you wanted me to do. I found a girlfriend."

"Can I meet her?"

"I don't think so."

"What does she look like?"

"She's pretty."

"Prettier than I am?"

"Aylin, please."

"Is she?"

"No. I'm sure I will never meet a woman as beautiful as you. But she cares about me, and that's what matters."

"Is that why you moved out?"

"Well, at first I just didn't want to go home to Nilüfer, but I like spending nights with Bobby."

"You mean, you sleep with Bobby, this woman with a man's name?"

"Isn't that what you wanted? Someone else in my bed?"

"I did not tell you to move into her place. Our agreement did not include falling in love."

"It was your agreement, not mine."

"Fine. Then go."

Mitch said, "You thought you could pull my strings the way you wanted, but I'm not your puppet. This masquerade is over!"

"You bastard! You have broken our marriage. I never betrayed you. But you . . . goddamn you!"

Aylin grabbed a vase and flung it at Mitch's head, followed by several ashtrays and her wine glass. He ducked, and the glass shattered against the wall, wine dripping down to the floor. Mitch gathered his things and walked calmly to the door. "You're reaping what you've sown, Aylin."

Aylin screamed as hard as she could and started to sob. An iron fist squeezed her heart. Thankfully, Hulusi and Tayibe weren't at home. Aylin finished a bottle of wine, and when her head began to ache she swallowed two Advils.

The next morning, Mitch called the apartment when he saw that Aylin had not shown up for work. No one answered. He asked Leyla to check in, and when she opened the door she saw that the living room had been turned into a battlefield. Hulusi looked equally dumbfounded. Aylin was still in bed and could not even lift her head. Leyla made a cup of dark coffee, dissolved a couple of Alka-Seltzers in a glass of water, and brought the glass to Aylin's lips.

"Mitch deserted me," Aylin whispered.

"You deserved it."

Aylin started to weep. "I didn't ask for this, Leyla!"

"Oh, yes you did. You thought you could treat your husband like one of your patients."

"What will I do now?"

"Listen to me for once in your life and don't put pressure on Mitch. Leave him alone for a while; don't speak of divorce or ask him to come back."

"Who speaks of divorce?" screamed Aylin. Her tears had left black trails of mascara on her cheeks.

Leyla said, "Pull yourself together and go to work. Try to be calm. Time mends all wounds. Mitch would not have sent me if he did not still care for you. He was scared you were hurt."

In the end, Mitch did not stay with Barbara, but he did not return to Aylin, either. She had offended him deeply, and he wanted to teach her a good lesson. When he came home, he slept in the children's room, then moved to Leyla's until he found a new place. Aylin was glad that he was close by and hoped Leyla and Ivan could persuade him to forgive her.

This arrangement was also convenient for Mitch. He was close to his office and would still have Hulusi at his service.

Hulusi visited Mitch every morning to iron his shirts and take his laundry to be washed at Aylin's apartment. Aylin often visited Leyla's place under false pretenses. In the end, it took months for them to really separate. Even after they finally divorced, separated their offices, and remarried years later, Mitch and Aylin would have lunch together once a week and continue to confide in each other.

When Aylin realized that she could not bring Mitch home, she decided to begin life anew. While she deeply regretted pushing Mitch away, she could not deny that she felt suffocated at the thought of living with him as before. The kids had grown older and stopped visiting them every week. Greg had gone to study abroad in Europe, and Tim had many girlfriends to attend to. Tayibe had started coming home quite late from the library because of her rigorous studies.

Suddenly, Aylin found herself all alone in a huge apartment. However, as usual, her uncle Hilmi was there for her. He and Rozi decided to come to New York to lend support to his beloved niece during a dark time.

Uncle Hilmi had quite a number of friends in New York and hosted many small parties at Aylin's place. One night, Aylin met Thomas Abbot, one of Hilmi's hunting friends.

Tom Abbot was a very charming gentleman of Hungarian descent. He was also seventy years old and a womanizer who favored pretty women. The moment he saw Aylin, he became infatuated with her. He thought that he had come across a very rare jewel. This woman was built like a model but was also intelligent, well educated, and well bred. By the end of the night, Abbot was ready to offer her the world.

Mitch had always noticed that Aylin seemed to electrify older men. One evening, Aylin went to Leyla's for a drink and told Mitch, "You won't believe it, but I picked up an old man again. He's taking me to Japan."

Mitch said, "Why didn't you just let him propose? You adore old men."

"If I was interested in marriage, I wouldn't have broken up with you."

"If you are after sex, passion, and excitement, go and find yourself a young lover."

Aylin said, "There's so much else in life that people can share. It's difficult to explain to people like you who are hooked on sex." She finished her coffee and left. Leyla noticed that Mitch had turned sulky and pensive.

She asked, "What is it, Mitch?"

"She's wasting her life."

"Oh, come on! She's only taking a trip to Japan."

"What is she doing with someone as old as her father? Couldn't she have found someone more appropriate?"

"I think you're just jealous that she may actually get involved with this man."

Mitch said, "Maybe you're right."

"So you still love her."

"Of course I do. I never wanted this."

"Why are you both so stubborn? Two people who really love each other and shared years of marriage won't put things right, just to get even! Shame on you."

Leyla knelt down in front of Mitch, took his hands in hers, and started to cry. She could not accept that they would throw it all away out of spite.

"Aylin has opened up many doors, but you have closed them all in her face. Now you're telling me that you love her. What kind of stupid joke is this?"

Mitch was astonished by her outburst.

Leyla said, "If Aylin moves on with someone else, that will be the end of it. Mitch, think hard on this."

"I don't think I have to worry about Abbot."

"Sure, maybe Tom just wants to travel with an attractive and intelligent woman in the last years of his life. But you have Turkish roots; you can't bear to think of your wife going off to Japan, even with an old man. Mitch, this is your last chance; think it over before it's too late."

Mitch said, "Fine. If she cancels this trip, I will take her back."

Leyla flew out to the elevator in her slippers and ran to Aylin's door, ringing the bell and knocking until Hulusi answered.

"What is it, Miss Leyla, is anything wrong?"

"Nothing's wrong! Where is Aylin?"

"Still in her room."

Leyla pushed past him.

"Aylin! We've got to talk!"

Aylin sat in front of her dressing table putting on mascara. One eye fluttered with long, full lashes, while the other looked small, sunken, and tired. She gave Leyla a bewildered look as she turned off her loud music.

"Listen to me, Aylin, and leave your makeup now!"

"I can't. Abbot is coming in half an hour to take me to the Russian Tea Room."

"Aylin, if you don't go to Japan, Mitch promises to come back home. Don't look at me like that—it's true! Now, finish your other eye and let's go. Wait, no! He can come here. That will be even better!"

Dumbfounded, Hulusi stood by the door, trying to hear the conversation inside.

Twenty minutes later, Leyla stormed out of Aylin's apartment. When she reached her own, she looked years older. Avoiding Mitch's eyes, she whispered, "She is going to Japan."

HULUSI

Saturday, June 4, 1977

From the airplane window, Hulusi kept his eyes fixed on the clouds for half an hour. They scattered and danced around him in vast layers. He wanted to reach out and touch them, but the window had no handle. He bent toward the little girl beside him and asked if there was a way to open it. Tayibe laughed so hard that Hulusi wished he hadn't spoken. *This family is too smart,* he thought. Still, he couldn't begrudge the people who changed his life.

He still could not believe his luck; he was flying to America. Just three months ago, had anyone predicted this, he would have replied, "You bastard, go pick on someone else!"

Hulusi was used to being teased for his milky skin, hairless face, and small stature. Suppressing his desire to press his face against the clouds, Hulusi tried to formulate the first letter he would write to his father back home.

My Dearest Father, he would start. First, I traveled to Istanbul by bus. It was a pleasant journey. The bus stopped at Bolu for lunch, and

I ate stuffed zucchini, pilaf, and a bowl of yogurt. I thought of my hometown the whole time.

When he thought of his family, Hulusi felt sad and lit a cigarette. A stewardess passed by and raised an eyebrow. Hulusi prodded Tayibe and pointed in her direction.

Tayibe chuckled, "How can she know how old you are!"

Indeed, this tiny, featherlight girl with long brown hair and the short, skinny boy made a very odd couple. Since they could not yet speak English, they had to communicate with the stewardesses by miming their requests.

What a long way it is from my town to America! Hulusi thought. He could not believe that God Almighty, who had not granted him a single ounce of testosterone, had given him this chance. Hulusi visualized the faces of the neighbors who had jeered at him his entire life. He had taken the trouble to go all the way back to his town to share his news, kiss the hands of the elders, and get their blessings.

The fourth son, Hulusi was a disappointment to his mother, who had hoped for a girl to help her with the housework. But Hulusi was a calm and pleasant child, and with his green eyes and long lashes, he had grown to be the most handsome of his siblings. But as his peers went through puberty, Hulusi did not change at all. His voice did not break, his facial hair did not grow, and his height stayed the same. Even stranger, he had no sense of smell.

First his brothers started to poke fun, then the neighbors, and finally the whole village. One by one, boys his age enlisted in the army, but he did not pass the test. Gradually, he became known as Hulusi the Girl. When his grandfather sold a piece of land, he gave Hulusi's father a small amount of money to take his son to a specialist in Ankara. This was the by far the biggest city that Hulusi had ever seen.

Unfortunately, Hulusi's operation was unsuccessful, and he spent a long time recovering. By the time he went in for a second procedure, he was twenty, but looked about twelve or thirteen. His body would not produce testosterone, but his intellect and his other senses worked like a clock. Instead of going back to the village where he had been the laughingstock, he decided to stay in Ankara and find a job. In Ankara, no one knew his age.

First, Hulusi worked shining shoes. Then a fellow villager found him a job as a waiter at the Hotel de la Palace. The hotel's clientele were mostly businessmen visiting from the inner Anatolian cities. When Hulusi served them, they were surprised by his intelligence and left generous tips. The clever, green-eyed, long-lashed boy soon became the hotel's unofficial mascot. When the regulars arrived, they asked for him.

For a while, Hulusi was content with this life. He had lost his inferiority complex and started to make money. But how long could he fool everybody? Hulusi was scared he would somehow reveal his real age and become the laughingstock of the hotel.

Indeed, over the next two years, his nonexistent facial hair and feminine voice started to attract some attention when people noticed he wasn't growing. This time, a fellow villager came to Hulusi's aid. A relative of his brother-in-law, Dursun worked as a gardener for a very prominent family. The G. residence was always teeming with visitors, and sometimes even five servants would not suffice to serve their guests. Dursun asked Hulusi whether he would be willing to leave the hotel and work for Mr. G. with him.

This offer came at just the right moment for Hulusi, whose friends had started to insist on taking him to the local brothels to lose his virginity. It was time to leave. Hulusi did not even ask about the salary. He knew very well that nothing would match the tips he earned at the hotel, but he did not care about money. He only wanted to leave the hotel before they learned the truth and started to pity him. He accepted and shortly thereafter moved to the annex of the G. villa that he would share with Dursun.

From dawn to dusk, there seemed to be no limit to the guests who visited the G. estate, not to mention the ones who stayed overnight.

Dursun told Hulusi that politicians were always eager to have a full house. It was good for their careers.

Hulusi started as an errand boy, but soon his intelligence and talent were discovered by the cook, and he was promoted to the kitchen. He became the cook's apprentice, cutting heaps of onions and peeling potatoes. In the meantime, he paid meticulous attention to the cook's techniques, although the cook was careful not to give away too many secrets.

One day, the lady of the house decided she would have this neat, clean boy attend the table. Hulusi had mastered service during his hotel days and surpassed all expectations. His confidence improved with every step he took.

Hulusi was happy with his life. His income was smaller now, but no one in the house bothered him about his height and bare face. Here, he was neither Hulusi the Girl nor Hulusi the Virgin. He was just Hulusi the houseboy.

One hot summer day, the cook was asked to prepare a dish specific to Ankara, to offer that night's special guests. The maid Halime took her time cleaning the bedroom floors that day. Hulusi was told to wear a clean shirt and tie. The staff had been bustling for days to prepare the house for Nilüfer's sister, who was visiting from America with her new husband.

The observant boy gathered that the groom would not be heartily received by the lady of the house. He was a Jew from Istanbul who practiced psychology, whatever that meant.

Despite Mr. G.'s talents of persuasion, his wife reacted to the news of their arrival as stubbornly as a mule. Her sister should not have married a Jew, and Nilüfer would never forgive her. Hulusi had never seen a Jew in his life and imagined an ugly hunchback with a terribly long nose. The tension in the house continued to build, and Hulusi waited excitedly for the guests, though he did not understand why his mistress had gone through all this trouble for someone she did not want to entertain.

Hulusi had heard them the previous morning as he served tea. Mr. G. pleaded with his wife. "I beg you to be sensible, madam. Mistreating your guest in your own home would not suit you at all."

Hulusi decided his mistress was definitely a bit strange.

When everything was ready, they set out the table for tea in the garden, and Mr. G. sent his car to the airport. Hulusi put on the serving jacket he had carefully ironed the day before and combed his hair with cologne. He brought the tea tray to the garden and positioned himself by the door to wait.

"Why are you standing there like a scarecrow?" said Halime. "Go and help in the kitchen. Off you go!"

Thanks to Halime's fussing, Hulusi missed the guests' arrival. Later, holding the teakettle, he passed through the door to the garden and thought he'd entered a dream. There sat the most beautiful woman he had ever seen—not just in real life but in the American movies, too. He stood paralyzed at the threshold.

"Why are you just standing there, boy? You're letting the tea get cold."

At the sound of Nilüfer's voice, Hulusi pulled himself together. He took a step forward, his eyes searching for the crooked Jewish husband. The handsome man sitting next to Mr. G. could not possibly be him. He did not look like a Jew at all. When Hulusi returned to the kitchen, he was still dazzled. He ran to the bathroom to comb his hair again. If God was responsible for this, Hulusi had surely done something right. Just as Aylin shook him with her beauty, so her husband impressed him with his height, broad shoulders, well-balanced features, and deep voice. To a boy like Hulusi, these were the attributes of a god. There should, would, and could not be a more handsome pair in the whole wide world.

Over the next three days, Hulusi made no attempt to conceal his admiration. He was at the disposal of both guests, trailing them everywhere they went. The only other person in the house who seemed almost as elated by their presence was Tayibe, the young daughter of his employers.

With the arrival of her aunt, Tayibe found herself flooded by a kind of love and attention she had not known existed. Nilüfer was disappointed Tayibe was not a son, and she neglected her even more after the birth of her younger brother. In keeping with Turkish tradition, Nilüfer's love, care, and attention were focused solely on her son.

Mr. G., on the other hand, was simply too busy to be much of a father to his daughter. Thus, Tayibe was growing up without the care she deserved. Though she loved her parents deeply despite the distance between them, she envied her spoiled brother, Mustafa.

But Aylin changed everything. The first time she glimpsed her niece, she felt the pure maternal instinct that Nilüfer had felt when she laid eyes on Aylin. Somehow Aylin knew that someday this girl would be as close to her as her own child.

For a long time, Aylin could not confess to her husband that she planned on inviting her niece to live with them. Tayibe would fulfill Aylin's yearning for the child she could not have. In the meantime, Mitch grew to love the sensitive little girl dearly. Aylin was relieved when he was enthusiastic about the idea. Now, they just had to convince Nilüfer and her husband. The first step was to invite Tayibe to summer school to see if she and her parents could cope with a temporary separation. This first wish was granted. In addition, Aylin asked her sister to recommend an eligible housekeeper to help out during her stay. With a child in their care, they would need someone to cook.

· · ·

And so Tayibe and Hulusi's wheels of fortune started to turn. Nilüfer chose Hulusi to accompany Tayibe to New York.

Mitch and Aylin collected Tayibe and Hulusi at the airport. Tayibe flew instantly into her beloved aunt's arms. Hulusi could not help but hug Aylin, too. He was wild with joy.

Tayibe and Hulusi sat in the backseat of the car as the city swam in an ocean of light. For the little girl, it was a fairy tale. But if Tayibe was in a fairy tale, Hulusi had been sent to heaven. When they arrived inside the apartment on the thirty-seventh floor, Hulusi froze. It was the most impressive view he thought he would ever see in his life. Only a god could look at the world as a bird would. All the flickering lights at his fingertips; he was brimming with glee.

He learned his daily rounds quickly—the grocer, the butcher, the cleaners—from Wilma, the maid. He had already perfected washing, ironing, cooking, and serving in Ankara. Soon he was able to manage everything by himself. In the meantime, he started to study English. He read the textbooks Aylin gave him and made sure to complete the exercises every evening when he was finished with his chores.

When it was time for Tayibe to return home, Hulusi suffered his first bout of homesickness. It was as if the little girl was his last tie to the home country. The night she left, he sequestered himself in his room and wept, trying not to feel desperately lonely. After all, the Nadowlskys had taken care to introduce him to the staff at the Turkish embassy, and he often met up with them in his free time. He never spent much, saving most of his money to send back to his parents. He had no expenses except for the cigarettes he had smoked since he was seven.

Hulusi was twenty-five when Aylin finally asked him why he did not grow. He had stopped thinking about it, but his mistress insisted on confronting the problem. She took him to two different doctors and three different clinics. He had X-rays taken and withstood multiple hormone tests. Although Hulusi knew it was hopeless, he still followed his mistress like a lamb. He knew that Aylin would persist no matter what.

Finally, Hulusi was diagnosed with Kallmann syndrome and given a concise therapy plan: three shots a week and one pill per day. Weekly prescriptions would cost 134 dollars.

Hulusi said, "Ma'am, if I could afford this, I would have done it a long time ago."

"I will pay for the medicine; you just swallow your pills on time," answered Aylin.

When he began the therapy, Hulusi had photographs taken, and the doctor noted his height and weight. At first, Aylin gave him the shots, but when she realized it made him uneasy, she taught him how to inject himself. Hulusi continued the therapy only to please Aylin. He was convinced it would not work.

But within eight months, Hulusi began to feel strange. His face was covered in pimples and he looked somewhat taller. In the evenings, he accompanied his friend from the embassy to a hotel, where the friend would meet a prostitute. Hulusi would wait in a coffeehouse until his friend reappeared, hot and flushed. He would ask, "How was it, buddy?" But it was only out of politeness. Why should he be forced to hear about pleasures he himself would never experience?

After Aylin, Hulusi was happiest to have Tayibe back with them in New York a year later. He saw himself as her guardian, which inevitably led to some clashing. "Tayibe, your aunt cooked the meat with wine tonight so stay away from it," he said one night.

"Hulusi, why do you keep harping on wine?"

"Muslims don't drink wine. If your mother hears about it, she'll be livid."

"My mother loves wine. You know that."

"Doesn't matter. It's my job to protect you."

"If you are so against alcohol, why do you drink whiskey and vodka?"

"Who says I do?"

"I've seen you. When my aunt and uncle are not home, you open the liquor cabinet, fill a big glass, add some ice, and drink. And you always pick the vodka with the Russian name."

"My dear girl," said Hulusi. "The Koran tells us not to drink wine; it says nothing about whiskey and vodka. And those drinks were purely medicinal, okay?"

Tayibe put her hands on her hips. "Listen, Hulusi, the Koran doesn't say, 'Don't eat a dish cooked in wine,' it says, 'Don't eat pork.' I will eat the steak cooked in wine. It's good for digestion."

Hulusi scoffed, "What a sharp tongue at this age! You're a little devil." Still, he did not go near the liquor cabinet for quite some time.

In the second year of his hormone therapy, he started to earnestly ask his friend for the details of what went on with women behind closed doors. A few whiskers appeared on his chin. One day, he told his mistress, "These trousers you bought me shrank when I washed them. Shall we return them?"

Aylin squinted at him. "Hulusi, come here. Take off your shoes and stand against that wall."

She penciled a mark above his head and measured it. Hulusi could have fainted when he heard he had grown—by a few inches, no less. Aylin remarked that his facial hair was growing, too. "Take off your clothes, Hulusi."

Hulusi sputtered, "I can't, ma'am."

"Don't be stupid, I'm a doctor! Now take off your shirt."

Hulusi took off his shirt and raised his arms. "Your armpits are starting to grow hair, Hulusi. Now take off your pants!"

"No, ma'am. I beg you."

Aylin said, "Okay, okay. Mitch will take a look when he comes home."

Hulusi had begun to resemble a man. He continued growing and shaved once every two or three days. Safe in his room, he started flipping through the pages of porno magazines and even started to masturbate.

He could not send all of his money home anymore. He needed it now for shaving cream, razors, dirty magazines, and dates with girls on his nights off, although he was still too shy to take one to bed.

Finally, toward the end of his third year of therapy, Hulusi felt like a handsome young man. He sent a picture to his village.

One evening, as he walked down the street with his friend, he saw a very pretty girl sitting cross-legged on top of a car. He wanted the girl but was too embarrassed to disappear with her in front of his friend. He made some excuse and rushed home to his stash of money before running back. The girl was still on the car, smoking her cigarette. His heart pounded in his throat.

"How much?" he asked.

"Ten dollars."

They entered a run-down hotel on Eighty-Sixth, where Hulusi handed an extra ten to the man at reception. The girl led the way as Hulusi slunk behind her. She sat on the filthy bed and said, "If you want the bra off, it's five dollars extra." Five more for this, another five for that. Hulusi's savings melted away in increments, but he didn't mind. He would have shelled out a hundred if she had she asked. All of his senses were concentrated on that single spot. He suddenly felt deeply ashamed.

The girl said, "Is this your first time?"

"Yes." He exhaled.

"You teddy bear!" The girl dragged him to bed and had his clothes off in a wink. Hulusi sat naked at the foot of the bed with his hands over his penis. He felt like dying of embarrassment. When the girl took him in her hands, Hulusi almost fainted.

"Ten bucks more for a blow job."

"Do what you want," he said. "Anything."

The rest was a blur. Right away, the girl was on top of him, then slid beneath him. She was everywhere—whining, touching, caressing, gripping, sucking, nipping him with her teeth. Hulusi was in another world; he fell back as cascades of exquisite sensation overwhelmed him.

The girl sat up, "Okay. You've come. Time to go." She dressed and then vanished with his money.

Hulusi lay outstretched for a few more blissful seconds. Dizzy, he put on his clothes and let himself out, the cold wind hitting his face. He ran the blocks home. It was past two and Aylin was fast asleep. Still, he knocked on her door.

His mistress yelled, "What is it? What's happening?" and opened the door. "Hulusi, oh my God! Has something happened to Mitch? To Tayibe? What is it?"

In the half-lit corridor, she saw Hulusi's smile widen.

"Miss Aylin, ma'am. I've done it. I've done it."

"Done what? Spit it out."

"I've done it. At last I have done it."

"Done what? Oh, you mean . . . *What?* Did you manage to?"

"I did it, ma'am."

"You lost your virginity?"

"Yes, ma'am."

Aylin grabbed her nightgown and ran into the living room. They whirled and cheered as tears fell down Hulusi's cheeks.

"May God bless you and grant you every happiness, my mistress. Had it not been for you . . ." Hulusi choked up, then fell into a fit of laughter.

Aylin yelled, "Come, we must toast to this." She took out a bottle of champagne.

"Ma'am, could I instead have the Russian vodka?"

Aylin laughed.

"Drink what you want. I must call Mitch and tell him."

"At this late hour? What about tomorrow?"

"No, it cannot wait. Bring me the phone, quick!"

A few days later, Hulusi passed Mitch in the hall and blushed profusely.

He said, "I must ask you something. It's very private."

"Go ahead, Hulusi."

"No, not here. May I come to the office?"

"Is it serious?"

"Yes. I want us to talk man to man."

Mitch managed to suppress a laugh and said, "Come to my office at six." Hulusi appeared at six on the dot and started to describe some strange symptoms.

Mitch stopped him. "I'm a psychologist, but I can send you to a specialist."

Hulusi paused. "Could you come with me? My English may not be sufficient."

"Okay," said Mitch, and they went to the clinic early the next morning. The specialist saw Hulusi first then called Mitch inside. He listened to the doctor and turned to Hulusi.

"Just as I presumed, Hulusi. You have gonorrhea. Do you know what that is?"

Hulusi nodded. "Of course I know it." He seemed almost proud.

Again, Mitch translated, "The doctor says there is no need to be scared. He'll solve the problem with a simple antibiotic."

Hulusi replied, "You tell the doctor that I am a Turk. We Turks don't fear such things!"

In the beginning of 1983, Hulusi sent a message to his village. The news fell like a bomb on the small community. Hulusi the Girl was looking for a wife. Still, no one trusted the pictures enough to send their daughter to America. It was Nilüfer who came to his rescue. She sent for Halime's sister and paid the dowry money to her family in Hulusi's name.

Out of spite, Hulusi planned the ceremony in his own village. He paraded his black-eyed, lovely wife Fehime through the square, and the unmarried girls shed tears of regret. Hulusi bought a small house, made sure his wife was settled, and returned to New York to save more money.

Things had changed in New York while he was away. Something was missing without Tayibe, Tim, and Greg filling the house with laughter. Mitch still listened to his music when he came home, but Aylin had started to sulk. They did not chat and giggle like they had as newlyweds.

One day, Hulusi came home and found it in total disarray. Vases, ashtrays, and plates lay shattered in pieces on the floor.

He turned to Tayibe, "It looks like a battlefield."

She said, "Mitch and my aunt had a fight. Mitch is staying with Leyla." She looked terribly sad and embraced Hulusi before leaving for school. "Please pray to God they will reconcile."

Hulusi whispered all the prayers he knew one after the other. He washed himself as an observant Muslim would and didn't drink a drop of alcohol that week so that his prayers would be accepted by God.

Mitch returned home a few days later but slept in the boys' room. Mitch and Aylin did not dine together, but at least the fighting had stopped. Hulusi hoped they would return to normal soon. In his opinion, they were made for each other.

One day, Aylin approached Hulusi with a serious look on her face. "I must talk to you. Please sit down." Hulusi heard the sorrow in her voice and instantly knew that something bad was about to happen. His hands grew ice cold. "Mitch and I have decided to get a divorce. He is moving out." She paused, as if she did not know how to go on. "I hate to say this, Hulusi, but I will not need you anymore. You need to try to find another job. Both Mitch and I will do everything we can to help. I promise, if I ever marry again, I will hire you back in an instant."

Hulusi stood by the window and gazed at the view for the last time. He recalled the moment he had first seen it, six years ago. He had felt like a god then, sitting in heaven among the stars. Now he was being thrown out into the hell of New York.

A few years later, the wheel of fortune turned once more for Hulusi. When Aylin fell in love again, Nilüfer traced him through the giant city of New York and put him in the service of the man Aylin was to marry. The year 1986 would be a good and prosperous one for Hulusi.

THE VAGABOND

Thomas Abbot and Aylin stopped over in London to visit relatives before continuing on to Japan. Aylin's cousin Semra lived in Sloane Square. Ayşe, Semra's cousin and Aylin's childhood friend, was also visiting for a short time. Aylin and Ayşe had not seen each other in twenty years. Semra wanted to have a special celebration for their reunion. She reserved a table for three at La Tante Claire.

Ayşe said, "Semra, must you choose the most expensive restaurant in the city?"

Semra replied, "Don't spoil it for me. Each one of us lives in a different corner of the globe. Who knows whether we will meet again."

Ayşe and Semra waited eagerly for Aylin to arrive. When Aylin finally rang the bell, Semra rushed to the door and the three women shrieked, falling into an embrace. They started to babble all at once about the years that had passed. Ayşe was the first to notice the panting old man in the threshold. She said, "I think these stairs have nearly killed him."

Aylin said, "This is my friend Tom."

Ayşe blurted, "You mean your grandfather's friend!" Semra prodded her with her elbow. Ayşe's laughter froze on her lips.

The old gentleman said, "I am Thomas Abbot," greeted the women by kissing their hands, and went into the living room.

Ayşe was mortified and ran into the kitchen. She was pacing when Semra followed her in.

Semra laughed. "That man is Aylin's boyfriend."

"Why didn't you tell me before?"

"I didn't know she was bringing him here."

"Do you think Aylin is cross with me?"

"Oh, Aylin doesn't care about such things," said Semra. "Come on, don't punish yourself too much."

When they headed to dinner, Abbot took his leave, claiming to have other plans.

When the first wine bottle was half-empty, Aylin turned to Ayşe. "Stop torturing yourself. I'm not cross. I know Tom looks much older than his age."

When they were halfway through the second bottle of wine, Ayşe whispered to Aylin, "Aren't you scared that Abbot might die on you?"

"No," said Aylin, "because he's never on me."

Aylin, Ayşe, and Semra burst out laughing. They had a blast telling each other every single detail of their lives, as if to compensate for the years spent apart. They tried hard to keep it down, but by the time the third bottle of wine was through, the restaurant had cleared out. Semra paid the bill, but they still had so much to say. The waiters flew around the table, collecting plates.

Semra said, "C'mon girls, let's leave before they kick us out." They could barely stand and clung to one another as they stumbled out into the street. When the cold air hit their faces, Ayşe suspected she would never have another night as warm, intimate, and sentimental. She was right.

After London, Aylin and Abbot went to Paris. The old man acquiesced to her every wish, took her to the most expensive restaurants, and reserved the best seats at the theater.

Aylin seldom let herself recall Leyla's heartbreaking pleas to stay in New York, but when she did she felt pain plunge somewhere deep in her heart. She tried to visualize herself at the end of a workday in their apartment on the Upper East Side. Mitch would be sitting with his feet on his desk, books piled up next to him, listening to his classical music, and Aylin would be nursing a glass of wine, her patients' case files piled up on her lap.

"This weekend, maybe we can go to Long Island," she would start, before her husband cut her off.

"Aylin, do whatever you want, but don't drag me into that weekend traffic again," he would say and still insist on making love before they went to bed.

My God, what a powerful libido! she thought, taking a sip of champagne. She blinked her eyes to sweep away the image.

Abbot asked, "Is there something wrong, beautiful? If the champagne is not chilled, I can send it back."

At the end of each night, Tom would kiss her fingertips, cheeks, and the corners of her mouth, before saying, "Good night, my beauty. See you in the morning."

Finally, they arrived in Japan. Exploring Asia and being spoiled like a princess felt good. Aylin had not been this pampered even when she was a true princess. She swam in a sea of pearls and silk kimonos and meandered the streets of Tokyo and Kyoto.

Upon her return to New York, Aylin learned that Mitch had left Leyla's and rented a small apartment. It was true that her trip had ended their marriage. She was torn by the bitterness of knowing she had spoiled a marriage for nothing. Aylin felt almost as lonely as she had when her mother died. Who would replace her companion now? Tayibe was still a child; she couldn't burden her with these problems. She was all alone with an adolescent girl on her hands. It was time to clip her wings and restore order and discipline for the sake of this child. At her age, Tayibe needed peace, security, and a mother more than anything else. Aylin realized what she had done and knew that the hardest days were yet to come.

As a board member of her high school's alumni association, Aylin took care to be present at its New York meetings. This association was an organic tie between her country, her youth, her past, and her present. She never missed the parties it threw for visitors from Turkey. One night, she happened to sit at the same table as Jeremy Barts, a member of the board of trustees.

Jeremy Barts may have exceeded most women's age limit, but Aylin had no limits in that regard. She was very impressed by his deep knowledge of Turkey. By the time dinner was over, Barts was bewitched. He bent over and whispered in Aylin's ear before they rose from the table, "If I were young and free, I would have fallen madly in love and proposed to you."

Aylin said, "You are free to make another kind of proposal, Mr. Barts. For instance, we could become friends. Neither our marriages nor our age gap would prevent us."

In time, Jeremy Barts and Aylin discovered they both had season tickets for the opera, where they kept bumping into each other at premieres. After four or five of these encounters, Barts made an offer to Aylin she could not resist. Why not enjoy the gala performances together? Perhaps they could even enjoy a light dinner in between acts.

Barts made a habit of picking Aylin up in a limousine. Aylin appreciated feeling like a princess, but she was careful not to let him pick her up at her office. After her last appointment of the day, she'd run across the road and wait for him in the entrance to her building. Barts could not help asking if she felt uncomfortable being seen in his company.

Aylin said, "My divorce is not yet finalized. Mitch is a jealous man, and I don't want to create any problems." Of course, she knew that Mitch would never make a fuss, but she was still sensitive about Mitch's possible misinterpretation. First Abbot, then Barts. She did not want him to think of her as a femme fatale out to hunt rich old men. In fact,

Mitch had not even started the divorce proceedings, and Aylin did not press him. It would mean dividing assets and breaking her last tie with him. She feared being completely on her own. Thank God for Tayibe. Whenever she was about to be overwhelmed by hopelessness, Aylin remembered her responsibilities to her niece and pulled herself together.

Once, Barts asked Aylin why she hadn't had a child during any of her three marriages. "Didn't you want any?"

"Didn't I want any? I gave up after seven or eight very painful miscarriages. I almost lost my life once. Then my sister gave me Tayibe."

"Tayibe must be a gift from God. Your sister did not have to entrust her daughter to you."

Aylin said, "But she did. And I will be grateful to her for as long as I live."

In those years, Aylin worked like a dog to fill the emptiness in her life and spent the rest of her time accepting Abbot's invitations to travel abroad or going to opera premieres with Jeremy Barts. But despite her crowded calendar, she was tragically lonely. She may have had elderly admirers, but her heart was empty, just like her bed. One day, through Uncle Hilmi, she met Roger Kinsky, a much younger man than her most recent beaus. He was nice, attractive, and intellectual. He was the publisher of an art magazine and a connoisseur of fine arts and antiques.

Roger and Aylin flirted for almost two years. Unlike her older suitors, he wanted Aylin to spend the night after visits to the opera, art exhibitions, or plays, and got upset when his advances were rejected. Furthermore, he did not fawn over her like most men. She magnified her charms, attempting to inflame Roger's attention, but Roger Kinsky was the only man who could read Aylin's soul like a book.

Not that he wasn't aware of his companion's value. Aylin was truly a fabulous, smart, talented, and attractive woman. It was impossible to sit beside her at any social affair and not have a wonderful time.

But even as she displayed a rich and inquiring mind, it was as if a little unsatisfied spot floated somewhere in her inner soul. Nothing could ever be quite enough.

It did not take Roger long to realize that nothing would guarantee Aylin's satisfaction, and so Roger stopped himself from pursuing a relationship that could easily become serious. Besides, Aylin was not inclined to attach herself to any man in those days. In the end, Aylin and Roger ceased being lovers and became close friends, without any hurt feelings.

In the meantime, Mitch went through a series of short-term relationships and finally decided it was time to remarry. Since he suspected that Aylin might make a fuss about the apartment and postpone the divorce, he decided to just let her have it all.

Aylin said, "We bought this place together. You really want to give it up to me?"

"If I ask you to sell it and split the proceeds, will you do it?"

"No. I live here, and you are the one asking for a divorce."

"What if I let you buy my half?"

"You know very well I don't have that much money."

"And that's why I'm leaving it to you."

Aylin was not the kind of person who liked to win without a fight. "But you own half."

"Aylin, it's thanks to your social skills that we have so many patients. I wouldn't have earned the money to buy my half if not for you."

"So that's it?"

Mitch said, "Yes. If you do sell it someday, maybe you can leave me a share."

Aylin nodded. "If I ever write my will, I will make sure Tim and Greg get their share, too."

Mitch also felt it was time to move out of their shared office. He knew Aylin brought men by to make him jealous, and his present girlfriend was tiring of the situation. Mitch found an office close by and moved out.

Aylin said, "You're so conservative; you belong to another era." Still, they made a point to have lunch at least twice a month to catch up.

One Wednesday, Mitch arrived at their usual place early. It was not like him to drink during the day, but he ordered a glass of white wine anyway. He finished it and sent away the glass when Aylin arrived. They caught up on Tayibe's studies and on Tim and Greg. Then Aylin told him the latest developments with her patient Lucy Crewe. Toward the end of the meal, Mitch said, "Aylin, how have you been lately?"

"I'm fine."

"Are you really fine?"

"What do you mean, Mitch?"

"I want you to tell me the truth."

Aylin fixed her hair with her hands. "Have I changed much? Do I look older?"

"I'm not referring to your looks; you're beautiful as always. But are you happy?"

"I'm not unhappy."

"I heard that your relationship with Roger ended."

"We are better as friends."

"Aylin, at our age, we cannot be content with friendship. Why can't you just find a relationship with a man your age and stick to it? Have you thought about this at all? Maybe you need help."

Aylin sat speechless. When she finally spoke, her voice trembled. "You are still angry at me, Mitch," she said. "You will never forgive me for tiring of our marriage."

"Aylin. I just want the best for you."

"If you really wanted the best for me, everything would have been different. You would have understood that I needed space. You wouldn't have run to a lover and asked for a divorce."

"Normal, ordinary people want to share their lives with someone."

"Well, I'm not an ordinary person. I'm extraordinary."

"Okay," said Mitch, "if you're so extraordinary, just go on running away from real life."

"I'm not running away from life; I'm running away from monotony."

Mitch did not answer. He had never succeeded in telling Aylin what she did not want to hear. She gathered her bag and rose. "Thanks for lunch, Mitch. The next one is on me."

Mitch said, "Give Tayibe a kiss for me."

After Aylin was gone, he called wearily to the waiter, "Another glass of white wine, please."

SAMUEL GOLDBERG

Before Aylin's colleague, Dr. Gordon, introduced his neighbor Sam Goldberg to her, he told him quite a bit about her. Sam had a problematic teenage daughter. Alice was not a naturally bright girl; it took her three times as long as the other kids to learn basics like reading and simple arithmetic. However, in other areas she excelled. For instance, no one else in the household could match her mechanical knowledge, and she could recite numerous telephone and license plate numbers by heart. Yet Alice's mother had abandoned her as a young girl, claiming she had never wanted children in the first place.

Despite her father's deep affections, Alice had always missed her mother. Now, she faced one of the biggest dangers awaiting youngsters in New York: puberty. Her father was terrified she would start to indulge in drugs or bad boyfriends. He asked her older sisters, Hilary and Pia, to keep an eye on her, but they had lives of their own.

Pia was an aspiring starlet married to the actor Kevin K. She devoted all her time to auditioning. Hilary had a master's degree in art history from Columbia and wanted to act on Broadway. Her husband had recently resigned from an advertising company to become a painter, but so far, his work had not sold well. In short, Alice had absolutely no hope for guidance from her big sisters.

Nevertheless, Alice needed help. As a child, she had drowned in a sea of psychiatrists, and now suffered a panic attack whenever she heard the word.

Dr. Gordon had seen Aylin work miracles on Lucy Crewe, the hopeless case. He had known Lucy for many years, heartbroken to find her in the emergency room after each suicide attempt. He had referred her to a different psychiatrist each time, hoping that they could cure her. He himself had tried, too, to no avail.

One night, Dr. Gordon found Sam and Alice in the emergency room. Alice's boyfriend had hit her and injured her ear. Dr. Gordon took his friend aside. "I know an excellent psychiatrist, Sam. I think she can help Alice. Would you like me to introduce you?"

"My daughter is a mess. I don't know if she can be helped."

"Trust me, Nadowlsky can work wonders. You must at least give her a chance."

"Fine, but I want to meet her before I bring Alice in. I need to warn her about Alice's boyfriend, too. I'm afraid that he's a drug addict."

Gordon nodded. "I'll invite you both over to my place. You can meet her and make up your mind."

True to his word, Steven Gordon invited a group for drinks one night. Sam could not escape the office and was the last to arrive. When he entered, he recognized most of the guests. There were only two women in the room he didn't know. The first was surely a model or a movie star. She couldn't be a doctor. Sam walked toward the second.

"Dr. Nadowlsky?"

The lady stared.

"Aren't you Dr. Nadowlsky?"

"No, my name is Peckwood."

Sam Goldberg said, "I'm very sorry," and headed straight for the host. "You said you'd invite her."

"I did, of course."

"Didn't she come?"

"Yes, she's right there." Gordon gestured toward the model.

"My God! *She* is the doctor?"

Aylin turned around and approached them with a smile.

"Aylin, I want you to meet Sam Goldberg. Sam is a film producer. He took you for a movie star just now. Maybe it's time for a career switch?"

"Well, I do need a change." Aylin extended her hand. "Aylin Nadowlsky. I might be too late to play the ingenue, but I play mother in real life. Do you have a role for me?"

"Do you have children?"

Aylin said, "A daughter."

"Problematic?"

"Does any child lack problems?"

Sam said, "Come with me," and took Aylin by the hand, leading her to the armchairs at one end of the room. He couldn't help gazing at her shapely legs along the way.

An hour later, Sam caught Gordon in the kitchen.

He said, "I don't care if she's good for Alice or not, this Nadowlsky is going to do me some good. What a marvelous woman, Steven. Why the hell didn't you introduce her to me until now?"

When the party ended, Sam had learned everything he could about Aylin. In turn, Aylin had learned that Sam was the producer of the Tony Awards, that he had a son from his first marriage and three daughters from his second, that his youngest was mentally ill, that his son-in-law was Kevin K., and that his daughter Pia had appeared in the film *Lace*. Most importantly, Samuel Goldberg was rich and unmarried.

Aylin called Mitch the next morning.

She asked, "Mitch, what exactly did you want to tell me at lunch the other day?"

"I'm sorry, Aylin. I thought it over, and I don't have any right to interfere with your private life."

"I'm not mad, Mitch. I know you are the person who knows me best. Really, what were you trying to say?"

"Do you promise not to get angry?"

"Promise."

"I think that you have to work harder on your private life. Your professional success is not enough to make you happy. A woman your age needs a fulfilling relationship. You have many friends, and yet I feel that you're very lonely."

"Are you telling me that I should get married?"

Mitch said, "Not married, necessarily, but there should be someone with whom you want to share your life. At least, that's my opinion."

"Well," Aylin said, "I think I've found that person."

After she hung up, Mitch stood motionless with the phone in his hand.

Two days after the party at Steven Gordon's house, Sam Goldberg invited Aylin to dinner at one of the most popular restaurants in New York. Aylin had spent extra time getting ready and wore a very elegant dress. Sam could not take his eyes off her.

He said, "Are all Turkish women like you?"

Aylin said, "Like what?"

"Beautiful, elegant, smart, cultivated, humorous, pleasant, talkative . . ."

"Have you run out of adjectives, Sam?" Aylin laughed.

"It's not my fault, Aylin. You are dazzling."

"If you want to meet other Turkish women, I'll introduce you to some of my friends."

Sam replied, "I'd be honored."

A week later, Aylin and Sam went to Emel and Paul's for dinner. Sam was starting to believe that Turkish women were by far the most beautiful girls in the world. When the women were alone in the kitchen, Emel asked, "Where did you find this one, Aylin?"

"Steven introduced us. How do you like him?"

"He's very likeable but a bit fat, isn't he?"

"I love bigger men. They're cheerful and trustworthy."

Emel said, "Well, I can see you've got your reasons."

When they said good night, Sam whispered to Emel, "Talk me up to Aylin."

She closed the door, turned to her husband, and said, "Heavens! We've just met Sam, and he already wants me to put in a good word for him."

"Well, just do it," said Paul. "He's a rich, practical guy. Maybe this is what Aylin has been seeking all these years."

As it happened, Sam introduced Alice to Aylin over lunch instead of in Aylin's office. Aylin learned a great deal without the sixteen-year-old suspecting anything at all.

Later, she said to Sam, "Alice is much brighter than you all think. You have never trusted her with any responsibilities. If you had, she would behave differently."

"So you'll treat her?"

"Yes, but not in my office like any other patient. The child is sick and tired of the doctor-patient relationship, but if I can win her confidence as a friend, I think I can be very helpful to her. She's going through the most sensitive phase of her life. Watch out for her and be attentive, but don't make her feel controlled. Otherwise, you risk losing her."

Aylin succeeded in building a solid friendship with Alice, and Sam's admiration for her grew. Aylin had won Alice's trust without ever frightening her, and convinced her to open up about her drug-addicted boyfriend, even helping him enroll in group therapy sessions. Moreover, with Aylin's support, Alice started working at a music shop, and her self-confidence bloomed overnight.

Before long, Aylin had not one but two admirers in the Goldberg family. Alice trusted Aylin like she had never trusted anyone else in her life. She also clung to Tayibe, who warmly embraced her into her own circle of friends.

When Christmas rolled around, Sam took Alice, Aylin, Tayibe, and Mustafa, Tayibe's brother, to a ski resort in Switzerland. Aylin had not been back to Switzerland since university. She felt very nostalgic and gave them all a tour of her campus and old neighborhood. They even looked for Jean-Pierre but could not find him. All they learned was that he had remarried and lived somewhere in the United States. Aylin and Tayibe returned home very relaxed and content. Tayibe liked how Sam treated her like his own daughter. She asked, "Auntie, wouldn't you like to marry Sam?"

"You know that I cannot seem to make my marriages last, Tayibe. Maybe not getting married at all is the best course for me." Yet in her mind, she heard Mitch's words, *The years are flowing fast, Aylin. You must settle down.*

She hated him for being so right.

Sam introduced Aylin to his son, Peter, his daughters, Pia and Hilary, and their husbands. Aylin and Peter immediately hit it off, but Hilary had not made a good impression at all. She seemed to blame other people for the fact that her painter husband could not find commercial success. Aylin sensed the negativity in her voice when she first said hello.

As for Pia, she was still riding high from her role in *Lace* and was a little cool when she met Aylin. Her husband Kevin K., on the other hand, treated Aylin with more warmth.

Still, all the family held a grudging respect for the woman who released them of their burden, Alice, who seemed smarter, calmer, and happier than she had ever been. Besides, their father, who had been a bachelor for many years, was surely not going to marry now. They could tolerate his friendship with a pretty, cultivated, and professional woman.

When school let out for the summer, Aylin, Tayibe, and Alice traveled to Sam's house by the seaside for vacation. The house had a huge porch and plenty of bedrooms, but it had not been repaired or painted for a long time. Still, it was an ideal place for a family to live comfortably.

The house reminded Tayibe of summers on Fire Island, and a slight pain pierced her heart. Did her aunt ever think of those times? They were no longer the same happy family from those years, but Sam did everything in his power to make them feel at home. It felt as if everything was slowly regaining the right balance. This big, sincere man was winding his way into both Tayibe and Aylin's hearts.

Toward the end of August, Sam had to shoot a film on location. Aylin and the children remained at the beach house. Aylin had met all of her neighbors and often invited them to parties or beach picnics. One evening, a neighbor named Stanley Cohen held a dinner party; Betty Ross, Kurt Miller, and Aylin were among the guests. After dinner, Stanley asked the group, "Well, what now? Shall we go dancing or take the boat out?"

Aylin jumped up. "I grew up on the Bosphorus. Boating in the moonlight is the thing I love most in life. Let's go!"

Everybody ran to Stanley's boat at the dock. Unfortunately, it was a cloudy night and the surface of the sea was as black as a raven. Even though he was tipsy, Stanley drove the boat at top speed. All the guests were cheering and singing as loudly as they could. All of a sudden, Stanley hit something, jerked in the air, and crashed into the water. Everybody lost their balance and fell across the deck. No one knew how to stop the engine. Luckily, the boat just drew large circles in the sea.

From the water, Stanley cried desperately, "I'm drowning!" Only Aylin and Kurt Miller were sober. Finally, Aylin took charge.

She shouted to Kurt, "Take the wheel and try to slow down the boat!"

He did as he was told.

"When we pass by Stanley again, I'll try to pull him in. Come here and help me."

Aylin yelled to Betty, "Stop that silly crying and wait at the other end of the boat!"

"I can't get up. I think my arm is broken."

"Well then, crawl over there. If we all stay on the same side, the boat will capsize and you'll drown." Terrified, Betty made it to the other side and stopped crying. Kurt and Aylin grabbed Stanley and lifted his soaking-wet body into the boat. Aylin laid him down, pressed on his lungs, and tried to get the seawater out of him.

Some of their neighbors spotted the accident and called the rescue team. When they arrived, Aylin had already given Stanley first aid. Kurt was in awe, and so her list of admirers got longer. Stanley was hospitalized, and Betty Ross sued him for damages.

Aylin told Kurt, "Turks never sue a friend for such a thing, even if they die. They are the most loyal people in the world."

After such a terrible night, Aylin was delighted to hear some good news at the end of the summer. Nilüfer had finally tracked down Hulusi in the city. He started working for Sam as a butler and a cook.

That winter, Hilary and Pia finally began to suspect that their father's relationship with Aylin was becoming more serious. Sam had started to spend most nights with Aylin.

Mitch called Aylin when he heard she was ready to speed up the divorce proceedings.

He said, "What is it, Aylin? Do you have good news?"

Aylin said, "Didn't you tell me to find a man? Well, I did as I was told."

"I'm very glad to hear it. Can I meet the groom?"

"Of course. At the first opportunity."

Mitch said, "Tell me a little more about him."

"His name is Sam Goldberg. He's a film producer."

"A Jew?"

"Yes."

"What about Nilüfer?"

Aylin said, "She has matured. She likes Jews now."

Mitch asked, "So it was my fault, then?"

Aylin said, "Who knows? Maybe she was envious of our love."

"Well, don't you love this Sam Goldberg?"

"Every love is different."

This time, Aylin loved her fiancé for the secure, peaceful life he could offer her. She would never again worry about her bills or finances. She spent to her heart's content and took great pleasure in treating herself and the people she loved. She often made significant financial commitments without a second thought—like Hulusi's lifelong therapy or Tayibe's wardrobe, pocket money, and education. If she saw a rare medical text at an antique shop, she bought it for Greg without even asking its price. Many warned her it was unsustainable, but her husbands had always covered any debts. Still, ever since her divorce from Mitch, Aylin had been struggling. She often fought with her former patient, Irene, whom she had hired to help in the office and to manage the business side of things. Irene took a tough-love approach to Aylin's finances.

Irene would say, "Stop spending, Aylin. We have bills to pay and you have tax debts," but Aylin didn't listen. Life was for living, loving, buying, and giving. Sam gave her that freedom again. She could shop at expensive boutiques as she chose. She thought maybe she would limit how many patients she saw and devote more time to worthy causes and the arts. She would have a more interesting life than the one she had led until now. She would befriend movie stars as she traveled the world with Sam. She had worked tirelessly for years and was fed up with it. It was time for some fun.

Sam had a contemptuous brother who had always sneered at Sam's marriages. Why did he always indulge in affairs with exotic beauties that would never last? Now, not only was Sam more renowned as a producer than he'd ever been before, he was marrying a doctor. Specifically, a beautiful, erudite, well-bred, and funny doctor who could speak several languages and had a sound understanding of art.

Sam's daughter Alice made great progress working at the music shop. Feeling more at ease, he transformed his bachelor pad into a home, enjoying the services of his new Turkish butler. He hosted important guests in a finely decorated house, all thanks to Aylin. Sam was a businessman. He knew an opportunity when he saw one, and had no intention of missing out on the chance for a good wife. He just needed to convince Hilary and Pia.

In the meantime, Aylin once again became obsessed with Lucy's case. As Mitch had warned her, Lucy was a difficult patient—the most difficult of Aylin's career to date. Lucy now felt trapped. She had been suffering from an all-consuming nervous breakdown for many years. No doctor had been able to help her. After yet another suicide attempt, the hospital made her describe the sort of doctor she wanted.

Dr. Wieszner had thrown up his hands. "Lucy," he had said, "such a doctor does not exist. This is a fantasy. But I do happen to know someone who might come close." He scribbled on a piece of paper. "Try Nadowlsky. If she can't help you, no one can." And so their relationship began.

LUCY CREWE

The first thing she noticed was Aylin's skirt. The doctor was wearing a long, flower-patterned pastel skirt. She sat at her desk and looked at Lucy with her hazel-green cat eyes for a few moments.

Then she said, "So, tell me."

"Tell you what?"

"Why you hate yourself."

"I'm the shithead daughter of a loud, degenerate, uneducated, greedy, conservative Jewish family."

"I've got you beat."

Lucy thought she had heard wrong. "What the hell are you talking about?"

"I'm a shithead Jew, too. I converted."

"I don't believe you."

"It's true."

"Why did you do that?"

"To convince my Jewish husband to have a child."

"And did you have one?"

"No, Lucy. I had many painful miscarriages, each time more dangerous than the last. Finally, I gave up."

"So?"

"So, you are not the only hopeless case in this room."

"Hey, I'm not here to listen to your problems."

"Then tell me yours."

"Why would you choose that lousy religion?"

"I don't care about labels. I just wanted to have a baby. Converting doesn't change your heart. Mine is always the same."

The girl asked, "Is it Christian? Buddhist?"

"If a person believes in God with all his heart, he won't discriminate. Religions are all the same."

The girl said, "Not true at all. You don't understand because you're not a real Jew."

The doctor said, "The Jews that I know are all very savvy, talented, warmhearted people. Now tell me about the terrible ones you know."

Lucy said, "Let me start with my father." She tried to mimic her father's ugly face and accent. "Here, Lucy. Here, Lucy. *Bang! Bang!* I'll give you another spanking now, Lucy. I'll squeeze the life out of you, Lucy." She began to bang her hand on the desk.

The doctor said, "Stop that, you've made enough noise."

Had Lucy heard right? "Did you tell me to stop?"

"Yes. What did you do to deserve those spankings, anyway?"

"I will break this desk into pieces."

"Do it. Everything in here is insured."

"I can also shatter your skull."

"That's insured, too."

"I can tear up that lousy skirt."

The doctor said, "Oh no, don't do that. It cost me too much."

At that, the girl started to laugh.

The doctor said, "How old are you, Lucy?"

"Isn't my age scribbled in the folder in front of you?"

"That's your chronological age. I'm asking you how old you feel."

"One hundred and twelve."

The doctor said, "You're two years older than me."

For the first time, Lucy felt like she was in the right place. Her doctor was one hundred and ten and had beautiful eyes. She was smart. She was funny. Yes, this finally felt right.

The doctor tilted her armchair and looked at the wall in front of her. The girl drew her legs up to her chin and rested her head on her knees.

She had been talking for an hour. She recounted how she'd been cursed by that goddamn father of hers, and how her illiterate, timid mother could never protect her. She cried out the basest curses she knew. Yet that nice-looking woman in front of her did not blink an eye once. She did not fixate on the girl's problems; she tried to discover her talents. Her secretary appeared at the door when the hour was up.

The doctor said, "Irene, would you make us coffee? Do you want milk, Lucy?"

The girl said, "Don't you have any booze?" *She'll roll her eyes,* Lucy thought. I know these people. I've chewed up and spat out nineteen shrinks.

"Would you like gin, whiskey, or wine?"

"Gin."

"Irene, get us two gin and tonics, will you?"

That silly cow of a secretary just stood at the door, stunned.

The doctor said, "Pour one for yourself, while you're at it. It's almost six thirty. In my home country, this is happy hour."

Then she spoke in a foreign language.

Lucy asked, "What language is that?"

"Turkish."

"And what's that?"

"The language Turks speak."

"Who?"

"The people who live in Turkey. They're nice people. Maybe you'll go visit someday, who knows?"

The girl said, "If I live."

The doctor said, "Oh, you will live. Had you really wanted to die, you would have done it already."

The girl said, "I'll cut my wrists now and show you."

"Well, don't do it here. I just changed the carpet."

What have I gotten myself into? thought Lucy.

Their drinks came. The secretary had adorned the glasses with a slice of lemon. Lucy took a sip. It was good.

The doctor said, "Your time is up, but you can stay as long as you wish."

"Won't you charge me for the extra time?"

"No. Nor for the gin and tonic."

The girl said, "You Turks are a bit strange."

The doctor said, "Yes, we are. I'll tell you about us one day if you're interested."

Lucy refrained from saying, "I don't give a fuck about the Turks" merely because she didn't want to be rude to someone who had offered her a gin and tonic. She just nodded.

She talked for another half hour until her throat became sore. She stopped. The doctor wrote her a new prescription for her pills. Lucy stood up. *That gin was good,* she thought. She felt much better.

She smiled and said, "You know what? I wasn't going to tear up your skirt. Actually, it's a very nice skirt."

"You really like it?"

"Yeah."

The doctor undid her zipper. *What the hell is she doing now? Is she nuts?* Lucy thought. The skirt fell to the floor. Her legs were barely visible under her slip.

Lucy said, "I'm not a lesbian."

"Me neither," said the doctor. "How nice, we have that in common."

She took the white doctor's coat hanging on the hook and put it on.

"Take this, Lucy." She handed her the skirt. "The colors are far too youthful for me. Take it; let it be a symbol of our friendship and your confidence in me. You trust me, don't you?"

The girl said, "Well, I don't think of you as my enemy. Compared to all the other shrinks, you're pretty okay."

She took the skirt, feeling numb. *This doctor acts faster than I do; she checkmates me with every move,* she thought. A feeble inner voice told her to let go. Lucy wanted to listen to that voice. She held the skirt to her waist, "Can I wear it now?"

"Sure."

She took off her slacks and put on the skirt. The soft, slippery silk felt like summer rain against her skin. She twirled, feeling fantastic. When she left the room, she came face to face with Irene, who balked at the skirt and ran back into Aylin's office.

Silly cow, she thinks I've killed my doctor just for a skirt, thought Lucy.

When she left, her skirt floated in the air and embraced the cool wind. She approached an old woman whose dog was peeing on a tree trunk and said, "I will not commit suicide. Neither today nor tomorrow."

The old woman gave her a bewildered look as she walked away.

A year passed. Lucy shed all of her tears in Aylin's office until there was not a single drop left. It was possible she wouldn't cry again for ten years. She told Aylin of her first disappointment; first depression; first love; first screw; her wounded heart; her father's spankings, insults, scoldings, humiliations; her first, second, third, and fourth suicide attempts on pills; the family meetings where everyone spoke without listening; her shrieks of joy when her father abandoned them; and her relatives who looked at her with hate because she was the only child in the world elated by her parents' separation.

She recounted how she had to start working with her father after college because there were no other jobs, how she had put up with his degrading behavior, her first wrist cut out of anger, her second wrist cut for the sake of love, her stomach pumped over and over again because of the pills she swallowed, and her eighth, ninth, and tenth suicide attempts. When all the poison flew out like a stream, Lucy was left alone with her clumsiness and vulnerability.

During these sessions, Aylin started to uncover Lucy's talents. How could such a sharp intellect go so unused? Once she said to Lucy, "You must have some wit in that head of yours. Schools don't give scholarships easily."

The girl had replied, "You're right. Why have I never thought of that?" She also grew less ashamed of being a Jew.

Aylin said, "Some people voluntarily choose that religion, Lucy. Even Elizabeth Taylor is a late convert."

Lucy said, "But you haven't seen the women in my family with a ring on each finger, brooches on their collars, and tasteless earrings! Those potbellies gossiping and munching on anything they find. It's a disgusting sight!"

Aylin had said, "Is it really worth dying for these things you despise? If you hate the Jews, don't meddle with them. If your boyfriend betrays you, kick him out and find a new one. I was also betrayed by my husband. So what?"

Lucy had to agree with her. Moreover, her doctor always saw the funny side of things. She loved this about her best. One day, she became bashful. "I'll tell you something if you promise not to laugh."

"What is it?"

"Do you know who my stepfather is?"

"Who?"

"The ex-husband of my father's new wife."

"Oh, how intriguing!" said Aylin, "It's just like a Woody Allen film."

Isn't there anything that startles this woman? thought Lucy. "You mean, you don't find that embarrassing?"

"You keep complaining about your ordinary Jewish family. Well, here is something extraordinary. Why be embarrassed?"

Lucy was beginning to see the world from Aylin's perspective. People were born to survive adversity. Anything could happen. Therefore, it was wrong to blame people or to punish them. Tolerance was a must.

Once Aylin said, "You can try anything as long as you don't hurt others. When it's time to say farewell to life, don't leave a single broken heart or unfulfilled desire behind."

"Have you not broken any hearts?"

"Of course I have. Too many."

"Then why preach what you can't do?"

Aylin said, "Don't be silly. Can I not listen to the piano just because I can't play it myself?"

Lucy had stopped cursing. With Aylin's assistance, she found a job at an art marketing firm. She was going to be independent, away from her father for the first time. She also had a friend. No, Aylin was definitely much more than a friend; she was a mentor, a mother. She had a smart, beautiful, and sweet mother with whom she felt at home. That made her happy.

Aylin gave Lucy silver bracelets to hide the scars on her wrists. Lucy had worn the flower skirt until it crumbled away, and then bought a new one. During their sessions, they discovered that Lucy had always wanted to have a pet. Aylin encouraged her to buy a horse, but horses were expensive, so she suggested she start with horseback-riding lessons. Lucy went after work. A year later, she considered buying her favorite black horse with the commissions she had earned from selling paintings.

Aylin said, "Don't wait a second. Buy it right away."

"But I live in New York City. It will take all my savings."

"Lucy, for once in your life, do something you want to do. Go ahead and buy that horse."

Lucy thought of her mother and father, who had denied her wishes all her life.

"Aylin, I'm buying the horse."

"Do it. Don't think twice."

His name was Black Jack. Lucy went to the stud farm every day after work. Black Jack neighed and reared when he heard Lucy's voice. She made him gallop for at least an hour until he was soaked in sweat. When she raced with the wind at her back, she felt amazing. The death wish that had gnawed her soul for years fell away. One day, as she was riding at full gallop in Central Park, she caught herself crying out, "Life is beautiful! Death, keep your hands off me! Stay away from me! I want to live, live, and live!"

THE FOURTH MARRIAGE

"Even Muslims are not permitted to have more than four," said Mr. G. to his sister-in-law. "See to it that this will be the last."

Aylin said, "This is going to be the last. Even Nilüfer does not object to Sam."

"But what about those horrible daughters!" interrupted Hulusi as he handed Nilüfer her coffee.

She said, "You mind your own business and return to the kitchen, will you?"

But Hulusi had overheard the conversation between the girls and their father and reported it to Aylin the next day.

Hilary had said, "This woman is marrying you because of your money, dad."

"Ninety percent of women do the same, my child. Maybe if you had considered money when you married, you wouldn't be after mine now."

"So you don't mind her loving you for your money."

"Don't you love me for my money?"

Hilary had banged the door and left. Sam had tried to tell Pia, "I also want her for her values, because she has a career and because she's cultivated and elegant. Is that wrong?"

"But she wants you for your money."

"Aylin is not a beggar in the streets. She has enough money to have all the luxury she could want without me. She has a magnificent apartment in the best neighborhood in Manhattan. She has an office and can pay its rent. She is respected in her field. You must free yourself from this obsession. Besides, I'm not a Rockefeller."

Pia changed course. "She drinks."

"And why shouldn't she? You also drink. Your brother drinks, I drink, too."

"She's an alcoholic."

"Don't be ridiculous."

"She gets drunk."

"No, she doesn't. She has a social personality. She loves dancing, laughing, and having fun. I only wish you and Hilary could get so much zest out of life."

Hulusi could not bear to hear all this about his mistress; he dashed into the room and shouted in his broken English then banged the door into the kitchen. Father and daughter had not understood a word of what he said.

Pia said, "Turks are crazy."

"Maybe, but I'm marrying Aylin whether you and Hilary like it or not. If money is your only concern, I have prepared my will and you're in it. You need not fret." These were Sam's final words on the subject.

Aylin spent her last single days at her Upper East Side apartment. She had put it up for sale when Sam proposed. They were to begin their married life in a brand-new house, where there were no traces of their former lives, ex-wives, or ex-husbands.

Sam had found a big three-story brownstone on Seventy-Fourth Street between Park and Madison Avenues. They planned to transfer Aylin's office to the first floor. Hulusi and his wife would settle in the housekeeper's quarters. The top floor was for Tayibe and Alice. Turkish carpets were laid in the halls. Aylin and Sam had bought most of them in Istanbul over the summer. There was a mystical Ottoman atmosphere in the house. The guest room looked stately and serene with its dark flooring and navy and burgundy rugs.

Back at her apartment, Aylin looked out of the window. She was moving from this bright and spacious place that was hers alone to a dim and gloomy house that was completely alien to her. Was she doing the right thing?

Hulusi fanned the flame when he said, "What the hell will we do with the daughters?"

Aylin had been smoothing relationships for a long time. She had managed Nilüfer somehow, despite all her hostilities. Now, she faced a new challenge. For the first time, she understood how awful it must have been for poor Mitch to tolerate Nilüfer. Fortunately, the girls had softened toward Aylin. Aylin had organized dinners and bought them gifts, but she was getting sick and tired of trying so hard. Both of them were grown women. Why she bothered them so, she never knew.

Nilüfer said, "Everything will be fine when the girls get to know you better."

Almost four hundred wedding invitations were sent out. Three days before the wedding, Aylin was settling at the house on Seventy-Fourth Street. Sam came home in the evening with some documents for Aylin to sign.

Aylin said, "What are these?"

"Read them."

"Don't make me read boring things, Sam!"

"It's a prenuptial agreement."

"What?"

"A prenup."

"What does that mean?"

"It details your rights and limitations if I die or we get a divorce."

Aylin froze. "Sam, I have been married three times and I've never signed something like this."

"I have children, Aylin."

"Mitch also had two kids."

"Please just read it."

"I won't read it, and I won't sign it. We are getting married. If either one of us dies, the law will decide."

"If you don't sign it, we can't get married."

Aylin said, "Okay, we won't get married." She grabbed her bag, banged the door, and strode to her apartment. She felt absolutely degraded. She called Nilüfer's hotel, but no one picked up. She called Emel; she wasn't home, either. Aylin didn't want to talk to Leyla, who was still disappointed about her divorce from Mitch. There was no one to confide in. She dialed Kurt Miller's number; thank God, he was home. She began to cry when she heard his voice.

"We're not getting married, Kurt. The wedding is cancelled."

"Aylin, what are you talking about?"

"Sam has humiliated me."

"Where are you now?"

"At my apartment. Thank God, I haven't signed the contract yet."

Kurt Miller said, "Wait for me."

Later that evening, Nilüfer, Kurt, and the lawyers tried to persuade Sam and Aylin not to make a big fuss over nothing. In the end, they reconciled. Sam repented and Aylin apologized for her harsh reaction. However, the joy had been spoiled.

Three days later, in June of 1987, Aylin and Samuel Goldberg wed at one of the most elegant hotels in New York, with all their closest friends in attendance.

Aylin looked incredibly beautiful. Jeremy Barts said, "Aylin, being a bride suits you."

She replied, "That's why I get married so often." She looked radiant with her glittering eyes. There was not a trace of the tension of the past three days. She was starting life anew and was hopeful.

Sam and Aylin went to Turkey via Paris for their honeymoon. After visiting family members in Istanbul, they traveled down to the Turkish Riviera to spend time on Betin's boat. Sam was in awe.

Nilüfer and Mr. G. gave a party in honor of the newlyweds at the Anatolia Club on Prinkipo Island. The night was overloaded with memories, and Mr. G. gave a sentimental speech, wishing his sister-in-law limitless happiness and a lasting marriage.

Life at the brownstone on Seventy-Fourth Street was even better than Sam and Aylin had expected. Tayibe had embraced Alice, who was happier than ever. Alice was like a younger sister she had taken under her wing, even though they were the same age. Like her aunt, Tayibe got along well with Sam's eldest, Peter. After his parents' divorce, Peter was brought up with different values than his half sisters. Tayibe had been accepted to Harvard University and had just started her freshman year. A new school, a new house, new friends, and a new family. It was a year full of excitement.

Aylin never stopped hosting her traditional Thanksgiving dinners. She invited Mitch's sons, Tim and Greg, along with all the other kids. Sam loved big family gatherings, when even Hilary and Pia were cheerful.

There were also a number of famous actresses, actors, and singers who swept through the house. Jill Clayburgh and David Rabe,

Kate Edelman, Neil and Leba Sedaka, football player Frank Gifford, and actress Kathy Lee Gifford were among the more frequent visitors. Aylin liked the comedian Robert Klein best. Johnny Cash and David Copperfield had also become Aylin's close friends.

And of course Sam's poker games figured prominently into their social life. Sam met his friends a couple of times a week, and they played for hours. On such nights, Aylin generally went to the opera or to the theater with Kurt Miller. Sam always said, "Every woman must have a Kurt in her life."

How Aylin managed to balance so much social activity with her work was difficult to understand. It was as if she were pumped with a special kind of energy. Her patients were beyond satisfied, and at night, she was surrounded by admiring friends. Life was like a windmill spinning in a storm, and Aylin was going just as quickly. She didn't have time to listen to her inner voice.

As summer approached, Aylin decided to buy a house in Westhampton with the money from her apartment. Sam said, "I already have one there. Why should we buy a second?"

"Your house is falling to pieces, Sam. Restoring it will cost much more than a new house."

But after the taxes were paid, she didn't have enough money left, and so Sam pitched in. He always supported Aylin but never stopped talking about it. His constant whining about money started to get on her nerves. Once, he even complained that Hulusi used too much detergent. Another time, Sam and Aylin invited a couple of foodie friends to Coff, an expensive French seafood restaurant. Sam chose the cheapest wine. Aylin heard her husband ask the waiter to bring a "blanc de blancs" and yanked the wine list away so angrily that it scraped the waiter's chin. She looked at the list herself and told the waiter to bring a bottle of Puligny-Montrachet, which was two hundred dollars more. Sam sulked for the rest of the night.

Aylin said, "These people are real connoisseurs of wine, Sam. We can't offer them just any brand." The whole evening was spoiled. As they were putting on their coats to leave, the man whispered in his wife's ear, "I don't think that this marriage will last long. The Aylin I know cannot live with a stingy man."

In the meantime, Aylin started having problems at work. A Cornell med student who had attempted suicide had been hospitalized and sent over to Aylin. Mitch told her, "You've made a reputation for yourself. God help you."

Samantha had come to Aylin with depression. Aylin put the girl on antidepressants and treated her for about a year, until she felt she was ready to go back to school and complete her internship. Aylin wrote a report supporting her patient's wishes and sent it to the school's psychiatric clinic, Payne Whitney. A commission of three specialists examined the girl, decided that she was not ready to go back, and rejected her request. Aylin scheduled a meeting to tell them that no one could evaluate the girl's condition better than herself, and that they risked her mental health by closing these doors to her. The doctors were all shocked by her outburst.

The dean said, "Samantha has been evaluated by the three most distinguished specialists in this field. Are you telling me that we have erred, Dr. Goldberg?"

"Yes, you are making a mistake."

"And how did this happen?"

"You have surrounded yourself by unskilled and uncaring doctors."

The dean stood up and walked to the door. Aylin followed.

She said, "I will not change my report, sir. Samantha is cured." She charged out.

After this, doctors at Payne Whitney stopped referring patients to Aylin.

Aylin did not return home when she left the meeting. Instead, she did a little shopping on Fifth Avenue, then went to a movie to calm her nerves. It was dark when she came out, but she felt like walking home. When she reached her stoop and opened her bag to get the keys, she realized there was a man behind her. He grabbed her bag and started to pull with one hand, holding a knife at her neck with the other.

"Gimme the bag or I'll kill you, bitch!"

Aylin aimed her high heel at the man's groin and kicked him. He staggered for a second, and she turned to see he was wearing a ski mask. She held her purse tightly with one hand and started to hit him with the other. He managed to grab one of her arms and twisted it behind her back, choking her. She kicked at his legs and yelled at the top of her voice. When he heard footsteps, he took her bag, pushed her hard, and ran. Hulusi opened the door and saw Aylin coiled on the sidewalk.

"Oh my God, Miss Aylin, are you hurt?"

"Run. Leave me and run after him. C'mon, Hulusi."

Hulusi said, "Run after a thief? I'm not ready to die yet."

Aylin said, "Damn bastard, he took my bag!" Hulusi helped her stand. She was soaked in mud and already her neck was bruising. Her chest ached. She leaned on Hulusi and went into the house. When Sam heard what had happened, he was stunned.

"How much money did you have in your bag?"

"Forty dollars in cash, my credit cards, some makeup. I had just bought a new lipstick."

Sam said, "Aylin, are you mad? How could you wrestle with a thief over forty dollars and a new lipstick? What if he had killed you?"

"What should I have done? Handed him my bag?"

"Of course. Are your things more precious than your life?"

Aylin said, "You Americans are all cowards!"

Sam replied, "And you Turks are all mad!"

"I'm not," said Hulusi. "I would never put my life at stake for a bag."

Hilary and Pia's friendliness did not last long after the wedding. They were livid to learn that Sam had sold the house at the seaside without consulting them. Their father said, "Girls, I'm not going to consult you when I buy and sell my properties."

Aylin tried to stay positive. "Now that we have a new house, you can all come and stay as long as you wish. You don't even need to ask."

Hilary replied, "That's your house, not ours."

"What difference does it make who owns the house, Hilary? We are a family."

"If it doesn't make any difference, why are you the owner?"

"Because I paid for it."

"Do you have that much money?"

Peter said, "You don't need to answer these rude questions, Aylin."

"But I want to. Your sister is obsessed with the idea that I am after Sam's money. If I can prove her wrong, it'll be better for all of us."

"I admire your patience." Peter patted Aylin's shoulder and left the room.

In the summer of 1988, Aylin and Sam went to Turkey for a boat trip along the Aegean coast with friends, then visited Uncle Hilmi's summer house on a little island in the Sea of Marmara. It was the first time that Aylin had acquainted herself with country living. She suddenly realized how fed up she was with ugly, concrete cities. Walking among the Mediterranean greenery and the tangerine and olive trees, and inhaling the deep thyme and jasmine scents kindled a desire to return to nature.

"We waste our lives among these skyscrapers without seeing sunrise or sunset, Sam," she said. "Wouldn't you like to live a healthier life?"

"Shall we settle in Turkey?"

"It doesn't have to be Turkey. We can find nature in America, too."

Sam did not take his wife too seriously. He knew that Aylin would never part from New York; her patients would not let her go. But instead of quarreling, he let her play out the fantasy. Indeed, after a few months, she forgot the dream of buying a ranch in the middle of nowhere. But then Aylin began to chase a dream that was much easier to realize. There was nature to be found in the many suburbs of New York. For instance, in Westchester County.

"Sam, we're both getting older. Wouldn't you like to live in a peaceful place away from the roar of the city?"

"What about your practice?"

"I can commute a few days a week, and so can you. You don't want to rush to work every day at this age anyway."

"What will we do with this huge house?"

"If we find a house we like, we can sell this one."

Again, Sam decided to let it play out. "Well, if you want it so much, find a few houses to see."

He thought that this dream would fade away like the others. But he was wrong. Within a few months, Aylin presented five houses on large plots of land just a couple of hours away from the city. All the houses were magnificent and surrounded by lush forests. Especially one in Bedford, which was situated on eight acres of hillside. If they sold their brownstone for a good price, they could buy this house plus a pied-à-terre downtown. Suddenly, the country house started to haunt him as much as it had haunted Aylin.

Meanwhile, Aylin had devoted herself to a new patient.

SISTER NANCY

She sits facing the secretary like a stone statue. Her large bag lies on her lap. Her hair and her eyes are brown, though she looks as colorless as a mouse.

She does not answer Irene when she asks her name. She does not complain when Aylin is fifteen minutes late. She is wearing a gray skirt and jacket. Irene wonders why the nun does not wear the traditional habit. The nun is aware that she has disappointed the woman sitting behind the desk. She is used to it. But she does not care anymore. She does not care about anything. She is only here to gain time. The church has given her one more year of psychiatric treatment. It is the last hope for a nun who has not spoken a word in four years, and who suffers from chronic depression. If Nadowlsky's treatment proves futile, Sister Nancy will be sent back home. Nancy is determined to make the most of this year. She'll see what happens next. Although the church is meant to be a last refuge, she has not found it to be so. Still, she has no other place to go. She lost her friends and relatives long ago. Only God is left. She cannot take the life He gave her with her own hands. But even this reason for staying alive hangs by a thread.

The green light on Irene's telephone blinks.

Irene says, "Dr. Nadowlsky is ready. You can go in now."

She turns the knob and stands, bewildered. Nadowlsky, whom she thought she would find sitting at her desk, stands right behind the door, there to receive her. But this woman cannot be Nadowlsky. This woman is tall, slim, and very pretty; she has blond hair and amazingly bright eyes. This woman does not wear a formal suit, but a light-green skirt and blouse.

"Sister Nancy, welcome. I'm Dr. Nadowlsky." She takes the sister's hand and holds it tightly in her palms.

"You are my first patient from the church, you know. I'm very excited. Please take a seat, Sister. The armchair is a little uncomfortable; allow me to put this cushion behind your back."

Sister Nancy sits. The room looks like a living room rather than a doctor's office.

"Sister Nancy, can you tell me what has led to your depression?"

No answer.

"Or just anything you'd like to tell me."

Silence.

"Sister, you are Scottish. Scotland is one of the most beautiful countries in the world. You must tell me about the town where you were born. Did you grow up on the shore of one of those famous lochs?"

The sister's thin lips are clenched, her gaze fixed on the floor. Only her hands move, as though she is kneading a ball of dough. Aylin watches helplessly as she droops her shoulders and hangs her head. Mitch had warned her—no, begged her—to stay away from the nun. He had told her over and over that she was a hopeless case.

"Sister Nancy, you and I depend on each other. We will be sitting face to face in this room twice a week, for an hour each time, for a whole year. Just as you have taken an oath at the convent, I have taken one as a doctor. I don't have the right to refuse patients who are sent to me. I beg you, let's help each other. You don't have to answer my questions, but please, at least raise your head and look at me. Now, I'll read your file out loud. Tell me if you have any objections."

The sister lifts up her head and looks into Aylin's eyes, then bows it again. It's just a moment, but Aylin hears her silent scream.

"Sister Nancy, you were the fifth of fourteen children, born in September 1942 in the town of Dumbarton in Scotland. Your name is Mary."

The nun shakes her head violently. Aylin understands; she is Sister Nancy now. Could it be that she has not reconciled with her family identity? Aylin's senses are sharpened like a leopard following its prey; she is ready to evaluate every expression, gesture, or look. She continues to read.

"The family is not prosperous but not poor, and they usually get along with each other. Your most beloved sibling was your younger brother, Brian, who died of leukemia; however, the death of your baby sister also affected you a great deal."

The flutter of the sister's hands stops. She doesn't take her eyes off the floor. She is a block of stone.

"You have had many relatives fall victim to cancer. Three brothers, two sisters, your mother, and your father were all taken by it. I beg you; please look at my face, Sister Nancy." Does this woman feel guilty for surviving? Aylin wonders.

The nun lifts her head for a second before dropping her gaze once more to her wringing hands.

"You had a minor love affair before you entered the convent at the age of eighteen. A friend of your brothers fell in love with you. You entered the convent after you separated from that young man."

The sister's hands start to mold the invisible ball again.

"Your family, especially your father, strongly opposed the idea of your becoming a nun. You would not listen. You took an oath and joined the church after nine months of training and became a nurse." Aylin closed the folder. "This is the summary of your life. What made you choose this difficult path, Sister? Was it your sister's very painful death? Did that young man hurt you?"

You know nothing, thinks the sister. That folder does not even come close to the truth. That young man was not in love with me; he was in love with my older sister. Why should he have loved me, a mouse, when my sister had auburn hair and eyes as blue and deep as a lake? It was her he loved. Only I knew it, and I kept it to myself, just like I kept my sister's secret love to myself. It was like a soap opera; my sister loved a married man, Willie loved my sister, and I loved Willie. Even then, I was silent. Both my sister and Willie confided in me their hopeless and secret loves. I only listened and kept quiet.

"I'm prescribing you some pills, Sister Nancy," says Aylin. "Please don't forget to take them. You'll take the pink pills in the morning and the others at night when you go to sleep. They'll make you feel more at ease. I also take them now and again; they work very well."

The sister is surprised at the attention.

"See you on Wednesday, then. The bus stop is close by. Irene will show you the way."

Irene sees the nun out, closes the door, and goes to the kitchen. She pours a gin and tonic in a glass with a handful of ice cubes and a lemon slice, and walks into Aylin's office.

She takes a sip. "I asked you to give me gin, not tonic. Pour some more gin in here."

"Extra gin won't make the nun speak."

"I'm not in the mood to hear your wisecracks, Irene."

"Yelling at me won't make the nun speak, either."

"Bring me my gin!" Aylin roars.

Irene enters with the gin bottle in her hand.

"Contact the institutions and hospitals where she worked," Aylin says. "See if she has any relatives in New York or someone who knows more about her childhood. And leave the gin."

Irene ignores her and leaves with the bottle. Aylin does not react. She takes another big sip from her glass and starts to read the folder on her desk more carefully. She jots down her notes about the nun. She rewinds the tape and listens to the recording. It's her own monologue. She didn't even hear the woman's voice. But she won't give up.

She checks her watch. She is well aware that she has been neglecting Sam lately. She takes her frustration about his daughters out on him, but Hilary has been getting on her nerves more and more since last Christmas. Aylin is angry that this grown woman with a life of her own has become such a nuisance. Her latest obsession is Aylin's dream house in the suburbs. She whines that her father cannot live so far away from New York. The friction between them finally exploded last weekend, when Hilary delivered a particularly boring lecture on her husband's art, and Aylin could no longer hold her tongue. "David is as much of a painter as I am a gardener."

Aylin's gardening failures were the subject of much mockery by the whole family. She could never keep a plant alive longer than two weeks.

"I think you're mistaken, Aylin," said Sam. "David earns his living with his art."

"We all know he cannot sell his paintings."

The hatred in Hilary's eyes deepened.

"You're not being fair, Aylin." Sam's voice was ice cold.

"Facing reality is an important part of therapy. It solves many problems."

"David does not paint pictures for money; he paints because it brings him satisfaction."

"There is no satisfaction without success."

"Why do you provoke us, Aylin?" said David.

"I am angry that your wife repeatedly inserts herself in matters that should concern only me and my husband."

Sam looked stunned, and Aylin regretted hurting David, but she also felt a deep joy knowing she had hurt Hilary.

Aylin has lost track of herself. A spoiled brat has almost made her into a witch. She will have to discuss this with Mitch at the first opportunity.

Aylin takes another big gulp from her gin as Irene enters. "Some people count to ten to calm down. I drink ten sips of gin," Aylin says.

At their next appointment, the sister sits like a stone block again, the big black bag on her knees. Aylin talks and she listens, but the sister says nothing. Or maybe she's not listening. Today she won't even raise her eyes from the floor.

"Sister Nancy, your baby sister died at the age of eleven. You stayed at her side throughout her entire illness. This must have had a profound effect on you. Maybe your inclination to care for the ill formed in these early days?"

Nancy's hands start to knead that invisible ball of hers again.

"Your mother was extremely fond of her dying daughter. I wonder what her attitude was toward you. Your grief must have brought you two closer. Please look at my face, Sister. Allow me to see your eyes."

Nancy bows her head lower.

I will not allow you to see my eyes, she thinks. *I have hidden away my feelings for forty years, Nadowlsky. Do you think that I'll reveal them to you? Death brought me and my mother closer? Nothing brought us closer. I was her dullest daughter. My hair was not red, my eyes were not green. I resembled a brown bedbug. Pimples appeared on my face as my beautiful blond sister lay on her deathbed. I can never forget the look my mother gave me: "Why her?" My sister dwindling like a candle each day. I would have gone gladly in her place. Maybe only Johnny would be sad over my death. I was his little squirrel. But God does not leave that choice to us. I was spared so that I would witness Johnny's death, too. Cancer is a horrible agony. But how would you know that?*

Aylin's hands start to perspire. *This brick wall of a woman!* she thinks. She does not leave the slightest crack for any light to stream out.

"Sister Nancy, seeing our loved ones in so much pain leaves very deep scars on our soul. It can take years for those scars to rise to the surface. You have lost too much to cancer. No one can know your extreme suffering. My mother died of cancer, too. I was very young. That I could not ease her pain has influenced my whole life, believe me. It's why I wanted to become a doctor."

Nancy lifts her head and looks at Aylin for just a second. Aylin sees a faint glimpse of warmth in her eyes.

"Here is your prescription refill. Don't forget to take the pills. We'll meet again on Monday. Sister Nancy, it will take time, but I promise you I will find the worm inside you and I will destroy it."

That week, Irene manages to find someone in the Bronx who knew of Nancy's childhood.

The elderly lady with blue eyes and white hair sits calmly opposite Aylin. Aylin listens attentively, evaluating each word. The woman has a heavy Scottish accent, and Aylin makes her repeat the words she doesn't understand.

"The McCinlops were like any other Catholic family living on the outskirts of Dumbarton. They had little money and a lot of kids. Of course, the father drank too much, but who didn't? The poor man had seen his children die all his life. Mary was a bright and hardworking girl, a little plain. She had very skillful hands, always repairing every broken thing at home. She was even better than her brothers in that respect. Mary loved her brother Johnny most. She shared her secrets with only him; that is, whatever secrets a child can have. Everybody knew that her sister's death had an immense impact on her. Johnny even heard Mary pray to God to take her instead. Mary never left the sick girl's side; she was holding her hands when her sister breathed her last.

She became strange after her sister's burial. She appeared very detached and composed and never again said a single word about her sister. She remained silent. Maybe silence was her fate. Oh, her first love? That was nothing important. Willie was a friend of her brothers. It was only a brief romance. Not even a year. Mary joined the convent immediately after the affair ended."

After the woman left, Aylin read her notes over and over again. She brought the pieces together like a jigsaw puzzle and rearranged them anew. But it was all in vain. Aylin pressed Irene's button. Irene popped her head around the door.

"Gin or champagne?"

"Neither!"

"What happened?"

"We'll try her relatives in Scotland."

The sister sits opposite Aylin. She has covered her legs with her bag again. She is always exactly on time for her three o'clock appointments. Aylin has nicknamed her "the Swiss train."

"Sister Nancy, you had your oath ceremony after nine months of training and became a full nun in habit and headdress. They appointed you to a hospital in New York, and you worked hard for three years. You always volunteered for harder tasks and more work, and preferred the operating theater. That is one of the most demanding jobs. What were you avoiding? In my opinion, you believed that you had sinned. Was it something about your dead sister? Did you envy her beauty and wish her dead? Look at my face, Sister Nancy. Look me in the eye!"

Oh, how far you are from the truth, Nadowlsky, but I don't pity you. I don't pity anyone. I was ready to give my life for the sister you think I

wished dead. How soft and naive I was at that age. Look me in the eye!
Read my eyes if you can!

Another hour spent in vain.

At their next appointment, the sister sits opposite Aylin in her usual seat, her gaze fixed on the floor, wringing her hands. Aylin has been talking to her for forty-five minutes, and her throat feels sore. She has started to make the sister her last appointment because she feels so drained by the end of it. This tiny, silent woman sucks up all her energy. Aylin does not remember any case like this in her long career. She is about to give up all hope. It is as if Sister Nancy comes just to collect her pills. At the end of yet another fruitless session, Aylin writes the prescription.

"Sister Nancy, it's a pity for both of us. The world is too beautiful to be wasted on the problems you've buried in your heart. Whether you speak or keep your silence is entirely up to you. Do whatever you want. After you leave, I'm going to have a very large gin and tonic and relax. What will you do? When you go home, sit down and think about whether you're the only person who has problems. See you on Wednesday."

She walks to the door with the sister as she always does. Irene is in the kitchen. When the nun leaves, Irene calls out, "Your gin's ready. Shall I bring it?"

"To hell with gin. I want you to get me clay."

"What?"

"Clay or mud or whatever. To make a statue."

Irene looks at Aylin with astonished eyes. "What the hell does that mean?"

"Irene, no questions, please. Just go now, find it, and buy it."

Irene says, "You know what? You're getting to be more and more eccentric every day."

When Sister Nancy comes in again, Aylin puts the huge heap of clay on a tray in front of her.

"Sister Nancy, you keep kneading your hands, so I got you some clay. Try it; I know that you have very skillful hands."

She notes the sister's startled eyes and swivels her chair, pretending to read a medical journal. She watches the woman in the reflection of the glass cupboard. Her heart is pounding. The sister sits motionless for ten minutes then slowly extends her hands, clasping the clay. Aylin continues to peer at Sister Nancy, too scared to incline her head, take a deep breath, or move a muscle lest she spoil her concentration. She knows that the smallest sound will destroy the magic. Half an hour elapses. The clay between the sister's fingers is expertly molded and shaped in a variety of forms. Slowly, Aylin turns her chair around. The woman's cheeks are ablaze. The material in her hands seems to be gradually assuming the form of a horse. Aylin's stress has been unnecessary; the sister would not have heard a cannonball; she is in another world, a little girl running through the country where she was born, the pines reflected on the lochs.

My heart's in the Highlands, my heart is not here;
My heart's in the Highlands, a-chasing the deer;
A-chasing the wild-deer, and following the roe—
My heart's in the Highlands wherever I go.

Twenty, thirty, forty more minutes pass. Irene will know not to connect a call. Aylin rises softly and creeps out of the room.

It is seven thirty. Irene has left when the sister puts her last piece on the table. A horse, something like a bird, a crucifix, and a heap resembling a child's head. The sister's hands are crossed calmly, inert on her lap.

"Sister Nancy, these are magnificent. You really are very talented."

She handles the objects, studying them.

"What is this? Is this a head?"

"A head."

Was Aylin dreaming? A word after all this time, a single word. Aylin grasps the edge of her desk. *God, help me take the right step,* she thinks. *I mustn't scare her. I must act as if nothing important has happened.*

"Of course, it's a head," she says. "A child's head." Her voice is quivering, and she places the sculpture carefully on her desk. She mustn't show any reaction. But was there ever a time when Aylin controlled her feelings? She shoots up from her chair, falls on her knees, and takes the woman's hands—the nails filled with clay—to her face and kisses them. "Sister Nancy! Thank you for trusting me."

She then gently raises the nun from her chair. She embraces the sister and holds her to her heart. The sister lets go and hugs Aylin back, but soon stiffens again.

At home, Sister Nancy turns her kitchen into a workshop. Her big table is covered with carving tools, clay, and wood. The moment she finishes her breakfast, she hurries to her table. There are times she even forgets to have her meal. She chips, kneads, and forms things for hours. Her hands and outfits are covered in clay and dust, but the moment she starts to sculpt she forgets everything.

At each session, Nadowlsky gives her some books on the art of painting and sculpting. A library gradually emerges in Sister Nancy's house. Now, the pair spends one of their weekly sessions at the Museum of Modern Art or small galleries. Nadowlsky has insisted on her attending a course in sculpture. She even found her one, but so far Sister Nancy has refused the offer. In fact, she is so talented that she produces works of original beauty just by reading the books. She gives most of her creations to her doctor as a gift, but Irene finds a stall for her in the artisan market at Union Square, and her birds and horses become very popular.

Aylin is well aware that she has made great progress since introducing the sister to sculpture. Now, there is silent communication between the sister, Aylin, and Irene. They understand each other with nods or shakes of the head. Her therapy and her prescriptions go on.

One day, Aylin does not bring her patient an art book; she brings her a novel about a real woman.

"Sister, this book is about a woman who loved to make statues more than anything else in the world. I came across it the other day and bought it for you. I think you'll like it. Maybe we can even discuss it when you're finished. What do you think?"

Sister Nancy throws a glance at the book lying on Aylin's desk, *A Woman: Camille Claudel.*

She doesn't even reach out to take the book. Aylin is a bit nervous today. She is running out of time. The year is almost up. She has tried everything in her power but still has not gotten the result she desires. She has begged Mitch to meet her for a consultation. They are having lunch on Thursday with another colleague. It is her only hope now. She needs support to prescribe a new medication, but Mitch believes that nothing can cure the woman; he believes her to be beyond help.

At the end of the session, Aylin says, "I was going to invite you to my house to show you where I've placed your statues. Shall we go up? We can have coffee." The sister nods and Aylin reminds her to take the book lying on the table. The sister puts it into the black bag.

"Sister Nancy, I have wondered since we met. What do you keep in such a big bag? Maybe you'll show it to me someday?" Sister Nancy bites her lips to suppress a giggle.

Aylin quickly jots down a note about it. S.N: She can hardly suppress her laughter. She's amused at something. 12 September 1988.

Upstairs, Sister Nancy studies the pictures on the walls in admiration. She has never seen such a beautiful house. She feels as though she is in a palace. Nadowlsky has elegantly placed her statuettes on a round table covered with a floor-length velvet drape near the couch. This house does not look American. It has a unique atmosphere, almost oriental.

"Sister Nancy, do you like the place I chose for your statues?"

The nun's cheeks redden with embarrassment. She shakes her head. Her art is the first thing to strike the eye when one enters the room.

"What? You don't like it? Oh, I see! You thought that I would put them in some hidden corner. No, ma'am, these works belong front and center. Just look at the strength in that bird's wing. Set him free and he'll fly away. Just like me."

The sister takes the horse from its place and puts it on a shelf.

"No, Sister, that horse belongs here. Such humility! When everyone asks, I will say a patient of mine did it—with pride. I do have the right, don't I?"

All of a sudden, they hear a noise at their back. The sister jumps and turns around. A plump, middle-aged man appears.

"Sister Nancy, this is my husband, Sam Goldberg. I've told him a little about you."

"Yes," says the man, "I have followed your fantastic development."

When he sees the sister's bewildered look, he corrects himself. "I mean your sculptures, of course. You have become a professional."

"Thank you, sir."

A thin, shaky voice. Sam and Aylin look at each other. Aylin holds her breath. Did she hear right? Nancy's voice?

She looks at Sam with wide eyes to make sure he doesn't do or say anything wrong; Sam gulps.

"I . . . I want to toast to our meeting today, Sister," Sam says. "We must celebrate with champagne."

Sam leaves. Aylin walks toward the sister as if nothing extraordinary has happened and puts her hand on her shoulder. "I keep telling you, Sister Nancy, you've made great progress in sculpture. I trust Sam's opinions of art very much. He is an expert and says that you must start working with bigger dimensions. Maybe you should start cutting stone. I'll do a little research on the matter."

Sam returns with Hulusi behind him, carrying a tray with a bottle and glasses. Sam uncorks the champagne, pours it in glasses, and offers two to the ladies. The sister hesitates for a short second and then takes her glass. Sam raises his glass and says, "To meeting a talented sculptor."

Aylin hopes this quivering thank-you signals a step toward the beginning of the end. Almost four months have passed since she heard the first word. If she waits that long for each new word, she'll be finished.

Sister Nancy cuts the block of stone Irene sent her with an electrical cutting tool, making a thunderous noise. She knows that her neighbors will complain, but she doesn't care. The poor sister's hair, face, eyes, and clothes are coated in thick layers of tiny white particles that scatter as she cuts the stone. This is a totally new adventure for her.

That night, Sister Nancy lies on her stiff, narrow bed. A beam of light falls on the book that has been lying there for months, *A Woman: Camille Claudel.* Her bones are aching and she is sleepy. Is there anything in this book that could be of use? She shuffles the pages. Suddenly, her gaze falls on a sentence.

> *A tiny statue she has warmed up in her palm: Her heart hidden from the world . . .*

She skips ten or twenty pages and reads another page.

> *It was as if she spoke of a rendezvous, of another love, of an anxious, elusive, infatuated, and wild love story as she spoke of her God.*

She sits up in bed. Who has written these lines? Who has verbalized the secrets she hides away in the depths of her heart? She reads and reads, her senses on edge. Who is this Camille? Who is this woman who has suffered pains identical to hers? It's twelve o'clock, then it's one, two, three, five o'clock; it's the break of day. The first glimpse of sun fills her room. Camille and Nancy are intertwined; they have become one. The moment she finishes, the sister starts reading the book again. Her hands are trembling, her soul quivers. A woman, a woman dies as she herself is being born. She knows everything Mary has lived and felt.

> *Sacrificing your life for your beloved indicates the greatest of all loves.*

Didn't she sacrifice her life for her beloved? Camille had loved Rodin. Mary had loved Willie. She had opened up her life to him. She had opened up the most secret corners of her heart, her body, her soul to him. When she had to replace him with God—she had to replace him with something; so much sacrifice cannot be wasted for nothing!—didn't she give her whole life, her whole essence to her God?

> *Rodin takes her by the waist; she's just prey in his trap. Camille wants to see it all; her eyes are wide open . . . She thinks she is molded, she opens her mouth, she cannot wait anymore, when he lets go of her, she molds herself, she grasps her breasts. She feels his organ touch her body, its palpitation; she opens up wider. She had never learned it, but she knows its language now. She wants it, she wants it to take her everything.*

A fire burns in Mary. A blaze starts in her groin and consumes her whole body. Something breaks in her and pours out. She presses herself tighter to Willie's body. She had never learned it but knows it all; her gushing joy directs her man. A wind lifts her up and beats her, presses her to the ground; a river flows burbling within her. Her lips, her hands, her veins are on fire. She is like an offering on an altar; she has opened herself up, she is ready to give herself; she leans on Willie's ebbing member. Willie moans, his warm breath throbs behind her ear-lobes; and her own sister's name is a feeble shriek on his tongue. Willie groans her sister's name, and Mary turns into stone. The flame within her dies, the rivers dry up, her soul freezes, and her heart turns to dust.

"My God, what a merciless punishment this is for the sin I committed!"

> *It was as if a pain had pinned her down to that spot. A pain without bitterness, a fist bumping on her belly; it was something which resembled desire, a desire which gave her the drive to roll on and on into madness. The madness to say, "Monsieur Rodin, please place your hand inside me."*

A deep pain had pinned her to the ground. The moonlight fell on Willie. He leaned against the tree trunk in the garden to peep into her sister's bedroom. Her Willie, the man she had loved since she was conscious of herself, rocks to and fro, rejoicing in his pain with sweat on his brow and lids half-shut. It was as if he was carving her insides out. Willie, please hold me. Love me.

> *The fat woman sits on the man's lap with her legs wide open, as the man sits clumsily. Camille sees Pan's horns on his head. One of his arms is underneath her right calf. With the other, he holds her left hand as it moves back and forth on his shaft. He is submerged in her. Camille stands inert like the groups of marble around her. Monsieur Rodin pants behind the white shoulder . . .*
>
> *Camille is dying. She covers her breast with her hand. Her heart and her body take her far, far away.*

She watches from where she stands, like a tree rooted in the ground. A pain has anchored her. Mary holds the heart that belonged to him; her body takes her far, far away.

> *Then the priest reached out. He took off her bonnet. A nun approached her with scissors in her hand; the girl's locks started to fall to the ground. I remember her face was flatly lost like yours. I remember, they put her bonnet on her lockless head, and she turned; only that face was left, pulsating beneath the headdress.*

Her hair fell at her feet when the nun cut it. It formed a brown heap on the ground. Until then, she had always thought of her hair as colorless. At the ceremony, she saw only her father's eyes, bottomless pits. It was only Johnny, her beloved brother, who had begged her not to join the convent, who shed tears. They made her wear her bonnet. At that instant, she gave her soul to them. Only her wounded heart was left for herself.

> *Camille does not know anymore where she goes and what she does. She works. White are her eyes, her hands, and her face. Her heart pounds. Very fast. She is tired. She feels hot. Some evenings she can't even stand up. She staggers back home, drunk with fatigue, with dust, mud, earth, and stone splinters in her hair.*

Sister Nancy works at a mad tempo. She does the work of three people all by herself. She volunteers for more shifts. She is so insistent that they have assigned her to the surgical ward. Her face is chalk-white, but her eyes are like red-hot cinders. Her clean-white apron is stained with clots of blood, urine, and pus. She staggers back home, drunk with fatigue.

I'm very late to write to you, but it was freezing cold. I could hardly stand still. It is so cold, my fingertips are too numb to hold the pen. I couldn't get warm the whole winter. I'm freezing; the cold penetrates to the marrow. It divides me into two, it is unendurable. I cannot describe the cold in Montdevergues.

New York is frozen. A white blanket of snow covers everything. Mother Superior forbids central heating at night. She will send any spare penny to the orphans' fund. On some nights, I can't sleep because of the cold. The tips of my fingers and toes go senseless with cold. It is intense and sharp like an unbearable toothache. Bitter pain.

Monsieur, these are my working hours, questioning hours, the hours when my soul is on fire. When you were guzzling and gulping and devouring life, I was alone with my statue, and I poured my blood, my years, and my life into the depths of this earth.

Mother Superior, I submitted my life to you. My youth and my whole being, my essence was yours. My innermost, purest feelings and that deep, aimless love I gave. I gave without asking anything in return. It was my whole life. Then I begged you; my Johnny, my dearest brother, was dying; my beautiful sister was dying. My mother and my father were dying. Each time, I asked you for just a few days. You did not grant me the time. You told me that people also died here, people in need of my care. You were like a wall. Your eyes did not reflect the deep compassion and sympathy Jesus radiated. My heart was dead, but you killed my soul. I sought shelter at your side—I took an oath to serve you. But now, I'm deserting you. There is only God left for me.

Camille is within four walls. The pain is sharp and strong around her heart. She bangs against the walls, screams out his name to the mirrors. Weariness, rejection, when will she ever confess to herself that she's defeated? Yet, in the eyes of the whole world, she knows that she will remain only the sad reflection of her lover.

They put me in a cell. They interpret my silence as a revolt against God. I will sit in my cell and pray. I will pray. I am forbidden to work as long as I don't speak. Here I am, between four walls, not thinking, not moving, and finally not praying. I will never speak again. And I will never pray again.

O, youth! The incomprehensible! That which crosses our lives within a second.

My youth lasted only one night. A single night. In that night, when Willie loved me, I was young and I was old. O, Youth! That which crosses our lives within one fleeting moment!

Camille doesn't envy anyone, she doesn't repent; neither being deserted, nor living in silence. She doesn't covet her sister. She does not have a husband, she does not have a child, and she does not have a lover. She is the taker, she is the one who decides, and she is the one who creates the statue with her own hands. A woman who will give herself to whomever she wishes, suddenly, joyfully, beautifully, and freely!

I don't have a husband. I don't have a child, I don't have a sweetheart, I don't have a mother, a father, sisters, brothers. I have no one. I have no belief. I fear nothing. I have no past, no future. I'm free and totally alone. No, not anymore. *I am not alone.* There's Camille. I have my Camille, who suffered my pains, grew numb in my cold, who burned in my fires.

Her hands tremble, her lips tremble. She now holds Camille's tiny heart hidden away from the world and warms it in the palm of her hand.

Mary Sarah McCinlop, Sister Nancy, closes the book and presses it to her heart. Camille must exist in other worlds, even though she doesn't exist in this one. Her loneliness is over!

"Sister Nancy? You don't have an appointment today."

She dashes in without knocking, her eyes red like pots filled with blood; it is obvious that she hasn't slept. Her uncombed hair looks like fleece. A button is missing on her gray blouse. *My God, what the hell has happened!* Aylin has never seen her look so disheveled.

"Don't stand there, come in and sit down. What's wrong, for God's sake?"

The sister waves the book in Aylin's face.

Aylin cannot understand at first. She feels sick. She should have read the book herself. Oh God, what can be in it? She doesn't know what has moved the sister, but she must make the right guess. And she must not lose time; she must make it here and now.

She leaves her seat and approaches Nancy, whose eyes are bulging in their sockets. Aylin grasps both of her hands. She looks deep into her as if to read her soul. "Sister Nancy, no torture can be endured forever. Come, let's set it free."

She wants to hold the sister up as she falls to her knees, but cannot manage it. Now, they are both on their knees. Aylin presses the woman's head to her bosom and softly caresses her head, which shakes with the force of her deep sobs.

·   ·   ·

This is the third time that Mary has felt stark naked. The first time was the night she took off her clothes for Willie. The second was the year the nuns took off her veil. After years of wearing a long habit down to her ankles, she felt terribly naked in a skirt. She had used the big black bag to conceal her legs. Now, she is stark naked in front of Aylin. She is cold and Aylin is like a devil possessing her soul. She must tell her everything. Absolutely everything. The sister staggers to the armchair in her doctor's arms. She lets herself go like an empty sack. She is only vaguely conscious as Nadowlsky places a cushion at her back and gives her a cool glass of water. She stretches her legs on the stool in front of her. She hears Aylin repeat the same sentence in a weary and trembling voice, "Thirty years in the asylum. My God, what a terrifying injustice is this! What a terrifying injustice is this!"

They have taken their place at the long table, but Hulusi's dishes have yet to arrive. Sam fills the champagne flutes. Irene, Tayibe, Alice, Peter, Pia, Kevin, Hilary, and David are all there. This is a very special day. Even the witch, Hilary, looks well behaved. Sam is so proud of his wife's success that nothing can spoil his and Aylin's joy. A hopeless case has found her cure on Aylin's couch. The report will redeem her in Cornell's eyes and restore her career.

Sam stands up and holds out his glass.

"I've arranged this dinner in honor of my wife, who has succeeded in a very difficult task. Aylin is the most magnificent psychiatrist in all of New York. Sister Nancy is cured. You wouldn't have believed your eyes had you seen this woman on her first day, a year ago."

"Did you see her on that first day, daddy?"

Could Hilary ever suppress her jealousy? Irene snaps, "I don't know about your father, but I did, Hilary. She was like a wounded animal."

Alice says, "The sister came to this house. We've all seen her."

"You invite mentally ill people into your home?" Hilary says.

Aylin says, "Hilary, dear, I'll call you up and ask for permission before I invite anyone here in the future."

Sam sulks. Why does his daughter always create problems like this? Maybe Aylin has a point.

He says, "Don't be such a spoilsport, Hilary. I don't want to quarrel today. We're celebrating Aylin's victory." He turns to Aylin. "A toast to your future victories, Aylin. You deserve a gift. Now tell me, what would you like?"

Irene says, "Ask for a trip to Asia."

"Auntie, what about that emerald ring we've seen at Tiffany's?"

Pia says, "Perhaps you want a face-lift in South America."

"I'll have a face-lift when the time comes, Pia," replies Aylin, "but I want something else from your father."

"And what's that?"

Aylin looks into her husband's eyes as he waits for an answer.

"The house in Bedford, Sam."

EROSION OF RELATIONSHIPS

Sam and Aylin bought the house in Bedford in 1988 but did not move in until the end of the year when the renovation and decorating was complete. They planned an office for Aylin in the basement of the house.

By the time they finished, they were both physically and mentally exhausted. Both their marriage and their relationship had begun to crumble. Had Aylin predicted the stress a new house would bring, she never would have urged Sam to buy it.

Hilary and Pia continued to add fuel to the fire; they were especially angry about the house. They depended on their father's money, even though Sam often tried to bring his daughters to their senses.

He said, "Listen, girls, I'm selling my current house to buy another. There's no money wasted or lost. If anything, this is an investment. I'll make money on this deal."

"You're a city person. How can you live in a suburb, Daddy?"

In fact, Sam had been asking himself the same question.

"I'm getting older. I look forward to a restful life in nature. I want to do some gardening. I want to raise dogs, or hens and rabbits."

"C'mon, Dad, don't make me laugh," said Hilary.

Aylin had started to lose the patience that Sam's son Peter had so much admired. She had given up once she realized her good intentions would get her nowhere. Because she was smarter than Hilary, her step-daughter was usually silenced by Aylin's well-targeted remarks, although this had the effect of making the girl even more peevish, damaging their relationship further, and Hilary found all the support she needed in Pia.

Aylin rarely saw Peter. The young man had his own family and a separate life. Aylin had only Alice on her side. She loved Alice, but it was not possible to confide in her and expect any real help. As for Tayibe, she didn't want to burden her when she was already struggling to pass her classes at Harvard. Aylin felt very lonely. If it were not for Lucy and Irene, she would have felt totally isolated.

Lucy had become deeply attached to Aylin and was always at her side in times of crisis. Aylin had invited her to the wedding when she married Sam, but Lucy never established a close relationship with him. She had never particularly liked him, but when she recalled how she had hurt Aylin the last time she voiced her opinion, she flushed with shame and guilt.

Aylin had said, "Sam looks handsome tonight, doesn't he, Lucy?"

"You're the good-looking one."

"Still, he is good natured, cute, and—"

"Rich," Lucy said.

"Yes, he's rich, too. I don't think that is a fault."

"You don't need money."

"Everybody needs money. In any case, I don't love Sam for his money; I love him for his personality. He's a nice person."

"Nice and fat."

"I personally find plump men sexy."

"I don't."

Aylin had said, "Lucy, I know you object to Sam because he's Jewish. I'm disappointed in you. I thought I had cured this bias of yours. Now I see that I have failed."

Lucy had thought, She's upset because I don't like her husband. But how can I like him? He's Jewish and fat. Stupid, stupid woman.

Still, Lucy tolerated him so she could keep visiting their home.

She had learned to cook Turkish meals from Hulusi and given him some recipes for kosher dishes. Aylin mocked her and said, "I see that you must have reconciled with your identity."

Lucy replied in the same tone, "Yes, you've shaped me anew! My creator, my mentor, my goddess! I owe it all to you."

Aylin said, "Well, honey, that's what shrinks are supposed to do. Why else should we take your money year in and year out? Seriously, though, Lucy, you're completely cured. You don't need my help anymore."

"I will always need you. Till death do us part."

"You can need me only as a friend. And I need you, honey. But our doctor-patient relationship is over."

"That's not true. You're my mother, my friend, my doctor, my everything."

"Mothers and friends don't charge money for a chat. You don't need a doctor anymore. At the moment, you are psychologically healthier than I am."

"Why do you say that? Do you have a problem?" asked Lucy. "Maybe you need to go and see a shrink, too."

"A shrink cannot sort out my problem; Sam is the only person who can do that. Only a father can tell his daughter that it's time to grow up and live her own life. And Sam does not do it."

"Well, maybe he is the one who should consult a shrink."

Aylin said, "He's already got one at home. I doubt he wants to meddle with a second one."

Irene, too, had been Aylin's patient before she'd become her secretary and closest friend. For some reason, Aylin felt much closer to the people whose brains she had picked than those whose personalities she could not read. She could not open her heart and confide her most vulnerable worries to her husband. She wished she had her old school friends at her side, but unfortunately, they lived far away in Istanbul.

To distract herself from the mounting tension in her marriage, she decided to concentrate her thoughts and energy on a new cause. She had become a member of the Republican Party after she married Sam, so she began to devote her free time to party meetings, campaigns, and speaking engagements. Aylin was a natural. Sam was pleased to follow his wife's deepening interest in politics. He accompanied her to parties at the White House and became acquainted with senators and the secretary of state. Aylin enjoyed showing off her friendships with the president and other power brokers, and her husband started to dream of doing business with them. Although their motives differed, both Aylin and Sam were happy with the situation.

Besides the excitement of decorating their new house and becoming more politically involved, there was something else that made Aylin happy in those days: Sister Nancy. She had made a full recovery. Aylin had called Nilüfer soon after she cured the woman of muteness.

"Listen, Nilüfer, I've been entertaining your guests in my house for years. Now it's your turn to host one of mine."

"Who are you sending me?"

"The sister."

"And who is that?"

"Sister Nancy, the nun I cured."

"The mute sculptor?"

"Yep. That's her."

"What will I do with her? She'll get bored."

"You don't have to do anything. Just give her a room to sleep in. Nancy will work in the fields."

Nilüfer was speechless, but Aylin was so insistent that she couldn't say no. Shortly thereafter, Nancy went to visit with her worn-out brown suitcase and settled into the first floor of the farmhouse. She woke up at daybreak, milked the cows with the peasants, collected fresh eggs, laid the breakfast table, and chatted eagerly with Mr. G. as she drank her coffee. In the afternoons, she climbed up on the small tractor and went to the fields to collect cotton wool next to the peasants. For the first time in years, she put on weight and got a tan. She began to absorb some Turkish words, which sounded very amusing when pronounced with a Scottish accent. The peasants doubled over with laughter. Her hair, which she had detested her entire life, shimmered with gold streaks in the morning sun.

Mr. G.'s gardener, Hüseyin, had never met such a hardworking and sweet woman before. Though she was a Christian, an infidel, her skirts almost touched the ground and her sleeves reached her elbows. She always wore neat, plain dresses. Hüseyin's wife had died two years earlier. His children had married and settled in big cities. He felt very lonely.

One day, he asked Nilüfer, "Ma'am, do you know whether Miss Sister has a husband back in her country?"

Nilüfer replied, "No, she is not married."

After that, Hüseyin came around the farmhouse often. Ten days before Nancy was due to leave, Hüseyin approached Nilüfer with his head bent and his eyes cast down.

"You are my mistress; you will understand me."

"Come, Hüseyin, tell me. What is it?"

"This Miss Sister has grown used to our farm. And she has such talented hands." He grew quiet and waited.

Nilüfer said, "And?" She suspected what he might say but was enjoying the situation so much that she let him continue.

"I mean to say, maybe Miss Sister would like to stay—"

"Through the winter?"

"If you will consent, mistress, I want to marry Miss Sister." The gardener stopped again.

"Hüseyin, are you proposing to our sister?"

"If you give your consent."

"Well, it's not up to me. You need to ask her yourself."

Hüseyin said, "I don't speak English. Perhaps you could ask her on my behalf?"

When Nancy first heard the gardener's proposal, she couldn't believe it. Then she roared with laughter. She had not laughed so heartily since she was a child.

No one could make Hüseyin understand what it meant that Nancy was a nun, that she was married to God and could never give her hand to anyone else.

He kept saying, "How can that be? If she doesn't like me, if her heart doesn't love me, I can understand. But married to God? Good Heavens!"

Sister Nancy left Adana much happier and healthier than she had ever been, though she felt sad to know she had left a broken heart in her wake. When she returned to New York, however, she saw that Aylin was not her usual self. She looked pale. Apparently, there were many problems with the new house they'd been so excited to buy.

Sam, used to noisy, hectic life in New York, could not acclimate to suburban life. He missed his poker friends and sulked all the time, watching old movies for hours. Aylin could handle his moping but could not bear to hear him whine about the house she had bought in Westhampton. He wanted to sell it, claiming they didn't need the extra home.

Exasperated, Aylin repeated, "One of the houses is in the woods and the other by the sea. You are not broke. Why not keep them as they are?"

Sam continued, "We pay so much in taxes and maintenance costs for a house that's empty most of the time. It doesn't make any sense."

Aylin and Sam fell into a pattern of constant bickering about money. Sam complained endlessly of their unnecessary expenses. Aylin grew weary listening to the same old arguments day in and day out. Then a strange twist of fate introduced a new problem that inevitably led to a fresh round of quarrelling.

They had decided to buy a small apartment in the city with the profits from the sale of their previous apartment. Aylin encouraged Sam to buy an office with a small two-bedroom apartment upstairs on Seventy-Fifth Street. Sam had liked that idea very much, until his daughters popped up with a new list of objections. Aylin was at the end of her rope with those girls, and Sam was no help. He simply stood by as they blamed every inconvenience on his wife.

Another source of stress was the fact that business was slow at Aylin's office in Bedford. Maybe no one there needed a psychiatrist. Was it possible that everybody in Bedford was mentally sound? She realized that in order to build a clientele she would need to advertise, but advertising meant expenses. Expenses meant still more arguments with Sam, especially since her income had dwindled after the move. She was already having trouble keeping up. She regretted referring some of her patients to colleagues when they moved to Bedford. She knew her patients would gladly have her, but to take them back from her colleagues was unethical.

Her husband had always said, "You may be smart, but you're completely hopeless when it comes to money and business matters." She supposed that Sam had been proven right yet again. He had told her repeatedly not to refer patients elsewhere until she found new ones in Bedford. But of course she hadn't listened. She never listened.

Aylin was suffering. Her career was moving in the wrong direction. Her relationship with Sam and his family was becoming more tense. She began to rely more and more on alcohol. White wine and gin and tonics helped her to relax, but only temporarily. As for Sam, he had become numb to his wife's worries. He believed that his contribution to Aylin's expenses, on top of Tayibe's tuition, was more than enough evidence that he was a good husband. Yet it was precisely this attitude that angered Aylin the most.

Then there was Tequila, Aylin's new Chihuahua, who seemed incapable of learning that she could not pee wherever she wanted.

Even worse, Ashley, Sam's longtime accountant, began to hang around the house. She had grown more possessive of Sam since his marriage to Aylin, as if she would lose influence. Besides, Ashley and Hulusi detested each other. As chef, Hulusi, became furious when Ashley went in and out of the kitchen as she pleased, poking her nose into everything, opening the fridge for Cokes or beer without asking, and brewing coffee or tea for herself at all hours. He was ready to snap.

One day, Tequila peed on the financial records that Ashley had left in a corner of the living room. The household erupted in a huge fight. Sam blamed Hulusi for not taking Tequila out on time, and Aylin for failing to train her dog. Hulusi, in turn, griped that Ashley had consumed all the beverages in the fridge. Aylin ranted that she never had any peace. The dog, upset by the tumult, peed once more on the carpet.

Three days later, Hulusi rushed into the dining room just as Sam and Aylin were sitting down to dinner; his face was white.

In Turkish, he said, "Miss Aylin, something terrible has happened."

Sam asked, "What did he say?"

"The dog has been run over!" Hulusi exclaimed. "Tequila! A car has run her down!"

Aylin and Sam jumped up and ran to the scene. Hulusi had covered the dog with a piece of cloth so Aylin wouldn't see her.

Hulusi said, "That woman must have done it." Aylin was so sad that she lost her appetite. She would no longer have anything to do with Ashley.

Sam said, "Ashley had nothing to do with this. You can't really think that?"

She replied, "I know, Sam, but I can't help it. That woman gets on my nerves."

Shortly thereafter, Ashley quit and never saw the Goldbergs again.

"Tequila left this world too soon," said Aylin, still grieving the animal.

Irene couldn't help scolding her, "Aylin, I lost my only son. You fretting so much over a dog is insulting." Aylin felt as though Irene had slapped her. Two weeks later, Tequila was replaced and Aylin never mentioned the dog's name again in Irene's presence. Aylin named her new curly-haired white dog Toby von Schweir, after her old friend whose bangs had covered his eyes.

The only times Aylin and Sam got along well again were on their trips abroad. When they were away from home and the girls, their relationship seemed stable. Besides, traveling did both of them good. Partly for this reason and partly to cheer up his wife, Sam asked Aylin to join him on a trip to Monaco. He had been visiting Monaco for years to film the Circus Festival, which went on for almost three weeks thanks to the patronage of Prince Rainier. When he invited his wife to join him, Aylin shook her head. "I cannot leave my patients for that long."

Sam said, "Well, come for just the last week. All the parties are around that time anyway." Aylin liked this solution. She could reschedule her appointments, take her time, do some shopping, and go. But she had not predicted Hilary would lay a trap guaranteed to make her feel angry and miserable.

One day, Hilary called and asked, "Aren't you going with my dad, Aylin?"

"No, Hilary. I'll go in two weeks."

"But why? Will it take you two weeks to buy new dresses to wear in Monaco?"

Aylin replied, "Yes. And I will do all my shopping with your father's credit card so he pays for it all." She slammed down the phone, her nerves rattling. She called Mitch immediately.

"This girl will drive me mad. I'm almost tempted to take a sedative."

Mitch replied, "Don't do it. You're not that kind of person. What's wrong? Are you getting old or something?"

Aylin went to the mirror and took a close look at herself. Yes, she was getting older. Though she did not often worry about it, she was definitely aging. It was a fact that could not be avoided. She could have a facelift or get silicone implants, but she would get older even with those procedures. Would she, too, need to consult a psychologist to face up to this reality?

Maybe an early death like her mother's was the best way to go for women. Lucy, Alice, and Tayibe could not understand this; they were still very young. Betin would understand, but she was far away. Suddenly, Aylin felt absolutely alone.

Aylin thought that she would have a peaceful week away from her problems in Monaco. Indeed, her first days were very pleasant. There were parties every night, and she ran from one affair to the next with Sam. Finally, the big day came—a formal dinner hosted at the palace by Prince Rainier. Sam was placed at the table of circus directors, but Aylin was seated at the end of Prince Rainier's long table. The guests at the table conversed in French, and Aylin was introduced to her neighbor, who happened to be a minister in the government.

She said, "I visited Monte Carlo a couple of times with my father when I was in my twenties. He insisted that I had to see one of the most beautiful spots on the planet. I, like him, fell in love with your country."

The minister asked, "Haven't you been back since?"

"Unfortunately, I never had the chance."

"Well, how do you find Monte Carlo after so many years? Has it changed much?"

"Yes, very much so, I'm afraid. Buildings have been built on top of each other. The casino is overcrowded with the nouveau riche. Was it worth all this damage for the sake of tourism?"

The minister's voice became ice cold. "Had the French given us a little more space, it wouldn't be like this."

Aylin said, "Or maybe they did the right thing. Who knows what you would have done with it."

A deathly silence fell over the table.

The following day, an American friend of Sam's who had been at Aylin's table the night before approached their table at breakfast. Aylin had left to fetch some food from the buffet.

He said, "Goldberg, the prince is upset about what your wife said to his minister last night."

"I apologize. I'm also upset, but I'm not responsible for my wife's words, Turner."

"It's your job to control her."

"How can you say that? Can the prince control his own daughters?"

Aylin returned to the table.

Turner said, "I think your words were probably misunderstood yesterday, Mrs. Goldberg. I'm sure you didn't mean—"

Aylin interrupted him. "I meant every word I said. I get very angry at those who destroy nature with uncontrolled urbanization. I simply spoke my mind."

"When your husband's business relations are at stake, maybe you shouldn't speak your mind so loudly."

Aylin said, "My husband may be a businessman, but I'm a doctor."

It was as if the Monte Carlo trip was jinxed. Sam kept grumbling, "You've probably cost me at least a hundred thousand dollars."

Aylin argued with him, "Can't you ever think of anything besides money? Don't you value anything else? Money has become your God!"

When they returned to America, they were still fuming, and their squabbles continued at home. New disputes arose. Aylin decided to organize a family dinner in order to soften the atmosphere and broker some peace. She invited all the children, but only Peter, his wife, and Kevin accepted her invitation. Pia announced that she could not come because of her rehearsals. Hilary and her husband did not even give an excuse. Aylin was livid. "Well-mannered people always give an excuse."

Sam said, "You insulted David. I think it's understandable that they don't feel like coming."

"When did I insult him?"

"Didn't you tell him that he was as much of a painter as you were a gardener?"

"Sam, that was a joke I made over a year ago."

As always, Sam played the diplomat. Dinner was rescheduled, and everyone showed up on time. The table was set in the garden, and Aylin prepared a delicious meal. On such a warm, sunny day, no one could have predicted the weather could turn so nasty on a dime. But all of a sudden, it started to thunder and pour. Everyone ran inside, shrieking and carrying the dishes to the kitchen. Lightning flashed across the hills as the rain got heavier still. The air had become humid and suffocating.

Aylin said, "C'mon, let's all go for a swim in the pool. It's lovely in the rain."

Sam said, "You're crazy. You can't swim in this!"

"In our childhood in Istanbul, we always swam when it rained."

Pia said, "You're not a child anymore, Aylin."

"If you kill your inner child, you can't enjoy life," said Aylin. "I'm going in. Will anybody join me?"

Tayibe and Alice shouted, "We'll come, we'll come!"

Hilary said, "No, Alice. We won't allow you."

"Why on earth not?"

"It's dangerous. What if the lightning strikes the pool?"

Sam said, "Your sister is right. There are too many trees around. Trees attract the lightning. Stay inside, dear."

Alice said, "Well then, they can't swim, either."

Pia said, "Aylin always does what she wants."

Aylin and Tayibe put on their swimsuits, went into the garden, and jumped in the pool. The people in the house pressed their noses against the windows and watched as Aylin and Tayibe had wild fun splashing around. When the rest of the group retreated to the kitchen, Aylin nudged Tayibe.

"Come on, let's play a joke."

They snuck out of the pool and stealthily took off their swimsuits and left them in the water before running inside through a side door. They could see the living room from Aylin's bedroom and turned off the light to wait. The people in the kitchen entered the living room one by one. The heavy rain held on with all its might. Sam walked to the window and looked out. He signaled to Pia to come to his side. Pia squinted and tried to see the pool clearly. The whole family clustered at the window in horror, the swimsuits floating on the surface of the water. They could not understand how Aylin and Tayibe had vanished. Alice's eyes were as round as balls. Aylin and Tayibe suppressed their laughter in the bedroom.

Tayibe said, "Auntie, they must think that we're dead. Come on, let's wrap ourselves in sheets and tease them more."

Only Peter, Alice, and Kevin found their joke funny. The others were appalled by the two crazy Turks. They, too, felt crazy for coming so far from the city just for dinner.

When Aylin realized that she could never curry favor with Sam's family no matter what she did, she gave up. This decision led to even more tension at home; Aylin read her books in her corner, Sam watched his films on TV, and no one invited the family over. They resided together but both lived alone. Aylin was drinking more, and Sam often grumbled about it, infuriating his wife even more.

As time went by, they learned to balance their life a little. Sam began to stay overnight in New York a couple of times every week to see his poker friends again. Aylin invited her friends to Bedford or went to plays with Kurt. Sam and Aylin met in Bedford on the weekends and gave dinner parties or arranged picnics for their friends. The space had done their marriage some good.

One night, they went to a party in honor of the Tony Awards. There were some famous New Yorkers at their table, including the mayor. Aylin had always loved dancing and danced to every tune the orchestra played. When they started to play the Charleston, she found herself in the midst of a younger crowd. She was having the kind of wild fun she hadn't had in a long time, but Sam suddenly pulled at her arm. She turned around to see his darkened face.

She yelled, "Come and Charleston with me!"

Her husband said, "You're making a fool of yourself."

"I'm only dancing."

"You're sitting with the mayor. Act your age."

"What, am I supposed to dance *Swan Lake* for the mayor?"

"It's better if you don't dance at all."

Aylin said, "Let's ask the table what they think."

Sam pulled her away to another table and said, "Wait for me here."

Soon he was back with Aylin's bag and shawl in his hands.

"Stand up," he said. "We're leaving."

In the car, she said, "Sam, have you lost your mind?" Aylin could not understand his anger.

"You are a doctor. You've been seated at the mayor's table. The Charleston! Swinging your skirts, at your age? Everyone will think you were drunk."

Aylin began to scream, "To hell with everybody, starting with the mayor! If your daughters had not labeled me as a drunk, no one would bat an eyelash."

"Don't involve my girls in this!"

"But they are involved in everything!"

"Aylin," said Sam, "I really cannot understand how you can be so smart and so crazy at the same time. How does someone who cures so many patients dance like a fifteen-year-old girl?"

That night she wondered: Was Sam slowly killing her lust for life?

Aylin needed someone to cheer her up. In the morning, she dialed Mitch's number.

Mitch and Aylin met for lunch at their usual place. Aylin poured out her problems.

"Are you getting sick and tired of married life again?" asked Mitch. "It's an old habit of yours."

Aylin said, "It's not my fault this time. I'm doing my best."

Mitch said, "I'd like to meet that husband of yours."

"Would you really?"

"Yes, but Sam might not like the idea."

"Why not?" said Aylin. "Sam knows your boys; they come over every Thanksgiving. I know your wife. I also know his ex-wife. Why shouldn't you two meet as well?"

Sam didn't object to dining with Mitch and his wife at all. Aylin also invited Emel and her husband, and reserved a table at a restaurant.

Sam seemed very impressed by Mitch. He knew that Aylin was friends with her former husband and respected it. Everybody was content with the evening until Aylin asked her guests whether they'd like to come over for some cognac.

Sam turned to Mitch, "Was Aylin always this much of a lush?"

Mitch was taken aback. The others at the table did not know where to look. Mitch said, "Aylin has always been an outstanding hostess."

Emel tried to make a joke of it by saying, "Maybe Sam doesn't want to part with his cognac."

"My wife drinks constantly," said Sam. "Bloody Mary or beer in the morning, whiskey or sherry in the afternoon, wine at dinner, and cognac after. What do you think of that?"

Mitch said, "We Turks have always been fond of wining and dining."

Sam said, "Mitch, may I ask you a very serious question?"

"How serious?"

"Very serious."

Mitch said, "At the dinner table? If you want to ask something professional, you can come to the office tomorrow."

"No, now. Do you think that Aylin has a drinking problem?"

Mitch was speechless. The atmosphere had become very tense.

"I'm not joking. Do you think Aylin is an alcoholic?"

"I'm not joking, either. Aylin is not addicted to alcohol," said Mitch.

Aylin regretted ever having organized the dinner. Thank God these were her closest friends. They would understand.

Mitch called Aylin the next day. "Sam must have a reason for wanting to embarrass you in front of us, Aylin. You should find it."

"I'm doing my best, believe me, but it never ends."

Mitch said, "Well, at least you'll have no time to be bored with this marriage." His voice broke.

"Mitch, don't throw stones," said Aylin. "I'm very stressed these days."

After the girls decided to skip Thanksgiving, Sam proposed family therapy, a new American trend. Sam would arrange the appointment. Aylin agreed.

A few weeks later, Aylin, Sam, Peter, Hilary, Pia, and Alice met at Dr. Goldman's office for the first session. Tayibe refused to attend. She reminded them that some time ago, following poor Alice's nervous breakdown, they had attended a session and it had been a disaster. What was meant to help Alice with her problems turned into an hour of Hilary and Pia blaming Aylin. Tayibe recalled that she had not known whether to cry or laugh at the sight of a grown woman wailing, "Daddy, don't you love us anymore? Daddy, you don't care about us like you did before!"

In this session, everyone was asked to say exactly what they thought, with the aim of having the parties reconcile after being unnecessarily harsh to each other. Unfortunately, what was supposed to be a peaceful session turned into a battlefield, one in which Aylin lay defenseless, beaten by all her family members.

The girls cursed Aylin for being a gold digger and an insane drunkard. Their stepmother made their father unhappy and thought only of herself. She harmed his business with her absurd behavior at parties and pushed Sam away from his daughters. She had even moved their home to a suburb in order to steal their father away from them. Even Peter, whom Aylin had so much faith in, didn't utter a single word in her defense. Alice stuttered a few times, but no one paid her any attention. Sam sat there with a smug expression on his face, as if to say, "See, this is what people think of you." Aylin was shocked. What had she done to deserve this? Why did they hate her so much?

In the end, Dr. Goldman turned to Aylin and said, "Now, it's your turn. Tell us about your feelings."

Aylin said, "I have nothing to say."

"Nadowlsky, you're a psychiatrist. You know the benefits of airing out what ails you."

Aylin said, "I've heard enough today."

That weekend, she told Tayibe everything with tears in her eyes.

Tayibe said, "I wish I had not left you so alone, Auntie."

Tayibe couldn't believe that Sam had left Aylin defenseless. When she saw Sam next, she said, "You've injured my aunt very badly, Sam. Why didn't you protect her?"

"Aylin must know what others think about her. That is the point of therapy."

Tayibe said, "In this whole world, only Hilary and Pia think badly of my aunt." She went to her room immediately so as not to say something she would regret.

Family therapy had opened Aylin's eyes. She had to do something. She had to break free from this loveless circle, rearrange her life, and win back the patients she had lost by moving to Bedford.

Sam saw that his wife was hurt and didn't go to the city for poker the next week. One evening, seeing Aylin had fixed her eyes on the fire, a glass of wine in her hand, he asked, "What are you thinking of?"

"I'm thinking of going away, Sam."

"Where will you go?"

"I'll go away, very far away."

"Do you want to go on a trip?"

"I want to go to the Gulf War."

"What?"

"The Gulf War. The war in Iraq."

"But you're not a soldier. They won't let you go."

Aylin said, "Want to bet?"

"How many glasses of wine have you had?"

"This is the third, including the ones at dinner."

"You've started to drink even more."

Aylin said, "I don't want to hear another word." She slammed the glass on the table and went to bed.

Sam didn't take this conversation seriously, chalking it up to a tipsy Aylin. He spent the following week in the city. When he returned to Bedford the next weekend, he had already forgotten their discussion.

A month later, over dinner, Aylin said, "I cannot go to the Gulf, but there's a slight chance I'll be sent to a hospital to treat the soldiers."

"What are you talking about?" asked Sam.

"I told you. I want to join the war."

"Were you serious?"

"Certainly."

"I've told you. They don't take recruits your age."

"They do, Sam. They'll probably ask me to work with trauma victims."

Sam said, "You're kidding!"

"I'm not, but I still have a long way to go. As I said, there's only a slight chance so far."

Sam thought for a second. "What'll happen if everything goes smoothly?"

"They'll appoint me to a VA hospital."

"Will you go if they ask you?"

"I will."

"So you're running away from our marriage?"

"No. I don't have any intention of being chased off by two girls half my age."

"Well, why do you want to go then?"

"For other reasons. I've been exerting all my energy on personal cases for years, trying to solve the problems of the rich. In the army, I can arrange group therapy sessions and deal with real problems. Besides, there are other projects I have in mind."

"Aylin, I understand, but what about me? Everybody will think that you've left because our marriage is not working."

Aylin asked, "Who? Pia and Hilary? I couldn't care less."

"Our friends, our families, everybody who knows us."

Aylin didn't answer. She didn't want to fight when nothing was definite yet. Sam hoped this would be forgotten in time.

Aylin could not hide all the correspondence from Irene. One day she couldn't help asking, "What's going on? What are these military papers?" Aylin told her what she was doing. Irene couldn't believe her ears.

"You mean, you'll really join the army?"

"Why are you so surprised?"

Irene said, "I've never heard such nonsense in my life."

"I appreciate your support."

"Why would I support this craziness, for God's sake? Does Sam know?"

"Yes."

"Did he consent to it? He'll allow his wife to enlist in the army? It's mostly men."

Aylin said, "You're so dramatic. I'll join the army as a doctor, not a stripper."

"Still, did he consent to it?"

Aylin said, "I don't know, Irene. I'm not going to ask him before I know for sure that I'm in."

Irene led Aylin to the patients' couch.

"Aylin, do you remember what you told me when I came to you as a patient?"

Aylin said, "It's been such a long time."

"Let me remind you, then. You said, when someone with a heart problem goes to the doctor, the doctor first asks the patient if he smokes. If the patient says yes, he first tells him to quit smoking. This is what you told me."

"So?"

"Then you told me, 'Now, go divorce your husband, and then come back to me, otherwise I cannot help you.'"

"Yes, I remember that. Your husband was a hopeless alcoholic who was beating you every day."

"That's right, and I did as you told me. I divorced him, broke free of the pills, and started to work, thanks to you."

"Why thanks to me? I saw your talent and offered you a job."

"Never mind. My point is this: I owe you my mental health. There are not many people in the world who believed in me as much as you did."

Aylin said, "Stop beating around the bush. I'm getting bored!"

"You were my doctor, I listened to you. Now, it's your turn. I'm your friend and you have to listen to me."

"Okay."

"Don't leave your husband to run off to some war. If you do, this marriage will end."

"Don't worry, Irene. It won't."

"I know that you're not very happy, but you still have a decent man at home. Please don't go."

Aylin's heart melted. She had real friends who loved her.

Lucy was just as irate as Irene when she heard about the Gulf War.

"You're not a soldier," she said. "This is suicide. Are you crazy?"

Aylin raised her eyebrows and smiled. "Look who's talking about suicide."

"Don't even go there."

"I won't go as a soldier; I'll go as a doctor. And it's not to the Gulf; it's to Oklahoma to work with war veterans."

"Are you doing this to run away from Sam? Didn't you always tell me not to run away from my problems? To face them and solve them head on?"

"I'm not running away from Sam. Until now, I've always dealt with rich New Yorkers' petty problems. I want to be useful to people who have come face to face with death, who really need a psychiatrist."

"I don't believe it. You're unhappy, and I can't help you. What will I do without you, Aylin?"

Aylin said, "Don't worry. Nothing is definite yet."

But the possibility the military would take her kept growing, and the more Aylin's hope grew, the more enthusiastic she became. She couldn't think of anything else but the army. Finally, she received the good news, although she was scared to tell Sam. The inevitable day came at last.

"The contract is only for two years," said Aylin. "You'll see how fast it'll fly."

Sam said, "If you want a change, pick something less dramatic."

"These two years will be professional gold."

"Aylin, no one will believe that. Everybody will interpret it as our marriage ending."

"I'm not concerned with other people's interpretations; I only care about yours. You know why I'm going, and that's enough for me."

"I don't want you to go. I don't want to be lonely in this house. I didn't get married to live by myself."

Aylin said, "Sam, eventually you will see that this separation will do as much good for you as it will for me. You'll have your peace of mind, though we'll miss each other. That will be great for our marriage."

FORT SILL— OKLAHOMA

Aylin slipped into her uniform for the first time on a cold January day in 1992.

She looked in the mirror and slowly slid her hands down the sides of her black jacket. The lapels were decorated with the stars of a lieutenant colonel. She wasn't dreaming. The woman in uniform in the mirror was herself; she was Aylin Devrimel Nadowlsky Goldberg. The uniform suited her long and slender torso. It was as if the uniform was her own skin, her personality, her identity, her very self.

Her friends thought she was fleeing reality. Maybe she was to a certain degree, but she was tired of dealing with the spoiled New York patients who couldn't cope with a little emptiness in their lives. She was also fed up with Sam. She and her husband had been drifting apart for so long.

They all thought that she was being crazy. They thought she was only playing soldier.

But Aylin had never played. Not as the good-hearted woman or ill-mannered woman, the princess, the hippie, the woman in love, the spoiled girl, the seductress, the student, the teacher, the doctor, or the mother. She had always inhabited her role, whatever it was, committing her heart, her mind, and her soul as long as necessary.

And now, there was only one truth: Lieutenant Colonel Aylin. The military was in her genes.

She yelled out, "I did it!" This was, of course, not her first victory, but now she had succeeded on a whole new level. To actually get to wear this uniform had not been easy. There had been applications, refusals, renewed applications, waiting, endless interviews, inquiries, written and oral exams. Her war with Sam. But she got there in the end. She had her uniform.

As a doctor of psychiatry, Aylin was not required to do basic training at Fort Sill. No one expected a fifty-four-year-old woman to complete it. Therefore, when the sergeant saw her jogging laps with a battalion, he couldn't believe his eyes.

He said, "You don't have to do the training, Lieutenant Colonel."

"But I can, isn't that so, Sergeant?"

"Certainly."

"Well, I want to, Sergeant."

"Just quit whenever it gets to be too much."

"Okay, Sergeant."

Aylin's unit fell into step and then marched to the training area, where the sergeant ordered them to run. The soldiers made a single line and started to run. When they'd been running for half an hour, the sergeant appeared at Aylin's side.

"Are you all right?"

Aylin said, "I'm fine. What about you?"

The sergeant muttered.

At a ditch, the sergeant took out his timer. The soldiers ran to the ditch and crawled on their stomachs. They used ropes to climb up twenty-foot-high beams. At the top, they jumped down onto the sand. Aylin stole a look at the sergeant's bewildered face and tried to suppress her laughter. There were two more women in the group, but they were in their twenties, and she was just as strong. There was only one difference; Aylin didn't utter a single word of complaint.

At dinner, the sergeant came to Aylin's table and said, "I want to congratulate you for your performance on the field today, Lieutenant Colonel Nadowlsky. We start at six o'clock in the morning tomorrow. Do you think you'll join us again?"

Aylin replied, "See you at six, Sergeant."

Aylin never skipped training. When new soldiers arrived, the sergeant proved to them that they could get through training by parading Aylin in front of them.

She passed the physical examination on November 9, 1992, and broke a record, winning her first Certificate of Achievement.

This was only one side of the coin. Aylin was developing skills that were much more important than running and climbing.

Lieutenant Colonel Doctor Nadowlsky was promoted to head of the Psychiatry Department at Reynolds Army Community Hospital a week later. She wanted to conduct light therapy on soldiers who had returned from the Gulf War with depression and insomnia, who were having difficult readjusting to life back home. The army had only applied this technique in Alaska, but they had faith in Aylin and allowed her to give it a shot.

Along with organizing a light-therapy program, Aylin was wildly successful in her group-therapy initiatives, helping countless veterans readjust to life off the battlefield. It was not long before Lieutenant Colonel Doctor Aylin Nadowlsky was awarded the artillery regiment's highest honor, the Honorable Order of Saint Barbara, in 1993.

The light therapy program had an incredible rate of participation and success. The devices Aylin had installed mimicked the rays of the sun. In fact, curing the mentally ill with sunshine was a method first developed by the ancient Greeks and Romans and had been applied many times throughout history. People's energy decreased during the dark days of the winter months, and they became inactive, needing more sleep and carbohydrates. It was as if some human beings went into a psychological hibernation period in the winter months. People who worked at night often had similar symptoms.

The beams reflected by the lamps radiated solar light through the retina, reached the glands in the brain, induced a chemical reaction in the hypothalamus, and thus cured depression, simply because the hypothalamus would secrete the right balance of hormones. Light therapy had absolutely no side effects. Furthermore, it didn't damage the body like antidepressants did. A group of soldiers could simultaneously benefit from exposure to a few lamps at each half-hour session. Aylin had therefore devised an economical method for the army.

Despite her success, Aylin had to admit that she suffered from an aching loneliness when she found herself so far away from her friends and her vibrant life in New York. She missed Tayibe, Irene, Lucy, Mitch, and even Sam. In the male-dominated military, she felt like a minority. They showed mostly sports on the TVs in the rec room. Most men at Fort Sill were not interested in the opera, music, museums, or elegant restaurants. New York felt like an illusion. She had taken her city for granted.

Aylin begged Irene to come to Oklahoma in October, and they had a lovely weekend together horseback riding and chatting long into the night. She made Irene catch her up on everything she was missing in New York. What was in the shop windows? Were the streets decorated for Christmas? Where would the best New Year's parties be?

Despite her loneliness, Aylin mostly abstained from alcohol and looked happy. Irene didn't recall another ever seeing Aylin so healthy. She had a nice tan and natural streaks in her hair. Her sleek body had been reshaped by the daily training, her muscles stronger and more pronounced, and her posture much improved. All her uniforms fit her so elegantly.

Irene said, "Aylin, you look so natural in that uniform. Was your father a soldier?"

Aylin said, "My grandfather's father was a soldier. They say that my crazy side comes from him."

Sam visited only once in two years, and that was with Tayibe on her first Christmas. Mustafa and Nilüfer were visiting at the same time. Aylin hosted Sam and her family in her big apartment, and gave a Christmas party in keeping with tradition. She invited the high-ranking officers she knew, her colleagues, her neighbors, and some of her patients. Sam had been a pilot in the Second World War and had won the Purple Heart award for his heroism. He had many memories to share. He had a great time, and felt so proud of his wife when they told him of her amazing success.

"That wife of yours is an incredible woman," said the army commander. "She holds the female target-shooting record. She manages whatever weapon we give her—pistols, rifles, whatever. She's a pro with them all. She's also very good on horseback and never complains about the camping beds. She's tougher than the majority of the men."

Sam left Oklahoma with a huge smile. They called each other often in those days; even writing occasionally. He followed her promotions with interest. Aylin faxed him every grade and evaluation she received, and appreciated his encouragement.

Sam's only problem was the boredom he felt alone in the house in Bedford. Thinking again of finances, he mentioned the possibility of selling the house in Westhampton.

He never went back to Oklahoma, despite Aylin's entreaties. "If I'm going to travel, it won't be to Oklahoma," said Sam. This attitude embittered her, but the space also made her come to terms with her own faults. She had made Sam, used to living in the most vivacious city in the world, buy a house in suburban Bedford. Then she had left him all alone there to join the army. Still, the separation was only for two years, and when it was over, she would return home and spend most of her time with him in Bedford, enjoying nature. After surviving training, she could probably even tolerate his daughters.

Eventually, however, their calls turned into an ongoing dispute about the Westhampton house. Aylin was fed up with Sam's insistence and his continual detachment. Finally, she relinquished the property.

Fortunately, Sam was not her only link to life in New York. She talked often with Lucy and Irene. Tayibe, who was doing her master's degree in London for the year, called her once a week. Her uncle and Rozi also called often. Even Sister Nancy had called her three times to ask how she was doing.

Lucy wrote her long letters. It was good luck that she'd bought the horse Aylin encouraged her to buy because she had met Norman, the owner of the stable where she went every weekend. According to Lucy's letters, Norman was blond, blue eyed, tall, and handsome. They went on long rides together, and Lucy was slowly falling in love with him. Each letter revealed something new. By the third, Aylin had learned that he was quite wealthy; by the fifth, that he was a good lawyer; and by the seventh, that he was deaf.

Aylin grabbed the phone. "Lucy, did you fall in love with a deaf man?"

"Yes," answered Lucy with her husky voice. "He's a wonderful guy, Aylin."

"You shouldn't have been left alone. If you have another break-down, I won't be there to help you until I can come home."

"A breakdown? I'm so terribly happy, Aylin."

"How do you converse with a deaf person?"

"Aylin, you'll love him. He's a fantastic person. He graduated from Princeton and has a master's degree from Harvard."

"But he cannot hear you!"

"He reads lips."

Aylin said, "Not when it's dark."

"We do something else when it's dark," said Lucy with a laugh.

When Sam went to the Pritikin Longevity Center for a diet program, he met Joan, a divorced woman in her mid-forties. She was there for the same reason.

Sam's letter came a few months later. Aylin had collected her mail and was walking back to the therapy room. She was surprised to see Sam's handwriting on one of the envelopes. She tucked her other letters under her arm and tore out the single page, reading it in an instant. It was a blunt letter. Sam wanted a divorce. He suggested Aylin contact her lawyer as soon as possible.

Aylin felt like she had received a violent slap in the face. The piece of paper trembled in her hand as she read it over again. *I've been unhappy for a long time. I have decided to get a divorce. Let's take the necessary steps.*

Aylin slid into her office like a ghost. Therapy was supposed to begin in half an hour. She collapsed into a chair in a corner of the room, holding her head in her hands, exhausted. She could not think. She could not believe it. She did not know what to do. She felt like scream-ing but couldn't. She felt like crying, but no tears came.

The patients came in to find their doctor sitting silently, an anguished expression on her face. Sergeant Friggs eyed Aylin for a sec-ond before approaching her.

"What is it, Lieutenant Colonel? Is something troubling you?" Aylin jumped as if waking from a dream. She pulled herself together and rose. "Yes, Friggs. I have received sad news from home. Don't worry; it's not something I cannot handle."

She turned to her patients and said, "C'mon now," in a cheerful voice. "Sit down. I've picked out a lovely tune for you today. Let's see if you like it."

As soon as she finished, Aylin ran to her room. She called home, but there was no answer. She called Sam's office. His secretary told her that Mr. Goldberg was not due in the office till the beginning of the following week, and she didn't know where he was.

"Don't lie, Charlotte," said Aylin. "You know where he is."

"Believe me, I've no idea, Mrs. Goldberg," said the girl. "He just said that he needed a week off. If he calls, I'll tell him to call you."

"Give me his number. I'm not kidding, Charlotte. I must talk to my husband."

"I don't know where he is."

"You must know. Dear, give me his number."

"I swear I don't. If he calls, I'll do my best—"

Aylin hung up. She lay on the bed for a time with her eyes fixed on the ceiling. She couldn't believe what was happening. It was a nightmare. She got up from the bed after about an hour, sat in front of the mirror, and scrutinized her face. It looked aged, battered by shock. She frowned and stepped into the shower, standing motionless under the cold water for a long time. Then she turned on the hot water, letting it burn her skin. Steam rose from her body, and the bathroom filled with hot mist.

Finally, she got out of the shower, sat before the mirror again, and put on her makeup very carefully. She smoothed on her foundation, patting the powder over it, blended the blush on her cheeks, put on eye shadow and mascara, lined her lips and filled them in with lipstick. She fluffed her hair, narrowing her eyes at the result. That old, beaten, weary woman was gone. Again Aylin had become an ageless and attractive woman.

She needed a drink. She always felt much better when she was settled among her friends at the bar.

"Wow, you look great today, Lieutenant Colonel Nadowlsky," said the tall and handsome Colonel Carlston.

"I have to look great from now on," said Aylin. "I need a new husband."

"Well, you don't have to go far to search. This place is full of men, and you can put me at the top of your list, Lieutenant Colonel."

Aylin smiled and told the officers that she was inviting all of them to have a drink with her.

One of the officers asked, "What are we celebrating?"

Aylin said, "A new era." They all raised their glass.

Toward the end of the evening, Aylin's buzz started to wear off. She developed a horrible headache and left. She lay down slowly on her bed. She had not had a headache since arriving at Fort Sill, or needed a painkiller, until now.

She gulped down two pills with some water and lay down again. Sam's letter started to dance before her eyes. The tears finally came and trailed down to her chin, leaving black tracks of mascara on her cheeks.

After her tears dried, Aylin called Irene. They had a long chat. Aylin told her that she intended to behave as if she had not received the letter.

Irene said, "You can't run away from his letters forever. I think you should face him as soon as possible and try to settle the dispute. Maybe you'll both forget this letter."

Lucy's opinion was more forgiving. She suggested that the letter might have been written in a moment of rage. She offered to come to Oklahoma with Norman for the weekend. She had wanted Norman to meet Aylin for a long time anyway. They would think together and figure something out. Norman was a terrific fellow; he would find a solution.

Aylin called her Bedford house all night. Sam was avoiding her. He had even shut off the answering machine, ensuring he would not hear her messages. Aylin suspected that there must be a woman involved. She was right, she later learned. A woman had been hovering since the first months of Aylin's absence.

It wasn't long before a new patient distracted her from her pain. Just a few days after receiving Sam's letter, she was summoned to a special meeting concerning a prisoner in the base's correctional facility.

The colonel said, "There's a distressing situation, Lieutenant Colonel Nadowlsky. Lieutenant Jones is a dangerous killer who needs to be kept locked up, but he's ill. He's having stomach pains, and by law, we have to transfer him to a hospital, but he refuses to communicate with anyone. We won't be able to tell the doctors what's wrong with him. We are hoping someone like you might solve the problem."

Aylin said, "I'll go see him this afternoon."

The colonel said, "Let me know how it goes."

"May I study his file?"

"His file is not here at the moment."

"Then I can postpone seeing him till tomorrow."

The colonel looked Aylin in the eye. "All right. I'll have his file sent to you."

Aylin didn't understand his hesitation, although she was a bit excited to go to a military prison for the first time.

In the afternoon, she left to see Jones just as the file arrived. The prison director had been informed about Aylin's visit. He received her cordially but opposed the idea of her being alone with the prisoner. "He's very dangerous. We think he's committed eight homicides, five confirmed."

"I will call for help if necessary."

"Lieutenant Colonel, I can't let you be alone with him. I'm responsible for your safety."

Aylin didn't want to lose time arguing with the director. She let the guards escort her downstairs. After winding through many narrow passageways, they arrived at a long room with a table and two chairs.

She waited for the young man anxiously. When they brought him in, she noted his prison jumpsuit, shaved head, and chained wrists. The wardens stood guard near the wall.

"Hello," said Aylin. "My name is Nadowlsky. Lieutenant Colonel Nadowlsky."

Jones cast a poisonous glance her way.

"I know that you don't like talking, Jones, but we have to know what's going on if we're going to ease your pain. Signal with your head if I give you the right information, okay?"

Jones didn't move a hair.

"Is the pain in the right side of your stomach?"

The man remained silent.

"The left side? Is it like gas? Or sharp, like being stabbed? Is the pain everywhere in your belly? Or localized? Oh, hell! You'd know if your appendix burst."

Jones nodded.

"You have appendicitis?"

The man shook his head.

"Oh, I see, you want to die."

The man nodded.

"If I were in your shoes, I would have chosen an easier death. Why should someone who's taken lives in the blink of an eye die in so much pain? You cut your neighbor's throat and shot your girlfriend. Do you know how an appendix bursts? It's not nice. In my opinion, you'd be better off in the electric chair."

The guards fidgeted.

Aylin took out a cigarette from her purse and offered him one. She said, "Don't look so surprised. I don't care about the murders. What I'm interested in are your motives, but unfortunately you will deprive me of that knowledge when you die here."

She held the pack of cigarettes under his nose. Jones took one. Aylin lit first his cigarette and then hers. They smoked in absolute silence.

"C'mon, Jones. Tell me what eats you up. Not just what's gnawing at your stomach, but what's devouring your brain, your soul, and your heart."

Aylin made the man stand and pressed expertly on his belly. She opened his mouth and checked his tongue.

She said, "I agree with the intern's diagnosis—probably appendicitis. I will prescribe one more medication. You won't be sorry if you take it. Well, good-bye. Don't miss me too much."

The director called two days later. Jones wanted to see Aylin again.

She called Lucy and said, "I don't want you to be hurt, honey. I miss you and want to meet Norman, but something has come up. I have to work the whole weekend."

"A new project, Aylin?"

"A new patient. He is my Hannibal Lecter."

"You mean a serial killer?"

"Yep, exactly. I have to meet with him every day."

Lucy was speechless. "Couldn't they have asked someone else?"

"I wanted him for myself."

Lucy exhaled, "Watch out for yourself."

Aylin and Lucy nicknamed Jones Hannibal, and Lucy called often to see how he was doing.

"He's fine. I had his handcuffs removed this week."

"How?"

"I gave him a pen and paper. They had to. He's very good at sketching."

"An artist and a sculptor. Aylin, I'm your only talentless patient. Why couldn't I turn out to be somebody?"

"You turned out to be a sweet, smart, and hardworking girl. Besides, you're my closest friend. Isn't that enough?"

"It's okay for the moment," said Lucy. "Give my regards to Hannibal."

Aylin continued to meet with Archibald P. Jones at least twice a week. She had become attached to the young man, tucked in a tiny cell with nothing but rattling chains.

Three months after Jones' appendicitis operation, his stomach pains started up again. By now, Aylin was allowed to be in the same room with him without the guards. They waited outside the iron bars and gave Aylin a bell to ring if she felt threatened. She doubted she would use it. A strange friendship had developed between them. It was as if she had extended her hands through a black curtain and played the piano without seeing the keys. She had pressed the correct notes until now, but a single mistake could trap her.

Hannibal gave her his drawings, and Aylin checked out books from the library, searching for answers.

"Archy, this picture. This is you, right? You're killing with a smile on your face."

Jones looked at her helplessly.

"Does killing give you joy, Archy?" Jones began to rock in his chair. He was restless.

"Let's take a look at this one. What is this? An egg?"

The young man scrawled some other images.

"A pillbox, pills. You drew a bullet inside the pill. And in that picture, you're killing somebody. Go on, Archy, what's in your belly? There's a pill in your belly." Jones rocked faster.

"Archy, are you trying to tell me that you swallow a pill before you kill?" Jones drew faster and faster. Then he quit drawing abruptly.

Aylin took the pencil and his sketches. "You can rest. You have told me a lot. Now, it's my job to find your secret."

At the base headquarters, Aylin told the superintendent that she wanted to study some of the archives. She sat at the computer for two hours. Her eyes started to burn as she took notes.

Back in the prison, she spoke to Jones. "Archy, listen to me carefully. I'm going to set you free. Both from prison and your stomach pain, if you help me."

Jones took the pencil, but Aylin snatched the paper away from him.

"No, you're forbidden to draw today. We have to talk. It's a must, Archy. If you don't want to talk, nod yes and no."

Archy stuck the pencil in his mouth and began to gnaw nervously.

"Did you take pills when you went to the Gulf? So you wouldn't be scared?" Archy bowed his head.

"This pill, whatever it is, is addictive. Killing becomes addictive. You want to relive that excitement, over and over again. You can't avoid it, though you know it's wrong. Is that it, Archy? Is that why you have these pains? You've been pushed to the point of no return. You are guilty, but the actual criminal is the person who made you take the pill and hauled you into hell."

Aylin's Hannibal stretched his hands toward his doctor's throat. She hesitated for a moment, her hand on the bell in her pocket.

"You won't enjoy it this time. Don't try to kill me, Archy. It would be useless."

But his hands were at her neck. She rang the bell. The guards appeared in an instant and pulled Archy to his feet. Aylin rubbed her neck.

"I won't give up, Archy. I'll come again. I know that you did this to scare me, not kill me. Go and rest and think it over. Wouldn't you like to kill the monster inside you, instead of a human being this time?"

.　　.　　.

Aylin went down to the archives again, but another superintendent had taken over, and he refused to let her access the computers. Aylin didn't accept defeat. She ordered him to let her pass and took her time.

She looked for Major Finch, her close friend and colleague, at dinner in the dining hall that evening.

"Do you have a minute, Finch?"

"What is it? Is anything wrong?"

"It's too loud here. Let's go over to my place."

"What is it?"

Aylin said, "My car's outside. I'll tell you on the way." She walked swiftly to the door, and the major followed behind her.

At Aylin's apartment, she quickly took out her notes and sat close to Finch, leaning into him. She did not want to miss a single word he said. She said, "Tell me, my friend. How does the army use its soldiers in experimental studies?"

Finch said, "In many ways. Do you absolutely need to hear it tonight?"

"I'm writing a paper. I must know."

"Research and development in the army happens on three levels: nuclear, chemical, and electronic. We work hard to outsmart the enemy. For instance, we're now developing electronic waves that bombard the nervous system, leading to disorientation and vomiting."

"What about nuclear experiments?"

"The army obviously does not conduct nuclear experiments on its own soldiers, but a technician may not always be aware of the danger he is exposed to."

Aylin said, "I heard rumors that several people were inadvertently infected in the course of an AIDS study."

"Aylin, these are only rumors. We shouldn't spread them."

"What about chemical experiments?"

"Aylin, couldn't all this wait until tomorrow? Did you really interrupt my evening for this?"

"I'm not finished yet. I have more questions."

Finch said, "Okay, but still, when I saw how jumpy you were, I assumed something terribly important was happening. You women! Always demanding immediate gratification."

Aylin poured some more whiskey in his tumbler.

A week later, Aylin finished her research and confronted the colonel.

The colonel said, "How did you attain this information, Nadowlsky?"

"I checked the files."

"Those files are confidential. Not everyone has access."

"Not even a doctor with the rank of lieutenant colonel? The superintendent certainly thought so."

"He was mistaken."

"What are you hiding?"

"There's nothing to hide. Every army conducts experiments. They serve the interests of the country."

"Maybe. Still, I was very impressed by some of the more daring experiments. For instance, I never would have guessed that extreme light exposure led to both temporary and permanent blindness."

"This is not your concern, Nadowlsky."

Aylin said, "I'm sorry, you're right. That's not my field of interest. I came here to talk about Jones."

He froze.

"Again, don't involve yourself in things that don't concern you, Lieutenant Colonel."

Aylin said, "Colonel, Jones has been permanently scarred by adrenaline pills."

"I beg your pardon?"

"Pills he was given to attack the enemy without fear."

"And?"

"The army wanted to create heroes, but it produced killers."

"Watch what you say, Lieutenant Colonel."

Aylin said, "Listen to me carefully now, Colonel." She felt the genes of the crazy Pasha coursing through her bloodstream.

Twenty minutes later, the soldier outside the door heard Lieutenant Colonel Nadowlsky say, "It's my duty to inform those involved," as she left the colonel's office.

Her contract with the army was set to expire. If she chose to stay, she would likely be promoted to colonel, but she had a life in New York, and a husband seeking a divorce. She decided not to renew her contract.

Shortly before she left Fort Sill, Aylin received an urgent summons to Captain Atleen's office. Puzzled, she hurried to meet him.

Captain Atleen said, "Lieutenant Colonel Nadowlsky, I'm sorry for calling you here on such short notice, but some documents have arrived for you to sign."

Aylin took the papers, put on her glasses, and sank into her chair.

Captain Atleen asked, "Can I get you some coffee?"

Aylin said, "No, thank you," unable to suppress the quiver in her voice. "Give me a pen."

Sam had sent the divorce papers to Fort Sill.

At home, she called Sam's office. "Charlotte, get me Sam."

"He is not here, Mrs. Goldberg."

"When will he be back?"

"I have no idea."

"This game again, Charlotte?"

"I'm only doing what I've been ordered, ma'am."

"Okay. Since we can only speak through you, tell my husband that I find him very rude, sending those documents to the base office. If he were a gentleman, he would not have sent them to my home. Or, even better, he would have waited another month and done it in person. Now, only three weeks before my departure; this news will speed through the base. They'll say, 'Lieutenant Colonel Nadowlsky's husband left her.' They will either pity me or mock me behind my back. Sam has disgraced me. Also, tell him this: he has made me suffer, and I will make him sorry for it."

Aylin began to weep as soon as she hung up. She knew that hard times awaited her. Two different wars would face her in New York, but she would not give up on veterans, nor would she leave Sam without a fight.

EXASPERATION

Aylin celebrated her homecoming with a big Christmas party. All her
New York friends, both Turkish and American, Tayibe's and Mustafa's
school friends, Uncle Hilmi and his family from Florida, where he'd
moved, all flocked to Bedford in 1993. Hulusi, his wife, and Handan,
who Aylin had hired to help clean her office, came to help with the
cooking and preparations.

Aylin didn't give her guests the slightest hint of any marital drama.
She seemed elated to be home. The guests assumed that Sam was on
a business trip. Aylin whispered to Uncle Hilmi about Sam's wishes.

Her uncle asked, "Where is he now?"

"I don't know, Uncle."

"Haven't you seen him at all since you returned?"

"No. He didn't call me, and he doesn't answer my calls."

Her uncle said, "Aylin, do you have a lawyer?"

He looked weary, fed up with Aylin's romantic troubles.

"I'm thinking of visiting Hunter this week."

"Is he a good lawyer?"

"The best in New York."

He sighed. "Well, don't delay." He felt such sorrow for his niece, who would never, it seemed, be happily married.

Hulusi and his wife did not move back to Bedford with Aylin. After years of saving, Hulusi had bought a cart and begun to sell fruits and vegetables in downtown Manhattan. Aylin kept her promise and continued to pay for his hormone pills. In return, Hulusi always ran to her side whenever she needed his help, no matter how busy he became.

Handan had continued to clean Aylin's Bedford office in her absence. Aylin had hoped to hire Handan full-time again, but Sam had made this impossible.

He closed their joint bank account and cut off Aylin's credit cards. Sam's accountant had evaporated into thin air along with her no-good husband. Suddenly, Aylin found herself with no knowledge of how much money or debt she had. She enlisted Irene to sort it out. Irene worked for weeks and eventually came up with a long list of debts. Aylin's credit card bills had not been paid since the bank account was closed. In addition, the taxes and fees for her properties had remained unpaid for almost two years. Worse, she didn't have any patients left in New York. She was suffering from a serious cash shortage. All of her funds were tied up in assets.

It was time to start over and tighten her belt. Aylin realized that she couldn't afford Handan.

"I'm sorry, Handan," she said, "but you know that I'm flat broke. I can't keep you on, even just for my office."

"Money is not important," said Handan. "I can stay until you balance your accounts."

Aylin would not accept her offer, but Handan insisted on tidying up the office at least once or twice a week. Finally, Irene came up with a bright idea.

She said, "Why don't you rent one of the office rooms out?"

"The second room is full of books," said Aylin. "I can't throw away my books."

Irene said, "Aylin, your books can stay where they are. You'll rent the room, not the shelves. The tenant will have to deal with them."

A rather strange-looking psychiatrist by the name of Dr. Coulton rented the room. He offered to pay Irene if she would be his secretary, too.

Irene agreed, but told him, "I can only answer your calls and arrange your appointments." Soon, both Aylin and Irene would have some extra cash in their pockets. With the additional income, Aylin paid Handan to clean the office two days a week.

In February, Aylin ran into Jeremy Barts at a cocktail party. Jeremy had heard she'd enlisted in the army and that she'd been in Fort Sill for two years. He was very glad to see her back in New York. Aylin told him all about Oklahoma and her light therapy. Then, all of a sudden, she said, "Jeremy, let's have dinner together."

Jeremy was very pleased to receive the offer, but asked, "Where is your husband, Aylin?"

"We are separated," she replied shortly.

"Oh, now we can reprise our opera dates. What do you think?"

"That would be great," said Aylin. "I've got a ticket for the premiere of *Aida* two weeks from now."

"Me, too. Shall I fetch you at home or at your office?"

Aylin said, "Coming to my house may be costly, Barts. I live out in Bedford now. You better pick me up at my office in the city."

Aylin failed to be as attentive to the divorce as she was to reviving her social life. In fact, she ignored it almost completely. Both Irene and Lucy warned her not to take the proceedings for granted. In the end, she decided to consult Hunter, the Hollywood divorce lawyer she'd met at the Tony Awards. Sam was alarmed to hear that Aylin had hired Hunter, who was renowned for getting the best settlements. On the other hand, he felt relieved that Aylin had finally accepted the divorce. Now all that mattered was striking a bargain.

Aylin did not yet have the means to put her life completely back in order, but she did find a girl named Amy to do part-time cleaning at her home. Still, the Bedford house was in poor shape. Sam had cancelled the propane and garbage removal contracts, so the house was ice-cold and hills of garbage grew by the garden fence. Aylin first had to pay past-due bills; her husband hadn't paid them. He had also taken away their king-sized bed and their artwork, days before Aylin returned home. Had Aylin not been confronted with such injustice, would she have been less furious? Behaved differently? But Sam had acted maliciously toward her, and she no longer felt very forgiving. He had cheated on her, and she thought his behavior was unforgivable.

Sam's ruthless attitude became even more apparent when she found photographs of her husband and his sweetheart on various trips. Half a bottle of cough syrup prescribed to his lover had been forgotten on Aylin's night table. Sam and Joan's hotel bill and plane ticket stubs had been left in the desk drawer in the den. A strange female voice called occasionally to ask for Sam. It was obvious that the woman wanted to inflame the situation and convince Aylin to divorce quickly. Aylin did not understand why Sam allowed his mistress to behave this way, not to mention to leave such private things lying around the house.

By the time Aylin showed up at Hunter's office, she was angry and depressed. She gave him both the power of attorney and strict orders: "Hunter, mutilate him. Destroy him, obliterate him, and make him regret everything!"

That winter, both Uncle Hilmi and Nilüfer traveled often to Bedford, rarely leaving Aylin's side. She appreciated having her family with her, but naturally, Nilüfer arrived with a companion or two. Aylin ended up hosting many of her sister's visitors, but did so without complaint. Thank God, there were a number of bedrooms in the house!

Fahri was one of Nilüfer's more frequent guests.

Nilüfer said, "I brought you a new Hulusi."

"Oh, well I hope this one doesn't have a hormone problem," said Aylin. "I can't take on another case right now, Nilüfer."

Nilüfer said, "Don't worry, he doesn't have any problems. He worked for me in Ankara, and I was very pleased with his performance. Aylin, you can't manage this huge house alone. Amy is helpful, but what you really need is a man to stay overnight, especially in the countryside."

Aylin refused to admit that she needed a man. Besides, she already had a few weapons hidden by her bed, just in case. Still, Fahri remained. Aylin never developed the same bond with Fahri that she had with Hulusi, but the man was so efficient with the housework and gardening that in the end she appreciated him. Fahri talked very little. His only problem was Porgy von Schweir, the puppy Aylin found after her beloved Toby passed away. He got mad when the dog scratched out the seeds he had planted. He often broke his silence to complain to Aylin, "Don't let this dog out without a leash. He destroys all the flowers."

Aylin said, "That's a dog, not a slave. He has to be free in the garden to play around."

"And what about the flowers?"

"The dog comes first."

Fahri sulked; he didn't understand why the dog took precedence over his garden. Aylin didn't take any notice of the man's gloomy mood because he was naturally silent and rarely smiled.

Aylin was inseparable from Porgy, leaving him only when she had to go on a trip. She didn't want him to suffer a crate in the plane's cargo hold, and so left him at home. When she went to meet Betin in Switzerland, she entrusted Porgy to Fahri and Amy. Before she left, she made sure to warn Fahri, "Even if he destroys all the roses, don't ever leash him or mistreat him. He should be in the garden for at least an hour every day." She also asked her neighbor to keep an eye on the dog every now and then.

A week later, Porgy disappeared. Fahri and Amy searched for him everywhere, from dawn to dusk. They questioned everyone in the neighborhood and searched the woods inch by inch. Finally, they called the police and gave them a description. Neither one of them knew what they would say to Aylin, who loved her dog like a child. That night, Amy was exhausted when she returned home. She had searched for the dog with Fahri for most of the day.

Two days later, when Amy went to clean the house, Fahri was not there. She wandered through the rooms of the house, calling, "Fahri, Fahri!" She wondered whether he had gone out to look for the dog, or if he'd gone out shopping. But the car was still parked in the driveway. When Fahri hadn't shown up two hours later, Amy went down to his room in the basement. She flung open his dresser; it was empty. She pulled out the drawers; everything had been removed—his alarm clock, his photos. Fahri had left. He had run away because he didn't have the guts to face Aylin and tell her that her dog was lost.

Amy paced the room, not knowing what to do. Should she also run? But Aylin was surely not going to kill her over a lost dog. She went upstairs, finished her work, and was about to change her clothes when she heard a howling outside. She flew to the kitchen door. There stood Porgy, smeared in mud and wagging his tail.

When Aylin returned from her trip, she was horrified to hear what had happened. Porgy may have gone on an adventure, but it never would have happened, Aylin insisted, if Fahri and Amy had paid better attention. She decided her employees didn't care enough about Porgy. Fahri was long gone, but Aylin dismissed Amy as well and hired another maid, this one a dog lover. Barbara was a Puerto Rican woman who lived in the same neighborhood as Aylin. She was a retired cop, so she didn't feel uneasy when Aylin cleaned her weapons, and treated Porgy as if he were her own dog. Aylin felt relieved at last.

Around that time, she received a call from Fort Sill. Archibald P. Jones had escaped the prison on family visiting day. They were searching for him everywhere and wanted to know whether he had contacted Aylin.

Aylin said, "He won't be able to get my home number; it's not in the directory, but my office number is."

"If he does call, try to figure out his whereabouts and inform us and the police immediately, Lieutenant Colonel."

"He might call. We were on good terms. When did Jones escape?"

"It's been almost a full twenty-four hours now. We think that he's still in Oklahoma, but you should be cautious, Lieutenant Colonel."

Aylin said, "I don't think he means me any harm. I almost wish all of my enemies were like Jones. At least I know where I stand and won't get stabbed in the back."

"I beg your pardon?"

Aylin said, "Forget it, Captain. No one understands me these days."

She warned Irene in case Jones did call her at the office. She wanted to make sure he got through without fail. But Aylin never received a call.

Hunter's divorce negotiations with Sam turned out to be extremely brutal. He was determined to get the best deal for his client. After all, it was Sam who wanted the divorce, and he was the guilty party with another woman in the picture. If he wanted to blame Aylin for abandoning him to go to Fort Sill for two years, then he should have said something sooner. He must have agreed to her enlistment, since she wouldn't have gone without his approval. Furthermore, he had visited Oklahoma and repeatedly told Aylin's colleagues how proud he was of his wife's choice. But shortly after, another young woman had taken Aylin's place in his life. Hunter had seen it happen many, many times.

Not one to back down, Sam gave Hunter a hard time in return.

Hunter said, "If you wish, we can always agree to disagree and let the judge be the one to decide."

Sam considered backing off. His mistress was putting pressure on him to finish the divorce as soon as possible. She had a teenage son who didn't approve of his mother's extramarital affair. They were a pious Catholic family; she had to be respectably married. Sam felt boxed in. Finally, he called Nilüfer and Mr. G. and asked them to convince Aylin to give him a divorce. For the first time in her life, Nilüfer gave Aylin some selfless advice.

"You can't have him by force, and you don't want him that way. Get what you can from the divorce and try to build a new life."

But Aylin had become so bitter that she resolved to use every penny she had to destroy Sam. She found a PR company, which booked her on a program called *Events*. She went to the studio in her uniform and told the audience that her husband, the film producer Samuel Goldberg, wanted to divorce her because she had joined the army. She did not forget to mention that she also happened to be the stepmother-in-law of the rising Hollywood star, Kevin K. Thanks to her PR expert, other TV channels and newspapers picked up the story.

Finally, Sam and Aylin began to meet in the presence of their lawyers to sort out the divorce terms. Aylin taunted Sam by saying things like, "Sam, did you watch the program last night? Did I look good? I simply can't understand why you're so angry. I didn't tell them anything bad. I just said, 'I love my husband; I know he'll come back to me, and I'm waiting patiently.'" She drove him mad.

Sam accepted Hunter's conditions just to get the whole thing over and done with, but every time he agreed to a request, Aylin came up with a new one.

Even Hunter started to tire of her mercurial demands. She wouldn't agree to anything without pushing him into another battle, often over minor issues.

"Aylin," he said harshly, "we cannot get anything more. He has given you the house in Bedford with all the furniture, the apartment above your office, and plenty of extra cash. You should sign the agreement."

Aylin said, "Give me a little more time to think it over."

"Well then, call me when you're ready, but there's nothing more to discuss. Make an appointment with my secretary if you want to sign the agreement, okay?"

Aylin didn't call Hunter for a long time. She knew very well that she couldn't get anything else from Sam, but that had never been the point.

When she did try to reach Hunter, he didn't answer. The secretary kept telling her that her boss was either out or in a meeting. Aylin left him one message after the other, but Hunter had meant it when he said, "Sign the papers!"

Every weekend, Hunter's office forwarded his calls to an answering service. After weeks of trying Hunter in his office, Aylin called the number. She put on a very heavy British accent and said, "May I please speak to Mr. Hunter?"

"May I ask who is calling?"

She replied, "I am calling on behalf of Princess Diana. Could Mr. Hunter call us back at his earliest convenience? We would like to consult him on an urgent matter of divorce. I'm sure you know that this issue requires your utmost discretion. Thank you."

Fifteen minutes later, Aylin's telephone rang.

Aylin said, "Hello Hunter, it's Princess Diana."

"Aylin! I should have guessed! The number seemed familiar. How stupid of me!"

"I'm sorry, but you didn't answer my calls."

"Because I can't do anything else for you. You just need to sign the agreement."

"Your office is too far."

Hunter said, "If that's really the problem, I'll have the documents sent to you."

"So Sam wins."

"No! Don't you know how much he cares about his money? He must be dying of remorse. We're doing what *you* want, Aylin, not what he wanted. Sign the documents."

Aylin remained silent.

Hunter said, "I'll have the contract sent to your office early next week."

The next morning, the headlines read:

WILL PRINCESS DIANA HIRE A HOLLYWOOD LAWYER TO DIVORCE CHARLES?

Hunter called Aylin, "Look what you've done! Someone in Hunter's office leaked the news to the press. What can I do now? Aylin, you've gotten me in major trouble."

Aylin said, "That's free advertising for you. You should thank me, not scold me!"

While Hunter claimed to be furious, shortly thereafter framed copies of the various headlines started to appear on the walls of his office.

A few days after Aylin's Princess Diana scandal, Nilüfer called her. "I'll be bringing a guest with me when I come to New York for New Year's."

"Who is it this time?"

"The mayor of Adana is a dear friend of ours. He has never been to the States."

Aylin said, "Bring him only if you will entertain him and not leave him to me. What kind of a man is he?"

"He's very dark."

"I didn't ask you that, Nilüfer. What the hell do I care about his color?"

Altan Kazova had retired from managing an oil company and now lived in Adana. He was a longtime business relation of the G. family. When he heard that the mayor was preparing to go to New York with Nilüfer, he asked to tag along.

Nilüfer said, "I can only host one person in my sister's house."

Kazova replied, "I have a place to stay in New York, but I would still be honored by the chance to meet your sister."

Later that night, Nilüfer said to her husband, "If Altan has hopes for Aylin, he'll be very disappointed. She won't take a second look."

Three days before the journey, the mayor's wife fell ill, and he had to cancel his visit. Altan Kazova sat near the back of the plane but didn't leave Nilüfer alone throughout the flight, bringing her newspapers, magazines, and chocolates. He also helped her with her luggage. They left customs together. Aylin had sent her sister a limousine to pick her up.

Nilüfer turned to Kazova, "Now that the mayor isn't here, there's enough room in Aylin's house. Would you like to come with me?" The man seemed to have been waiting for this invitation and jumped at the chance. They went on to Bedford together. Aylin was puzzled to see a blond man instead of a very dark one.

She whispered to Nilüfer, "Did the flight make him lose his color?"

Nilüfer said, "This is someone else."

Altan Kazova was given one of the bedrooms upstairs. He turned out to be such a helpful guest that Aylin ended up thanking her sister for bringing him along. He gave Nilüfer a ride whenever she wanted to go downtown, did the shopping, did odd jobs around the house, and even cooked when it was necessary.

Nilüfer had arrived in New York with quite a lot of money and kept all the cash in the zipped inner pouch of her bag. She put a small amount in her wallet each day. One day, when she counted how much was left in the pouch, she discovered that almost two thousand dollars were missing. She counted the money several times and then yelled to her sister, "Aylin, two thousand dollars have flown away from my bag!"

"Nilüfer, you keep that much money in a bag?"

"That's only how much was stolen."

"Are you mad? Haven't you heard of something called a credit card?"

"Money is money. You put it in your pocket and spend it."

"Or you lose it like this."

"Don't be smart with me. Just tell me what happened."

"It was probably stolen. Come to think of it, I noticed five hundred dollars missing from my purse the other day."

"Who could have done this?"

"Who else is in the house except you, me, and that man?"

"It can't be him."

Aylin said, "We will see."

They sent Kazova to New York on the pretense of an urgent errand. When he left, Aylin went into his room and searched his suitcase. She found soaps from her bathroom, her silver salt and pepper shakers, assorted silverware, and her army medals. He had also tucked Aylin's army belts and socks underneath the wardrobe.

When he came back three hours later, he had piles of shopping bags in his hands.

Nilüfer asked, "What are these?"

He replied, "Since I was already downtown, I decided to do some shopping." He then went to his room. Five minutes later, Aylin walked in with her army pistol raised. Kazova was busy placing his new purchases in the wardrobe. He jumped when he saw Aylin.

Aylin said, "Put your hands on your head and turn your face to the wall."

"Are we playing cowboys?"

Aylin said, "Do as I say, or I'll blow a hole in your skull."

It was only then he realized she was holding a gun. "No! You cannot do that!"

Aylin said, "Oh yes I can! I can easily claim self-defense. You've stolen quite a bit of cash. We've notified the police."

The man did as he was told and faced the wall. Aylin searched his pockets. Kazova didn't breathe.

"Pack your suitcase now, and leave everything you've taken from this house on the bed."

The man looked bewildered.

"C'mon, get going! Put it all on the bed. Keep the soap—you're filth." She leaned against the chest of drawers, the gun still trained on him.

"Miss Aylin, I'm ill. I'm terribly ill. I didn't do it to harm you." He started to cry. "Don't call the police. Please."

"Give us back the twenty-five hundred dollars you stole from me and Nilüfer."

"I don't have it."

"I'm not surprised. You probably used it all on your shopping spree. Then write a check and sign it."

The man did what she asked with trembling hands. He packed his suitcase, but he had shopped so much that some of his things did not fit.

"Could you lend me a bag, please?" he asked.

Aylin screamed, "You shameless wretch!"

Within half an hour, Kazova was in a cab with his suitcase and some stuffed plastic bags.

Aylin yelled out, "If you go near my sister and her family again, I'll crush that skull of yours. Got it?"

As the car drove off, Nilüfer stood in the yard. She said, "I swear, I'll never bring anyone else with me again. I swear."

Aylin said, "Don't swear, Nilüfer."

The Mysterious Call

Aylin and Nilüfer spent the next few weeks nervous that Altan Kazova might retaliate after being disgraced. Aylin figured he would at least call to either beg their pardon or threaten them, but they received no word from the man.

The call that ended up making Aylin uneasy came from the lawyer defending Archibald P. Jones. He was also an army officer and pleaded for Aylin not to publicize some of the details from her report, but faced with Aylin's unwavering stance, he insisted they meet in person.

"Are you asking me to drop everything to come to Oklahoma?"

"I'll be in New York at some point in the coming weeks. I'll let you know in advance so that we can meet."

"Great. We can even have dinner, but don't expect me to change my decision."

"Nadowlsky, I'm sure you won't still feel this way when you hear what I have to say. I simply don't believe that you would place the well-being of a killer over that of the army."

Aylin said, "If the army had cared even a little about Jones's well-being, we wouldn't be having this conversation."

"How can you be so sure?"

"I'm a doctor. I have taken an oath not to judge people, but to heal them and keep them alive."

"Fine, but you also took an oath as a soldier. Don't forget that."

"Will I be forced to choose between them? You should know that I would lean—"

"Enough," the lawyer interrupted. "Save it for when we meet in New York. There are some other things I can't discuss over the phone."

"My telephone is not tapped."

"The walls have ears," he said and hung up.

New Year's Eve was around the corner, and Aylin felt that she was on the verge of a nervous breakdown. The past year had been a hard one. Sam and Hunter were pushing her to sign the divorce agreement, and now this army lawyer was on her back.

She had told only Norman about their conversation. "They don't know what a tough cookie I can be. He thinks that he can convince me not to expose what the army has done. We'll see about that."

"Try not to create new problems for yourself; you've got enough as it is," Norman had said, stressing each word carefully.

Aylin laughed, "Great advice, Norman."

Apart from her legal fees, Aylin also had to deal with taxes, bills, and bank statements. She could pay them all off if she just signed the divorce agreement, but something held her back. Her close friends and relatives only made her more stubborn when they pressured her to end her stale marriage. In the end, she simply quit answering anyone who asked her about it, but she was starting to despair.

The first of the mysterious calls came one day when Aylin was feeling very fragile. She had come home early from the office to lie down on the couch by the fire, close her eyes, and listen to some soothing music. She was alone in the house and couldn't reach the telephone when it rang. She rose wearily, thinking about how badly she needed a full-time housekeeper to do such things.

She picked up the phone and said, "Hello?"

"I'd like to talk to Nadowlsky."

"You're talking to her."

"Are you Nadowlsky?"

"I've told you that I am."

"I just wanted to make sure."

"Well, you did. What is it?"

"I need to tell you something very important and personal."

"How personal?"

"Will you propose to me?"

She could hear the man breathing. She laughed, "Unlikely. I'm already unhappily married."

"Don't you ever take anything seriously? I told you this is important."

"Listen, either tell me who you are and what you want or leave me alone."

"My identity is not important."

Aylin slammed the phone down. She had no interest in entertaining maniacs. She turned up the music before going back to the couch. She had just lain down when the phone rang again. It rang ceaselessly. She rose, covered the phone with a cushion, and made the music louder. When it finally stopped, she fell asleep. Sometime later she was awoken again by the telephone. She walked to the kitchen, poured some water in a glass, and placed another cushion on the ringing phone. When it rang again ten minutes later, she realized it might be Nilüfer. She jumped up, dashed to the phone, kicked away the cushions, and picked it up.

"Hello?"

"Please, don't hang up." It was him again.

"Go to hell!" she yelled. "You've ruined my evening!"

"I have something important to tell you."

"Let's hear it."

"Are you alone?"

She said, "Right! That's enough. If you're out of your mind, call me at my office in the morning. One more call from you and I'll notify the police."

"Please, don't hang up," begged the man. "You need to watch out. Be very careful."

"Sure, will do. Thank you!" This wasn't the first time Aylin had encountered someone with a paranoid obsession. She suddenly felt as though she were carrying the weight of the world on her back. She was tired, helpless, and incredibly lonely.

"You're not taking me seriously, but I can't tell you anything more. Just watch out, okay?"

"Okay, I will. I'll wear a sweater. I'll watch what I eat. I already smoke less. I exercise three times a week."

"Watch your back."

Aylin said, "Thanks a lot for your advice. Good night."

She hung up and took a deep breath. Why hadn't she convinced Nilüfer to stay longer? She wondered how this delusional man had gotten hold of her number. Most probably from one of her patients. She had resolved not to give her home number out but didn't always stick to her word. What if they felt deeply depressed at night? What if they couldn't reach her? She went to her bedroom, undressed, took a shower, and brushed her hair with long strokes, a comforting habit from her childhood. When she was a little girl, her mother used to brush her hair before bed every night and say, "Well-brushed hair is strong and shiny." She had been thinking of her mother often lately. She went to bed and turned off the light, but the phone on her night table rang again. She jumped and picked it up.

"That's enough! You hear me? I told you I will be careful. Let me have some sleep, for God's sake!"

"How on earth could I know that you were already asleep? How rude," said Nilüfer angrily.

"Hold on, hold on, don't hang up. I'm sorry. I thought you were him. A madman has been calling all night."

"What does he want?"

"How would I know? He just kept saying, 'Watch out.'"

"Well, you should. Maybe he's Sam's man."

"Why would someone Sam hired call me?"

"To warn you?"

"About what?"

"Aylin, had I been in Sam's shoes, I would have killed you by now."

"Did my own sister really just say that?"

"Well, he has given you everything you asked for, but you're still playing around with him."

"Out of my deep love for him. If anything, he should feel happy. He must love showing his mistress how indispensable he is."

"It's not out of love, it's out of hate. You do it just to drive him mad."

"Nilüfer, why did you call me at midnight?"

"I spoke to Tayibe an hour ago. I meant to tell you right away, but your line was busy. She'll be coming to New York with the Turkish delegation right after New Year's. Emre is going to give a speech—"

"That's terrific! I've missed her so much," shrieked Aylin. "Nilüfer, I love you, you've given me just the news I needed."

"So you have no idea who kept calling you?"

"None. I'll unplug the phone now. I've already had my share of good news," said Aylin cheerfully.

Tayibe had finished her master's at the London School of Economics and returned to Turkey. Aylin missed her niece terribly. She had found marvelous jobs for her through her innumerable connections, but Tayibe had refused them all. She felt guilty about living so far from her parents for so many years.

Aylin had said, "There's no need for you to feel guilty. You were only a child when you came; it was not your decision."

Tayibe reminded her that her father was already in his eighties. She wanted to spend some time with him in Ankara while she could. She had applied to the foreign ministry but was refused because her Turkish was judged inadequate. However, a few weeks after she settled in Ankara, she could already speak fluently again. The chief advisor of the prime minister, who was a family friend, hired her to be his assistant.

Aylin was sure that Tayibe would not return to New York now that she had this very important position, at least not for quite some time. Then she would probably marry and settle in Turkey. God had given her the sweetest child for over a decade, and every mother eventually watched her precious bird fly from the nest, but Aylin couldn't help missing her. She considered settling wherever Tayibe lived when she retired.

She had forgotten the mysterious caller by the next morning, but recounted what had happened when she met Irene at the office. Irene immediately suspected Jones.

Aylin said, "He's in jail."

"What if he ran away again?"

"They would have informed me. His trial is in three weeks, and I'm due to give a report on him as his therapist. Anyway, that was not his voice on the phone."

"What if it's the guy you kicked out of your house?"

"He can't speak proper English."

"Maybe someone else was speaking for him."

"Why?"

"You should know, you're the psychiatrist."

"Look Irene, you're not a cop, you're not a psychiatrist, you're not a district attorney, right?"

"So?"

"So, keep your opinions to yourself!" Aylin walked into her office and slammed the door.

Irene stuck out her tongue and muttered, "Nutcase." Then she picked up the phone to do a little sleuthing. First, she verified that Jones was still locked up. Then she called the airport police and had them check all the departures to see whether Altan Kazova had really left. She worked solidly for two days before confirming that he had indeed departed on a plane to Istanbul three days prior.

When Aylin learned about her investigation, she said, "You're in the wrong office, Irene. You should work at a detective agency."

In the meantime, Aylin received two more calls from the mystery man telling her to watch out.

Irene said, "If he calls again, let's inform the police. They can tap your phone and find out who he is."

Aylin said, "Maybe. He may just be a harmless delinquent. Either way, answering his calls is getting to be a bore."

There was no need to notify the police; the calls stopped and Aylin began furious preparations for Christmas and New Year's. She was planning to throw a Christmas party at home like always. There were Christmas presents to be bought and a tree to be decorated. She also needed to prepare Tayibe's room. She wouldn't be staying at her aunt's house the entire time, but she could at least stay with her on weekends. Aylin was excited. She had felt much happier since learning of Tayibe's visit.

COUNTDOWN

Saturday, December 24, 1994: Hulusi

On Christmas Eve, my wife and I went to Miss Aylin's house with our son. We were planning to start cooking for the Christmas party the next day. We used to cook for her whenever she had a party. She loved my little boy, God bless her. Every time we visited, she would give him clothes, toys, and presents, and line our pockets with cash. I tell everyone that I owe my child to her. We would never have been able to conceive without her kindness. She had a large place in our hearts, and we always did whatever she wanted from us in return. She also asked us to stay overnight and clean the house before returning home.

Fehime and I had planted all sorts of vegetables in her garden. I had covered all the plants so that Porgy would not destroy them and so they wouldn't freeze. Tomatoes, cucumbers, dill, parsley, mint, chard, mushrooms . . . You could find whatever you wanted in her garden at certain times of the year.

Fehime was in the garden cutting chard for a Turkish specialty, stuffed leaves. I was in the kitchen. Suddenly, I heard her scream. Miss Aylin bolted from her bedroom and we ran to the garden. Fehime was frozen, squatting on the ground and panting like a steamship. There was a snake in the garden. I couldn't move. Miss Aylin quickly grabbed one of the chimney logs at her side and hit the snake once, twice, until she killed him. Fehime threw herself back and started to cry with relief. I stood still as a stone, watching.

She said, "Don't just stand there like a zombie. Help me look around to see if there's a nest." I pulled myself together. We did end up finding a nest, by the garden wall, and I killed the other snake out of embarrassment.

Fehime asked, "Why is there a snake here in winter?" That was a good point. What was the snake doing in the garden as the December cold slashed across our faces?

Miss Aylin asked, "Did the snake bite you?"

Fehime said, "I don't know. I was so scared, I don't remember anything."

"Did you feel any pain?"

"I felt fear."

Miss Aylin took her books from her library and read up on how to cure snake bites, but it was obvious the snake hadn't bitten Fehime. We worked in the kitchen for rest of the day and into the evening. We had a lot of guests arriving the following day. Ms. Betin had come from Istanbul with her mother, and they were planning to stay in Bedford for a few days. All of Miss Aylin's Turkish friends in New York were also invited to the party. We cooked many Turkish favorites in addition to the Christmas turkey. Miss Aylin came in to help us and said, "Good thing we found the snake before he bit Porgy or your son."

Fehime said, "The people in my village say that a snake in winter is a bad omen. Snakes belong to summer. Something evil is coming."

Miss Aylin said, "Enough evil has been done in this house. Maybe the snake signaled the end of evil." She always looked for something good in anything that happened.

Saturday, January 7, 1995: Aylin Gönensay

When Aylin called, I was busy unpacking in our hotel. It hadn't even been thirty minutes since we'd arrived in New York. I said, "How did you even know I was here? I haven't had enough time to tell anyone yet."

She said, "I always know such things beforehand. Come and stay with me this weekend. Tayibe will be here, too."

"Aylin, I cannot leave my husband alone. We can meet sometime during the week and have dinner."

She said, "Nope. Bring your husband. You're my namesake and my only friend who hasn't seen my house in Bedford yet. No excuses. You have to come."

"Emre cannot come; he has a lot to do. And I can't get there on my own—"

Aylin interrupted, "I'll send a car to your hotel. If you want to stay overnight after dinner, that's fine. If you don't, the driver will take you back. If you don't come to my house, I will not attend Emre's conference next week."

I sighed. "Okay."

On Saturday morning, I waited for the car at the corner of Madison Avenue. A small vehicle stopped in front of me and the driver asked in Turkish, "You are Miss Aylin, aren't you?"

I was startled. I got in the car. I said, "You must be Aylin's driver?"

He replied, "No, I work for Mrs. Nilüfer. When she visits New York, I drive for her, but sometimes I run errands for Miss Aylin, too."

He drove very fast. Soon, we turned off the highway and left the city behind us. An hour later, we came to a town surrounded by thick woods. A deep feeling of claustrophobia came over me, God knows why. We began to wind up a narrow road, and the trees, with their bare branches, seemed to hover over me. Finally, the driver pointed to Aylin's house at the top of a hill. It had huge windows. The car pulled into the driveway.

Aylin waved and yelled, "Come into the house through the garage!" The garage was filled with bales of hay. I didn't want to go that way and walked to the main entrance. The front door opened up to a big entryway that was dominated by a large picture of George Bush, signed, *For dear Aylin*, and a beautiful portrait of Aylin herself. Aylin and I embraced. Apart from the Turkish rugs on the floor, the house looked straight out of a Hollywood movie with its white marble floors, high ceilings, and wide windows. We entered the sitting room. Outside, I saw some very long, pale trees and a pool. A horse passed by the window and pressed his muzzle against the pane to look inside. For some inexplicable reason, this also made me feel nervous.

Aylin pointed at the horse and said, "Look, this is my latest boyfriend. His name is Charisma, and he came from Oklahoma with me. Who needs a husband when you have a horse? He's a beautiful animal, isn't he?"

A large chimney separated the sitting room from the dining room. Aylin walked me to the dining room, where the oversized table was covered with boxes of documents.

"I'm in trouble up to my neck," she said. "The accountant is coming today to try to settle this mess. I've been told that I have a lot of tax debts. I never had any idea about these things. In the good old days, Sam's accountant took care of it all, but no one has bothered with it for the past two years. We'll see what happens."

We walked into the modern and well-lit kitchen. The driver had changed his clothes and was now busy at the stove. Aylin whispered, "Another one of Nilüfer's never-ending men," gesturing at him with her head.

Tayibe, Nilüfer, Aylin, and I had lunch at the round table in the dining room. Aylin frequently got up to walk about. She seemed jittery and nervous. She had trouble focusing on our conversations. It was as if her body was present but her mind was elsewhere. The moment she rose from the table, Nilüfer told me Aylin was distracted because of her divorce.

She said, "Sam called my husband and me last winter to ask us to convince Aylin to give him a divorce. He has fallen in love with a woman who is close to Bill Clinton. He thinks he will do well in her circles. We have tried hard to convince Aylin to accept the divorce. Sam has left the house to her, just as it is. She also has an office in Manhattan. It is an excellent divorce settlement. I simply cannot understand why she is so upset."

When Aylin came back to the table, I waited for the right moment to say, "It's not your first divorce, Aylin. Why are you so upset? I am sure you will find someone much better than Sam before the year is even out."

Aylin replied, "This is a matter of pride" and stood up. "Come, let me show you around upstairs," she said, changing the subject. We left the table and poked around Tayibe's and Mustafa's rooms upstairs. "Did you know that I have started proceedings to name Tayibe my heir?" said Aylin. "This house and everything I have will be hers when I die."

I said, "But why speak of death? Death is still very far away for us both. We've only started to approach the end of spring; this is not the autumn of our lives."

We went into another room. Aylin said, "This is my army room. My uniforms, weapons, rucksacks, and all the other army paraphernalia are in here. I could go back to the army any time, and I must have those things at hand, just in case."

We continued to Aylin's bedroom.

"Aylin, aren't you scared of living alone in this house with those huge windows? They don't even have shutters," I said, feeling jumpy. "If a thief breaks in and hurts you, nobody will hear."

She pointed to the gun lying on her bedside table. "No one can harm me," she said, raising the gun. "I'm an amazing marksman."

I said, "Put that gun down, quick!"

At that moment, the doorbell rang. It was the accountant. Aylin had to talk alone with him in the dining room for a while. Another friend, Laureen, dropped in from New York later that afternoon. Aylin was much too preoccupied to entertain, so neither Laureen nor I felt inclined to spend the night. We decided to return to New York. Aylin begged us to stay, but we were adamant.

I sat next to Laureen in the car and waved at Nilüfer, Tayibe, and Aylin, who saw us off from the yard. We went down the steep slope encircled by those looming bare trees and their tall, pale trunks. I still felt filled with a strange, unnamed fear. It was such an ugly road.

Monday, January 9, 1995: Nilüfer

Aylin was incredibly tense. She came home tired in the evenings, quickly filled a glass with white wine, and sat before the fireplace for hours, her eyes fixed on the flames. We didn't even talk until after dinner. Then again, there were nights when we talked until three in the morning. I could never understand how she could wake up so early in the morning after we'd gone to bed so late the night before. She had grown thinner and her face looked tired. The divorce would be legally finalized in court in three days. Personally, I couldn't wait for it to be over. I truly believed this divorce was going to be Aylin's salvation. She could finally obliterate this tasteless matter from her mind, and I would return home that Sunday with a light heart.

We went to bed early on Monday. Aylin had a heavy schedule the following day. I retreated to my room and did a little meditation. I prayed for the divorce to go through without a hitch. Then I fell asleep.

I couldn't tell what time it was when I woke up suddenly to find Aylin hovering over me. At first, I was scared to death; I couldn't understand what was going on in my drowsy state. Then she turned on the lamp and sat at the edge of my bed. Her tears had drawn long, dark lines down her cheeks.

She said, "Nilüfer, I've got news."

"Are you crazy or something? What news can you have at this hour?"

"I changed my mind. I won't divorce Sam."

"What?"

"I'm not getting divorced."

"What kind of a joke is this? At three in the morning?"

"I'm very serious. Look, I've torn up the divorce papers."

I sat up in bed. She was holding ripped pages in her palm. My glasses . . . where were my glasses? Had she really torn up the divorce agreement?

"Aylin, have you lost your senses?"

"I've been thinking it over for so long. I have decided Sam and this woman still need to suffer. They should also be sorry; they should also have it hard. I won't make things easier for them. I'll go on fighting my war."

I just sat there, mute with astonishment.

"I have recorded a message on Hunter's machine, telling him that I've changed my mind. I told him to pass my message on to Sam."

"So there will be no court session on the twelfth?"

"That's right."

"Sam will be furious when he gets the message."

"I know."

"What if he tries to hurt you?"

"How else can he hurt me? He cancelled my credit cards, he left me to freeze through the winter, he made the garbage turn into a festering mountain. What else can he do?"

"I don't know why, but I'm scared. That woman frightens me more than Sam does. She's in such a hurry to marry him; what if she does something crazy?"

"Oh, c'mon, Nilüfer! Your imagination is running wild."

"We'll talk it over in the morning. Oh, Aylin, I was hoping to return to Turkey with a light heart!"

"Nilüfer, please don't leave. Stay a little longer."

"You've probably forgotten that I also have a life and a husband."

"Please. There is another flight next Thursday. At least stay till then." She begged me with those catlike eyes. Of course I would postpone my flight.

"Aylin, I'm exhausted. We'll talk in the morning, okay?"

Aylin began to weep, and I pushed the covers aside so she could lay down next to me. I hugged my sister, and she sobbed in my arms for a while. Then she fell asleep from sheer exhaustion. I freed my arm from underneath her head and whispered, "Oh, God, please don't let anything bad happen to her."

But I had a terrible hunch that my prayer would not be granted.

Tuesday, January 10, 1995: Tayibe

I met my mother at my aunt's office in the city. She insisted that I return to Bedford with them, but I had to stay with my friends. She said, "At least, let's dine together." I could not refuse. We waited in my aunt's waiting room for her last patient to leave. We could have gone upstairs to my aunt's apartment, but she had recently let Dr. Coulton, who also rented her office, have the place. My mother had been amazed that my aunt was not charging him any rent. "Have you lost your mind?" she said. "Why are you letting him stay there for free?"

My aunt had replied, "Out of pity. He had no place to go. He'll move as soon as he finds an affordable place."

But the guy had been in the apartment for the last two months.

When Mustafa had been in town in December, my aunt had told him to get the tape measure from the dresser in the apartment upstairs. Mustafa had gone up and come down with the tape measure and three hand grenades.

My aunt's eyes had popped out of her head. "What the hell are those? They look like hand grenades!"

"They don't *look* like them, Auntie; they're the real thing."

"Where did you find them?"

"I found them in the left drawer of the dresser."

"The left drawer belongs to Mr. Coulton. You should have looked in the right one."

"Well, how could I have known that, Auntie? I opened the left one first. There were men's socks in it. At first, I thought they were your army socks. Then I put my hand underneath and found these."

"Mustafa, are you sure those are grenades?"

"Auntie, I went to military school, and you were in the army. Please!"

"What could that guy be doing with grenades?"

Mustafa had said, "The sooner you find that out, the better."

Dr. Coulton had come up with some sort of explanation, but my mother had refused to go up there ever since.

She said, "I won't go up there where that nut lives!" That's why we were waiting for my aunt at her office.

My mother looked at Irene and said, "Did Aylin tell you that she has torn up the divorce papers?"

"Yes, she did."

"What'll happen now?"

Irene said, "Sam will fume about it probably. He hoped to be divorced and done with it all on the twelfth."

My mother said, "Irene, please get me Sam on the telephone. We have to tell him about Aylin's decision."

Irene dialed his number. She told Sam's secretary that Nilüfer was calling and gave the phone to my mother. I pushed the speaker button so we could all hear. It was a very short conversation. My mother tried to sound as nice as possible when she said, "It distresses me very much to tell you this, Sam, and I'm also very much against it, but Aylin still refuses to give you a divorce."

There was a long silence.

"Oh?" he said coldly. Another long silence. "So we have to start all over again." Sam's voice sounded like a snake hissing.

My mother said, "Give it a little time, and perhaps she will calm down enough to talk again."

Sam said, "Talking is over. I'll have to think of something else now."

He hung up. The three of us remained silent for a while.

My mother said, "Aylin should not know about this call." My aunt and my mother returned to Bedford that night. I stayed in New York.

Wednesday, January 11, 1995: Lucy

Aylin had cooked a huge chicken for dinner. We were at the dinner table with Nilüfer and Norman. Aylin told us that she had changed her mind about the divorce, torn up the divorce papers, and thrown them away. She said all this in a very flat voice, devoid of emotion. Norman and I exchanged glances.

Nilüfer caught our eyes. She said, "Tell me what you are thinking. Do you approve or not?"

"It's not a matter of approval or disapproval," said Norman, reading her lips. "The battle will start all over again. Is it worth it to keep fighting?"

I said, "Sam will go crazy when he hears this. We can't know what he'll do next."

"Actually, I don't think there's anything else to do," said Norman. "He's put Aylin through hell these last two years. He even left her without heat. What else is there?"

Nilüfer said, "I'm so sick and tired of hearing all this."

I said, "Sam's mistress must be fuming. I hope she won't do anything evil."

"What do you mean? Will she have me beaten or something?" asked Aylin. "I wish she'd try it."

"Well, she won't try it. Who could beat up someone with your army training?"

We all started to laugh. We devised various plots about how Aylin was going to be beaten by Sam's mistress and her son or by Sam's daughters, or how she was going to beat them. It was a lot of fun. Aylin also laughed, but I could tell she was nervous.

Norman said, "That woman will not have Sam's daughters and her own son beat you, Aylin, you should know that. She will go to people who specialize in that kind of thing."

"Will she hire Rambo?" Aylin was smiling, but I could see that her hands were trembling faintly.

I sharply said, "Enough. Norman, dear, you have a long way to drive."

Norman raised his hand saying, "Oh, all right. 'The husband is to his marriage bed as the villager is to his hearth,' as you Turks say."

I was planning to stay at Aylin's that night and go downtown with her in the morning. At the door, Aylin said, "Norman, dear, don't forget what I've asked you to do."

"What's that, Aylin?" Norman took care of so many of Aylin's issues.

"The will. Do it as soon as possible."

"Oh, that's ready. You just have to drop by my office and sign it."

"I'll come this week. Let's be finished with it."

Nilüfer asked, "What will?"

Since no one answered, I said, "Aylin wanted to change her will, so Norman prepared a new one for her."

Nilüfer looked dumbfounded.

Aylin said, "Why do you look like you've seen a ghost? You surely don't want Sam to be my heir."

Nilüfer said, "Of course not, but why are you dealing with such morbid affairs at your age? It's too early for you to talk about wills." She looked upset at the thought of her sister dying anytime soon.

"When I flew to Atlanta a few weeks ago, the plane shook so badly that I was scared as hell," said Aylin. "I realized that if I died in a plane crash, Sam and that woman would inherit everything. So I told Norman to write a new will. Tayibe will be my sole inheritor."

Nilüfer said, "Oh, do whatever you want!"

Aylin answered, "Well, I did. I just have to sign it."

Nilüfer said, "This nutcase hasn't let me sleep all week. I'm going to bed." She picked up her newspapers and went upstairs. After Norman left, I was alone with Aylin. She took the bottle of wine and settled in front of the fireplace.

I was awkwardly sitting beside her, painfully aware that I seemed unable to reach out and comfort her in the midst of her despair, as she had comforted and saved me from my own abyss of terror. It was she who had turned me into the happy, well-adjusted person I had become, and yet here I was, incapable of doing anything about the anguish or anger that seemed to overwhelm her. I could understand her bitter disappointment and wounded pride, and yet I couldn't do anything to ease her pain. I couldn't say, "The answer to your pain is not in the bottom of your wine glass." I couldn't say, "Give it up, kick him in the ass, and break loose once and for all." I just sat there, feeling useless. Aylin didn't drink much. She didn't even finish her glass. She kept dozing off.

She lifted her eyelids at one point and said, "You know what, Lucy? All the men, all my husbands—they have always deserted me."

That was a lie, and a big one at that.

I said, "No, Aylin. You paved the way for them to leave; you made it look as if they deserted you, but it was always you who left them."

Her eyes were shut. I wondered if she had heard me.

Monday, January 16, 1995: Tayibe

On Monday, Emre Bey and I came back from Washington. My meetings with representatives of both the Clinton administration and the World Bank had been fruitful. I couldn't wait to tell my aunt about the progress I'd made. We met at her office in the morning and had a long chat.

It was a placid, ordinary day. We talked about many things but didn't utter a single word about the divorce issue the whole morning. It was as if we had made a tacit agreement not to discuss Sam, but we both knew in our hearts that it was only a matter of time before we caught wind of Sam's retaliation. This was just the calm before the storm.

When the doorbell rang, we were about to go out for lunch.

My aunt said, "I don't have any appointments this morning. Who could that be?" It was Irene's day off, so I rushed out to answer the door. Oh my God! Right before me stood a very tall, unshaved man in rags.

I was about to close the door on his face when he said, "Is Aylin in the office?"

I thought that I had misheard him.

He said, "I want to see Aylin." The stink of alcohol on his breath pierced my nostrils.

I told him to wait and went inside.

"Auntie, a bum wants to see you."

"A bum?"

"He knows your name."

"What does he look like?"

"He's very tall, with blue eyes. He's absolutely filthy."

My aunt said, "Oh, it must be Dean."

"Auntie! You mean you know him?"

My aunt said, "Let me go and see." She returned with the bum momentarily.

She told the man, "Go into that bathroom and wash up." He disappeared into the bathroom. I was so confused.

"Auntie, who on earth is that?"

"That's Dean," said my aunt. "My bum."

Right then, the man came back. My aunt said to me, "I'll tell you later." She went to the kitchen and came back with a bottle of wine and a paper bag with something inside it, then pulled out a few dollars from her bag. She gave everything to Dean. She said, "These are chicken sandwiches. I know you like them."

"Thanks," said the bum and then turned to me. "This must be Tay . . . Teybi . . . Tayibe, right?"

My aunt said, "Exactly."

The man held out his hand. I didn't know what to do.

"Tayibe!" said my aunt harshly. We shook hands.

He said, "I'm Dean. Not a real dean, although my father would have liked that. It just happens to be my name."

I stared at him.

The bum said, "Well, bye now, Aylin."

"Take care of yourself, and don't drink too much," said my aunt.

The man left. I ran to the bathroom to wash my hands. When I came back, my aunt was ready to go.

I said, "Auntie, was that a dream? Was that man real?"

My aunt said, "I don't understand why you're that surprised."

"That man was a vagrant. A bum."

"So what?"

"Auntie, where do you meet all these guys? Aren't you ever scared? He might be a thief. And he's obviously an alcoholic."

"The man you saw is a human being, Tayibe. Furthermore, he is a philosopher. Yes, he has seen better days, but life has made him what he is."

"Okay, okay, but how did you meet him? Is he a patient of yours?"

"I was going to dine at the Park Café one evening. He was begging in the street. He asked me for change. I said, 'Will you use it to buy a drink?' and he replied, 'I'm hungry, I'll buy something to eat.' So, I told him that I would take him to dinner if he was really hungry. We went to McDonald's and he ate three Big Macs and two pieces of apple pie. He was really starving."

"And then?" It was like listening to a fairy tale.

"And then, that's all. We talked as we ate. He has an incredible story. We became friends. He sometimes drops in on Mondays for a sandwich and some wine. I occasionally give him some money."

"That's fine, Auntie, but how many people do you feed? Hulusi's pills, Handan's children's schoolbooks, the bum's sandwiches and wine. The list goes on and on. Why don't you just cure him?"

My aunt said, "I tried, but he doesn't want it. You can't force people to get help."

"Auntie, this compassion of yours, doesn't it wear you out?"

"Tayibe," said my aunt, "I might not have been able to handle this life had I not felt this urge to love and help people."

Tuesday, January 17, 1995, morning, noon, and early evening

Aylin and Nilüfer went to New York together around noon. Aylin dropped Nilüfer at a friend's house and headed for the hairdresser. Then she met Tayibe, and they went to the Plaza Hotel where the American-Turkish Society had arranged a lunch for Emre, Tayibe's boss and the other Aylin's husband. He was giving a speech. They went to the Terrace Room where the luncheon was being held. It was very crowded. Almost all of the New York-based Robert College alumni and Turkish diplomats were there.

Although Aylin seemed a little distracted, she was as jocular as ever. She talked to friends she hadn't seen for a long time, made people laugh at her jokes, and flirted a lot.

Tayibe and Aylin sat at the same table as the poet Talat Halman and his spouse. When Emre started to explain the economic crisis of 1994, and how the Turkish government had overcome it, to the American businessmen, Tayibe was all ears, but Aylin was almost indifferent to the topic. As a matter of fact, she and the Halmans were talking about art, music, and drama at their table. Aylin had asked for only one glass of red wine, and she didn't drink much as her mind was preoccupied by the divorce suit. She was scared of Sam's possible reaction, although she betrayed no sign of her fear.

Sam must have heard the news by now. What had he said? What had he thought of doing? He had surely been disgusted with her recent TV appearance, when she had declared, "I love my husband. I will by no means divorce him!" She had done it out of mischief, knowing it would infuriate Sam. She had tried to get him to see what a mockery it all was but was not able to make him laugh. A thick wall had risen between them. It was all because of that Catholic woman from Little Rock who was cozy with President Clinton. The White House! Sam certainly liked that!

She became aware that someone had been talking to her for a long time. At first, she looked at him with hollow eyes and then burst out laughing.

"You know what? My hearing must be starting to fail me. Can it be that I'm getting old? What did you say? Tell me again."

Her friend was bewildered, and thought Aylin was tipsy. But Aylin hadn't taken so much as a sip from her glass. Her absent-mindedness was for very different reasons. Only those who knew her very well would have been able to detect her flagging spirit or her preoccupation. Her old friend Ivan, whom she met there that day, was one of those people. When he returned home, he told his wife Leyla, "Aylin looked sort of strange."

Emre and his wife Aylin invited Tayibe and her aunt to dinner that evening. Emre's wife insisted on spending time with her old classmate, whom she might not see again for a long time, because the couple was returning home the next day.

Aylin said, "I'm going to the opera with Jeremy Barts. I can't possibly cancel. He bought the tickets weeks ago."

Aylin said to her namesake, "Why don't you find yourself a younger escort?"

"Younger men don't appreciate and respect us like older ones do."

After Aylin left the hotel, she returned to her office to see a patient. She slipped out of her suit and put on her doctor's coat. When the patient had gone, she freshened up her makeup, put on her lipstick, combed her hair, and sprayed her perfume; taking off her doctor's coat, she put her gray-and-pink blouse with the fringed neck and her gray suit on again. Then, from her bag, she took her antique crescent brooch, which she had worn at lunch, and attached it to her collar. She was already wearing her emerald Ottoman ring. She took a look at herself in the mirror. Aylin was ready for a night at the opera when Tayibe arrived.

Jeremy Barts rang the doorbell at ten past six. He had rented a limousine with a driver, just as he had always done on their previous nights at the opera. Oh, how nice it was! Aylin felt her heart lift with happiness for the first time in many days. She'd had a very pleasant day, and now she could settle herself comfortably into the limousine to go and listen to Donizetti. Life was beautiful in spite of Sam; life was worth living.

Tuesday, January 17, 1995, 6:10 p.m.–12:00 a.m.: Jeremy Barts

We met in Aylin's office on Seventy-Fifth Street around six o'clock. Her young niece, Tayibe, was also there. We exchanged a few words. Tayibe had turned into such an attractive young girl . . . Aylin told Tayibe to take her dog Porgy to the tenant in the apartment upstairs, and we left.

We were planning to go to the Metropolitan Opera to enjoy Donizetti's *L'Elisir d'Amour*. We enjoyed many nights at the opera before Aylin married Sam Goldberg. We were both opera fans and had a hard time getting partners to accompany us, so we had decided to use our season tickets to go to the premiere of every new performance together. We always had a light meal in between the acts and chatted as we ate.

That evening, we especially delighted in the voices of the tenors who sang the parts of Dr. Dulcamara and Sergeant Belcore. We made fun of the poorly dressed chorus of soldiers and had a laugh.

Aylin was as elegantly dressed as ever. She was wearing a shiny light-gray suit that gave the impression of a cloud. Her thinly pleated skirt moved beautifully as she walked, and I was aware that she was attracting stealthy glances of admiration from both the women and the men. The color of her outfit complemented her hazel eyes beautifully. In my opinion, Aylin's eyes, which always looked misty and catlike, were her most beautiful feature.

Her eyes had an effect on everybody, and clearly some remembered her from another night. I had once introduced Aylin to a friend of mine who was a retired diplomat. We had only chatted briefly. When I saw that friend many months later, I asked him whether he remembered the lady I had introduced him to at the opera. He had answered, "How could I ever forget a woman with such beautiful eyes?"

That evening, Aylin had let her hair down and left it loose on her shoulders. Though it looked beautifully natural, I knew it was the product of a skilled and expensive hairstylist. We had our dinner in the Belmont Room at the opera house. As usual, we started to eat before the performance, and had our desserts between acts. Aylin looked very joyful throughout dinner. She didn't say a single word about her husband and the divorce. In fact, I assumed that she had been through her divorce already. She told me that she would be meeting with someone from the army in New York the following day. She was evidently proud to have become the head of an army hospital and talked a lot about her achievements. She talked, too, of her horse at her house in Bedford and said that she wanted to move her New York office completely to Bedford so that she would be able to spend more time on her horse. I knew that she had turned the basement of the three-story house into an office.

In the midst of our pleasant conversation, she asked, "What do you think? Would I make a good diplomat?" I tried not to let on that I was startled by the question. Aylin was considering becoming an ambassador to Turkey if the Republican Party did well in the next election. She would likely have succeeded in attaining such a position. However, she was such a natural, open-hearted person, and so sentimental where her country was concerned, that I, after twelve years in the American foreign ministry, could not see Aylin as a suitable ambassador. Such positions require the total suppression of one's true feelings. I felt it might be better for her to return to the army instead. At least in the army she would be promoted to the rank of colonel. Achieving such a high rank in such a short time was unusual, especially for a woman. Still, I did not share these thoughts. I could tell she wanted my approval.

She drank only a single glass of wine at dinner. When I insisted that she share the champagne with me, she declined, saying that she had to drive to Bedford. She reminded me of her important meeting the next day.

We went back to her office as soon as the performance was over. She planned to collect Porgy and go home. I didn't think it was safe for her to drive all the way to Bedford at such a late hour and insisted that she stay the night in the city with her sister. But of course Aylin never changed her plans. So I accompanied her up to the door of her office and watched her enter the building. In her flowing, smoky silk skirt, she looked like a fairy princess. Before she disappeared, she turned and waved, smiling with those glittering, hazel cat eyes. That was the last time I saw her.

Wednesday, January 18, 1995: Nilüfer

Tayibe and I stayed overnight at the Harvard Club on Tuesday. Tayibe had not succeeded in persuading Aylin to come and stay with us after the opera, even though we had an appointment with Hunter the next day. Aylin had not met with her lawyer since she'd torn up the divorce papers. We were due to meet him at six o'clock in the evening to review the matter. Hunter had made it clear that he was fed up with her. He simply could not grasp the fact that Aylin was not interested in money. She was merely mortified by the fact Sam preferred another woman over her. I had high hopes that Hunter could still convince her.

I met Tayibe at Aylin's office around four o'clock. Irene had already left, so we waited for Aylin in the lobby. Half an hour later, Tayibe went to check on her and saw a light coming from beneath the door.

"Auntie doesn't like to be disturbed when she has a patient, so I didn't knock." She checked again at five thirty. "Look mom, I couldn't just walk into her room. She'll come out when she's finished."

Finally I went and knocked; there was no answer. I knocked harder and harder, but still there was no answer. We decided that she must have finished early with her patients, gone out, and forgotten to turn off the light. We called her house; no answer. We hoped she would be back soon and waited.

I kept dialing her number in Bedford, but there was no answer. The rush-hour traffic must have been very bad. I called Hunter; she hadn't been there, either. It was six o'clock. Then seven o'clock. God knows how many cups of tea and coffee I drank. I kept on calling Hunter's office and Aylin's house, all to no avail.

Tayibe said, "Mother, stop dialing. I've put a note on her door. She'll call us when she sees it," but I couldn't stop myself.

Hunter called us around seven thirty. He said, "I knew she wouldn't show up. I'm leaving."

Tayibe called Jeremy Barts and spoke to his wife. He wasn't home. I was very angry by then and knew exactly what I would say once I got a hold of her.

It was nine o'clock. There was still no news of Aylin. I gave up being angry; I was now terribly worried. My God, had something bad happened to my sister? I called Emel, Leyla, and some other friends of hers. None of them knew anything. Tayibe called Mitch. He didn't know anything, either. There was still no answer at her house. Where the hell was she?

Before we headed back to the Harvard Club, Tayibe left a message. "Auntie, has there been a misunderstanding? We're going back to the hotel. We'll wait for your call; we're very worried."

Had that goddamn Bedford house not been so far away, I would have headed there immediately.

Back in our room, I could tell that Tayibe was just as worried as I was, though she tried not to show it. We decided to go to Bedford the next morning if we had not yet heard from Aylin. But she was not at home; that we knew. Where was she? What was she doing? Had Haidar returned after all these years? Was she on her way to kill Sam's girlfriend? Had she had too much to drink and fallen asleep somewhere? She had not been in high spirits. In my opinion, she was on the verge of a breakdown. That fat Jew had destroyed my sister.

It was late in the evening, and not a word from Aylin! I was about to lose my mind.

Aylin

Thursday, January 19, 1995, 8:20 a.m.–8:50 a.m.: Barbara

The weather is ice-cold this morning. My fingertips are almost numb in spite of my gloves. I woke up with a bad feeling, as if someone was squeezing my heart. God knows why. My sister thinks depressive moods are normal at my age. All my life, I have always seemed to have more than my share of tragedy. Nothing has ever gone my way. For instance, if I miss the bus, like I did this morning, I wait twice as long for the next one. Then that bus is always crammed with people and I can't get a seat. The brats on their way to school push me back and forth and pinch my bottom. I never get angry; actually, they are the only ones who make me feel like a woman with this prematurely aging face of mine.

Miss Aylin frowns if I'm a bit late. Why does she always get to the office before me? Because I don't have a private car. Once I told her this just to see how angry she'd get, but she embraced me. My employer is a bit strange. She's unlike anyone else. She will scold people but then make up for it in a single breath. She's so softhearted; she can never be indifferent to other people's pain, and she is generous. But she is terribly miserable nowadays. This divorce has drained her completely. Her husband, it seems, took away some of the furniture while she was away. When my mistress returned from the army and found the house half-empty, she almost went crazy.

I said, "What will you do here all alone in this rambling house at the top of a hill? Why not move to your apartment in New York?" Does she ever listen? It went in one ear and out the other.

She said, "I won't be alone, don't you worry. I have a guest coming."

I thought, *At last she has found a man*, but what she actually found was a horse. One morning, when I came to clean, I saw a huge head looking at me from behind the window. She had tied up her horse right there, outside the living room. So yes, she is a bit strange!

I'm late again today. I must prepare myself for her temper. Shit, this hill is just unbearable to climb. Oh, Porgy, you naughty dog, what are you doing here? Did you run away from home again? No, you have your leash on. Are you going for a walk with the mistress? Why is the car right in the middle of the driveway? Where's the mistress? How can I get by? Miss Nadowlsky? Oh, there's someone under the car there. Someone is lying under the car. Oh my God! Under the car! *Oh my god! Miss Nadowlsky! Miss Aylin!* Answer me! Do you hear me? Why doesn't she move? Why doesn't she make a sound?

Thursday, January 19, 1995, 9:00 a.m.–9:30 a.m.: Tayibe

Last night, my mother couldn't sleep at all. I was also very tense, keeping my ear close to the telephone in case it rang. But no one called. My aunt had never been so inconsiderate. Sam would have been the person they called in case of any accident, because he was still my aunt's husband. We went to Sam's office early in the morning. No one was there yet. We lingered outside the door where Sam's secretary Charlotte was astonished to find us. We all went in and checked to see if there were any messages from the police, from anyone. But there was no news. We were almost comforted. Who knew? Maybe my aunt had run off with Jeremy Barts.

I was about to leave when Charlotte picked up the phone. She signaled to me with her hand.

I called to my mom, who was already heading out, "You go ahead, Mom, and I'll join you in a minute."

Charlotte was saying, "Oh my God; that can't be true." She looked utterly confused.

"What is it? What's happened?"

Charlotte said, "There's been an accident of some sort. The police in Bedford are dealing with it. They've called Sam at home. Sam will be here soon to pick you up; go down and wait for him."

My mother was standing by the elevator.

I said, "I think a burglar has broken into Auntie's, Mom." My knees were trembling.

"What did you say?" said my mother. "Well, that's why poor Aylin couldn't keep her appointment. How did the thief break into the house? I hope Aylin wasn't home. Otherwise, he'd have scared her to death."

Sam took a long time to arrive. The weather was icy; I was afraid of my mother catching cold.

As Sam pulled into a parking spot, I said to my mother, "I beg you, Mother, be patient with him. He takes his anger out on my aunt, and we don't want her harmed, do we?"

Through her teeth, my mother said, "Goddamn Jew."

I opened the door and made my mother take the backseat. I settled into the passenger seat beside Sam. He pulled out and started to drive.

Sam said, "The police called again. That's why I'm late."

My mother said, "What has happened, really? Did a burglar break into the house?"

Sam stopped the car, turned around in his seat to face my mother, and calmly said, "Aylin is dead."

Saturday, January 21, 1995: Westchester County Medical Examiner's Office

In the morgue it is very, very cold. Nilüfer is behind the glass pane that separates her from Aylin, standing on the borderline between life and death. She looks at her sister with hollow eyes. It is as if she has been given an injection and turned into a zombie. She cannot cry, cannot speak. She cannot feel anything.

They have wrapped Aylin in a white sheet and placed her on a pink cloth. Pink and white! Colors symbolizing happiness, purity, and peace. Nilüfer wants to stay there for hours and relive every day and hour she spent with Aylin since that Ankara evening when she held her in her arms for the first time.

She will never forget how her sister looked when she came home from her time away at school. The beanstalk of a child. She had worn a pink coat that tapered slightly at the waist, white knee-socks, and patent-leather shoes. Her reddish-blond hair was braided into two long plaits; her freckled face white from cold. When did this child get so tall? Had this really happened in just a single school year? Innocent and fragile, she stood amid the teeming crowd on the platform and gazed at her older sister as she got off the train.

Nilüfer hugged her sister tightly and kissed her. Aylin's cheeks were as cold as ice.

Nilüfer's heart swells with anguish and pushes against the ribs in her chest. Her red eyes are bone-dry. She has shed too many tears over these last few days. Maybe she has died but isn't aware of it. Is it possible to suffer agony and yet feel so calm?

Her delicate and beautiful sister resembles a snowdrop that has emerged from under the snow. Strangely, she feels an indescribable peace of mind. She speaks to her sister, enveloped by white and pink, just like she'd been many years ago on the platform of Ankara Station.

In her memory, Nilüfer bends down and presses her face against her sister's cold cheek.

"Aylin, why are you leaving me behind?"

Aylin looks as if she is smiling; if she could speak, she would say, "I wanted to surprise you, like always."

She takes her sister's long plaits in her palms, caresses her freckled face, moves her hands over the rough texture of her pink coat and pulls up her sister's white socks, so that her legs won't get cold.

Aylin's lips move. Nilüfer strains to hear her.

"Don't ever be sorry for me, Nilüfer," says Aylin. "The tempest has calmed; it is very quiet, very peaceful here. I was so tired. I need my rest now. Leave me be."

Nilüfer stands on the border between life and death, walking across life in the fog of the cold Ankara morning, transcending the years. She bumps into the reality of the present. Thousands of questions wing through her mind, questions that can never be answered. With her sister's dainty hand in her palm, she walks. She walks alongside Aylin in her vibrant and pulsating life, her longings, her successes, her failures, her joy, and her pain. She walks with a Mevlevi song ringing in her ears and Rumi's lines in her heart.

In this ocean there is no death
No despair, no sadness, no anxiety
This ocean is boundless love
This is the ocean of beauty, of generosity.

ABOUT THE AUTHOR

One of Turkey's most beloved authors, Ayşe Kulin is known for her captivating stories about human endurance. In addition to penning internationally bestselling novels, she has also worked as a producer, cinematographer, and screenwriter for numerous television shows and films. Her novel *Last Train to Istanbul* won the European Council of Jewish Communities Best Novel Award and has been translated into twenty-three languages.